THE CONVIC

THE CONNOISSEUR

The Connoisseur

Magda Sweetland

MACMILLAN
LONDON

First published 1986 by
MACMILLAN LONDON LIMITED
4 Little Essex Street London WC2R 3LF
and Basingstoke

Associated companies in Auckland, Delhi, Dublin, Gaborone,
Hamburg, Harare, Hong Kong, Johannesburg, Kuala Lumpur,
Lagos, Manzini, Melbourne, Mexico City, Nairobi, New York,
Singapore and Tokyo

British Library Cataloguing in Publication Data

Sweetland, Magda
The Connoisseur.
I. Title
823′.914 [F]   PR6069.W3/

ISBN 0–333–42241–4

Typeset by Wyvern Typesetting Limited, Bristol

Printed in Great Britain by
the Garden City Press Ltd, Herts.

Contents

Counter
Exchanges

Chapter One

On a Friday evening shortly before Easter, Innes Hamilton locked up his premises for the weekend and prepared to go home. The establishment – shop was too vulgar a word – was in Edinburgh's Grassmarket, an area that had been popular at one time and was to be more so in a year or two, but for the moment it was between fashions in a trough of neglect, awaiting the hand of the developer. His was one of the few smart frontages in the district. Not that smartness troubled him unduly. He did not care to be located in too much of a thoroughfare. The inscription above his door read

FINE ART AND ANTIQUE DEALER

but he addressed himself more to trade and specialist buyers than to the common herd. The strongest indication of his unwillingness to engage in trade was the fact that he persistently refused to open up on Saturdays. Professional gentlemen did not work on more than five days in the week.

He said good night to Mrs Forbes who did the serving, waited while she examined the weather and armed herself against it, then, when the door was closed behind her, reverted to a pleasant, single occupancy of the rooms where he carried on his business. The burden of her presence hung in the air like smoke after a party, an aura of invasion. He dispelled it quickly, solitude being his personal opiate.

He moved about the premises, methodically checking the windows at the rear and their safety catches, switching on the burglar alarm and finally, backing out of the door himself, padlocked a black iron grid in place.

He waited a moment, idling by the display in one of the windows. Only four pieces were arranged in stark precision on stands of oyster-coloured velvet. He specialised in porcelain figurines and statues, but it would take another expert to know that the pieces were arranged chronologically, top to bottom, were all from German factories in competition with one another at the end of the eighteenth century, and were united by their common theme – the pastoral. It did not matter that no passer-by was likely to appreciate the deliberate placing. He was content to please himself.

He specialised by accident. The previous owner was a horologist who kept some porcelain as a sideline. Innes bought the stock complete but like Markheim in Stevenson's tale, found himself daunted by the mechanism of clocks, winding them up each day, trying to keep pace with pendulum and escapement, measuring time as it ran out. When the hour struck, a hundred discordant celebrations of it jarred on him. He felt accosted by the temporal and the impermanent as time slipped relentlessly away. He even refused to wear a watch which had a hand sweeping the hours and had briefly gone digital, but the battery pulsed at him like his own heartbeat running down, and he abandoned timekeeping altogether. He sold the clocks at discount and concentrated on the porcelain.

It was a brief walk from the Grassmarket to the Waverley station, but the evening continued the steady drizzle of the day and he hurried through it. The portmanteau he carried was an impediment to his stride. It was weighed down by a statue which he was taking home to examine and he pressed on, partly in eager anticipation of the moment when he could unwrap it in the middle of his own living room and study it thoroughly.

The station was busy at rush hour on Friday. Businessmen poured onto the London train; students at the end of term dispersed out of the city, swollen by untidy luggage. Wet bodies. Rolled umbrellas. The dense throng of humanity. He wove his way among them, careful to avoid accidental contact with his briefcase, until he reached the North Berwick train, and was pleasantly surprised to find an empty compartment in the first-class carriage. He pulled down the blinds on the corridor side to discourage an intrusion and sat back to enjoy the peace in company with the morning's *Scotsman* once they pulled out.

But though he was adept at reading on the train, he found this evening his attention was blurred. He looked forward to a good weekend. An article he wanted to finish ready for posting on Saturday morning to the *Burlington Magazine*, the figurine in his case, the promise of a spell of fine weather so that he could enjoy his boat after a winter of dreary storms and go sailing for the first time that season: and these were the sum of happiness.

But behind the façade something nagged.

There had been a small incident at lunch time when Mrs Forbes, wife of a retired major, quite genteel, quite suitable, was out doing some shopping of her own. He had been caught by himself in the shop and was obliged to attend to customers.

It was a couple who came in, visitors in advance of the season who had time and money to spare. The man was not greatly interested in anything but price-tags, but the woman was a fingerer, touching the merchandise, picking up each piece on the display stands and handling it needlessly. He wondered, watching her uncomfortably from a bay where he kept a desk and tried to get some reading in, if he should point out two discreet notices he had inscribed himself in Gothic characters. *Please do not touch.* And at the other side of the chamber, *Breakages must be paid for.* It offended him to make such admonitions, even silently, though they were a necessary warning to hamfisted clients.

He restrained himself.

She talked over her shoulder to her husband, who would commit himself to pay but not to an opinion. Wedgwood, Bow, Stafford, it was all the same to him. To her repeated, Oh isn't this nice, he would grunt the non-committal noise. In one sense, Innes felt sorry for him, dragged round tourist spots and antique showrooms when he looked an outdoor man. He paid the penance of vacation – to be with his wife more than half of the waking day. On the other hand, Innes thought he should be firm and refuse to defer to the worst of femininity, acquisitiveness and the browsing instinct, though the woman did have a compelling insistence about her. Just as he could not brusquely say, "Please do not risk my stock by handling", in case she did not buy, so the husband could not curtail her attempt to involve him in the tenor of their marriage. In both contracts, she had the final say and so they waited for her favour to descend on one object or another.

She came at last to a Meissen haymaker, who held the fork with unaccustomed daintiness in her hand. It was only Marie Antoinette pretending to be a rustic down at the Petit Trianon. Hands not likely to blister from real work, but a pretty enough conceit.

"Now this is lovely," the woman declared, in a variant on nice.

5

The husband came and looked, examining the paper sticker which she exposed by inverting it. "That's all right," he confirmed.

But Innes underwent a pang. She had been a long time on the shelf, the Meissen haymaker. He had grown fond of her, though she occupied a space special to herself and did not want to see her go, especially to them. He noticed increasingly of late that in the barter between purchase and purchaser, the former often won. He was reluctant to sell certain things to certain people, for every one of his delicately featured figurines carried a personality to him. He knew them intimately, where they came from, how they were made, the history of their lineage and pedigree and cared, foolishly perhaps, how they were placed in the future. They were vulnerable to human damage and he hastened to protect them.

"I'm afraid someone left a deposit on that," he intervened.

"And hasn't come back to claim it yet?" She was swift in pursuing what might have been hers.

"I left it open till Monday." A lie. A bare-faced lie but it didn't feel like it. It was the form of response he had evolved for doorstep salesmen, pesterers all. He knew these blocking tactics very well. I have just bought a supply, to purveyors of the tangible. I am about to move house, to double-glazing firms and installers of anti-theft devices, or he was an adherent of another sect to religion pedlars. To agents who rang him on the telephone, he replied curtly, This is a form of advertising of which I do not approve. Good day. He obviated absolute rudeness in his dealings with those less subtle than himself, taking more pleasure in perfecting a rebuff than in slamming a door or a telephone onto the receiver. These were expedients, not lies.

"And still on show?" the woman queried, pressing further and further into the tissue of his make-believe.

"The customer had an option to buy," he parried, "just as I have an option to sell."

A wise woman would have seen there was uncommon spleen behind the eye, a flash of acid cutting through the bland habits of a gentleman, but as she opened her mouth to make a retort and argue with him about her rights to purchase whatever he had on display, he turned from stuffiness to persuasion. He smiled. The woman suddenly noticed how very personable he was, even

6

good looking. She settled herself down to be the recipient of his charm. A kind of wooing it was as he determined, come what may, that she would buy the ugly biscuitware piece he had not been able to unload for fifteen months. It was a pastiche of the Meissen and sure enough, she did not really know the difference between their country of origin, glaze or century. Though she was equally determined that before her husband wrote the cheque, the dealer would pay her half a dozen compliments – or some attention at least.

She started to tell him about her most prized pieces, a vase of cherubic fatness, a soapstone mourning ewer made to commemorate Prince Albert's death, or porcelain curiosities so that he found himself coerced into explaining the superstition of the broken candle on the statue used at wakes, or the reason why her biscuit figure was porous and in spite of its design, was not meant for holding water. He was forced to give away knowledge that had taken him ten years in business to acquire. He begrudged that, begrudged her boldly asking for a valuation on a piece he hadn't as much as seen. How was he supposed to put a price on it! It was her grandmother's. Been in the family for a century. Very old. But when it came to details that he might consult in his catalogue, she didn't even know the date of the figurine, or the factory that produced it, and described the subject with such gauche imprecision that he was thoroughly riled. He felt he paid too highly in forbearance, all to shift one nondescript item from his stock.

When everything was settled in exchange, the woman turned round and said condescendingly, "You must have such a lovely home."

This particular line was produced so often, usually as a palliative for non-purchase, that he had an equally stock reply. "Oh no. I find it is not good business to keep my wares at home."

She stuck. She could not follow this oblique witticism. "No, I suppose it would be a lot of dusting for your wife," she joshed him.

His head went up. She might buy his goods, wheedle his expertise from him, but no more. The personal was his own. "My lady wife? No, madam, that situation is vacant and is likely so to remain."

She was warned by his look and by his tone, and the archaisms

7

which sat on him like a pedantry she would only increase by questioning.

He sighed, going back to the front page of the *Scotsman*. He shouldn't let the customers weigh on him, but they did. They were less attractive than his wares, full of imperfections that seemed magnified in the context of his business. Greed, ignorance, a jealous envy of what he knew, faces distorted by cupidity – he saw these every day mirrored in his windows and his counters. Who would blame him for esteeming objects more than personages?

Underneath this disquiet was a more troubling one about the very intimate fact he had been stung into volunteering.

The situation of wife was vacant.

He was intrigued by the assumption the woman made that he was married. Did he have the uxorious air about him? Or at thirty-five was he automatically cast into the class of husband, because all men who were presentable became husbands in the end? Up to thirty he had passed for a rakish single, and he found her conjecture marked a significant evolution. He wondered what it was, that moulding brought about by union which she seemed to recognise. Something in common with her own husband, a man in tow? Was it because his hair was cut at weekly intervals and he kept his suits sponge-pressed, habits to which she felt her sex was indispensable? She was wrong. He could look after himself very adequately.

The rain fell slantingly on the carriage window and was driven in long runnels by the velocity of the train, so that it looked stormier outside than it was. He followed some of the droplets as they merged in movement.

Was the situation really vacant, he asked himself. There had been no end of applicants for the post, maybe too many. He was baffled by the choice. Beauty, that was the trouble. The search for human beauty, visual and tactile and mental. He was attracted to good-looking women, but equally to innocence, a kind of mental fragility, which good-looking women shed at adolescence. They became the victim of their own attractiveness, either pert or moody or downright obtuse, assuming their sexuality excused everything in their behaviour.

He had not met his match, that was the essence of it, or not a perfect match. Where was the woman who was a paragon, beautiful, sexual, chaste and clever? A Sheba, wise as he and every inch as regal. Perhaps she was a composite, this complexion, another's witty turn of phrase, that way of dressing. He admired something in all, and everything in none.

So? Was he the greediest, most ignorant, jealous and cupidinous to assume that he was worthy and even had the right to choose the elements he desired in one embodiment? It might be a presumption, but derived from self-awareness. He was not likely to be satisfied with less. It was a dire limitation to be born with many assets, not readily complemented in a mate.

So he went on making a compromise between external and internal womankind, bored by the bandbox lovelies, uncomfortable with the bluestocking, and saying of each of his escorts – She will do for now. Attempting to square these conflicting priorities, he was at times amused by his own predicament. All that copulation and no progeny. No family of his own to make it seem less effete and pleasure-seeking. He looked a hedonist, but admitted he was becoming tired of what was expended in the chase. A missing masterpiece in silver-gilt by Cellini. A salt-cellar for the banquet. Apollo forever in pursuit; Daphne forever fleeing.

He smiled at the imperfections of the metaphor, but thought behind its vanity, it held an uncomfortable truth.

The rain had eased a little by the time the train pulled into North Berwick station and he walked back the half mile to his house with increasing awareness of the imminence of his pleasure in reaching it. The prospect of the familiar rooms, the soft shapes that had evolved under his own hand, the fire in the hearth, and for two uninterrupted days, made a kind of singing lightheadedness in his ears. His step quickened as he went past the chain guards round the golf club and the open undulations of the putting green next to it, spurred on by his enthusiasm.

He lived in West Bay Lodge, a good nineteenth-century house that fronted the sea, in fact was separated from the shoreline by only the width of the road and twenty feet of grass, the tail end of the links. The house had a wrought-iron balcony and two semi-circles of railings set into the fronting wall. Really very fine against the stone. Elegant but strong. The position was exceptionally adapted to his taste and so was the building, one of the most exclusive properties in the town. Its disadvantage was that the house touched its neighbours on both sides, though this had some recompense. He was not required to overlook other forms of habitation when his public windows faced seaward.

He did grimace a little this evening to observe that the noticeboard on one of the houses adjacent to his had been changed. *Sold* replaced *For Sale*. It was rather a run-down place, not in the same class as his, and it was starting to detract from the crisp paintwork of the crescent as a whole. He hoped the new owners would bring it up to the mark.

After a meal, he sat down in front of the fire which by now burned bright and fierce. He closed the damper down and in a mood close to euphoria inculcated by warmth, retiral, almost secrecy behind the obscuring velvet curtains, he turned to the statue in his portmanteau. He handled it with the caution of an archivist working on parchment scrolls or a diver who carried the brittle lace of coral to the surface, gently and with respect. These hands, composed of moving bone, were like bone china, of a fragility that was deceptive. The human hand seemed delicate but it was incalculably strong; the mechanism of all making, the hand of the lover in caress, the hands that clung to wreckage for survival. It was implicit in agreement and in greeting, but also in anger was the instrument of aggression, and so he found he both admired and feared the multi-purpose but indiscriminate hand.

The statue which he revealed from paper, tissue, cotton wadding was an object worthy of this care.

It was a group of figures, about nine inches high. When he first saw it that morning, he had recognised the style which made it a product of the factory at Höchst near Frankfurt, dating from 1770 or thereabouts. Underneath, a wheel stamped in blue confirmed its origin. The modelling had the touch of one of the factory's notable designers, Johann Peter Melchior, and Innes guessed the title was "The Sleeping Shepherdess" from the identical piece in the British Museum. They evidently came from the same mould and were part of a series from the factory where pastoral groups were a favourite subject.

Three figures in a landscape, man, woman and child. Two sheep. The base was a knoll, a rocky knob of land which supported some grass for grazing and a hollow tree-stump on which flowers grew picturesquely. The negligent shepherdess was sleeping while her counterpart, seated and at ease, held up a finger maybe in admonition to the boy to let the woman sleep on.

Innes' eye travelled meticulously over the piece, picking out

10

the handsome details of drapery, the fine proportions, the modulation of the colouring which tactfully left the chief figures pale against a vivid setting. He could not tire of it. Round and round he turned it on a side table, observing that from every angle the figures achieved a harmonious symmetry. It was impossible to decide from which aspect it was most pleasing. It was complete only when it was seen in the round.

And the shepherdess. Lying with her bare legs slightly parted, the ruffled edge of her petticoat showing and an exposed breast; desire disincarnate. Desire calcified and perfected. He could not rule out, from his admiration of it, the elements of erotic beauty. Very little adjustment of the pose of each brought them into physical intimacy. Was this preserved moment before or after they made love? And who were they anyway? A youthful Philemon and Baucis living out an Arcadian idyll where in the flowery meads "shepherd boys pipe as tho' they never would grow old"? Or the revealed Rosalind by the sheepcotes of Arden with Orlando composing sonnets which he would fasten to the tree behind?

He found them exquisite, these timeless miniature people, mute and immutable. There was such delicacy in their gestures, such romance in their rococo attitudes. They were the quintessence of their model, retaining the human form without its innate limitations of ageing, coarseness or venality; they were creatures without vice.

The man who had brought the statue in that morning was an old and valued customer, one of the indigent gentlefolk who sold a little at a time to maintain their standards, to go on affording Baxter's marmalade at breakfast and a paper every day, someone who lacked the foresight to invest his income or insure against inflation and lived out his retirement on dwindling means. Innes Hamilton grieved at the necessary conversion of rare objects into common comfort, though his heart leaped at what was offered him. He was going to have it, whatever he had to pay.

They came to grips over pricing. What the old man proposed was ludicrously low, naively out of date, and the dealer realised he had the opportunity to make a killing. Innes had no intention of reselling the statue and a profit on it was therefore academic. Why shouldn't he have the advantage of his superior knowledge? He'd worked for it, earned it, that expertise. Why shouldn't he capitalise on it, not for gain but for his own self-rewarding pleasure? Its market value was neither here nor there.

Covetousness almost got the better of him, but a respect for the man's implicit trust supervened, something he would not abuse. Moreover, the worth of the artefact itself was a bond of honour he must fulfil.

"No," he said eventually, mulling over the opening bid, "that's too low."

He went over and found the catalogue which he used for reference, annotated on every page with personal comment and distinctions. He found Höchst and the date and the name of the modeller.

"See, this is what it is. It's very rare. It's very valuable."

"Is it so?" The old man, a little grey, a little sunk, looked surprised. "It's not my taste but my wife was always very fond of it."

"You could probably sell it to almost any museum or private collection in the world. I don't really know what it's worth because something like this comes up so rarely at auction." He ran his fingers down a column. "You see, it belongs in this group here. If I remember rightly, something similar went through Christie's two years ago and fetched a record price. Not such fine condition as this, either."

The vendor was not interested in the theories of value. How much was it worth now, over the counter, cash in hand?

Pressed, Innes volunteered, "I'll offer you what I think it would fetch, a dealer's price. But," he added, palming his conscience, "I'll ask another dealer's opinion and if he thinks it's worth more, I'll pay you the difference. I will get him to give you a valuation in writing."

This payment by instalments suited the old man very well. Innes Hamilton did not carry that much money but passed over two hundred and fifty pounds in notes and wrote a cheque against the Royal Bank of Scotland for the remainder. They parted well satisfied.

He was right. It was an important piece, the rarest if not the most valuable that had come into his possession. He felt a kind of fame had settled on him and a responsibility. He would have to record his ownership. He went over to the writing desk and composed several letters, one to the dealer he knew and the only man north of the border whose opinion he respected, asking him to call and give the valuation next time he was on the east coast, then to the ceramics curator of the British Museum, reporting the find and asking if a companion piece had previously been recorded, and a third to the administrator of the Frankfurt Museum, using his German dictionary. Two hours' work in all. He stamped them and put them on the hallstand ready for taking to the post office in the morning.

He stretched. He was not tired. Bathed in the glow of the fire and his acquisition, he went and put on a record of Mozart's clarinet concerto, the gentle dropping pauses of which did not impair the flow of his concentration. He went back to the desk and clearing it of practicalities, covered it again with the work relating to the monograph he was writing for the *Burlington Magazine*.

He had written a good many of these articles, published in *Apollo* or *The Connoisseur* or *Country Life*. Slim essays on single pieces or the occasional review of a country house collection, the sort of place he visited during holidays. Private or National Trust properties. Though he did it formally, writing ahead to the administrator to explain himself, and he took care to include a list of his published articles with every letter of self-introduction. This ensured that he was given private access when the building was normally closed to the hoi polloi and he could work in undisturbed tranquillity.

It was work of painstaking erudition, consulting his catalogues and illustrated specialist reviews, trying to track down an elusive marking or locate a piece after it had changed hands at auction. He was so patient in his research that his opinion had come to be sought, to be valued as an acknowledged expert in his field but one who had the advantage of handling far more merchandise than any curator saw in his cabinets. It was a working knowledge. Friends urged him to collect his essays in book form, but though he was tempted to a wider circulation, he knew that he chose from a very narrow range. He thought in publication his reviews might seem rather esoteric, and so far had declined to popularise to the general level of taste.

Chapter Two

The weather next morning was not promising. Lead-grey skies with hardly a movement of wind made the proposed launch look unprofitable. The enthusiasm Innes had whipped up for the slow and mechanical chores of getting his boat in the water, accelerated by the thought of sailing it, evaporated. But what was he to do with himself instead? The day seemed vacant without the task he had allocated to it and so he decided, as an interim activity, to wander down to the harbour and see what other yachtsmen were making of conditions.

In the early-morning state, depeopled, the streets evoked a minimal regard from him. He'd lived there a long time, buying the house and business in one year, so that his occupation and his abode seemed inseparable, twin gestures of stability.

The streets were simple in plan, cottages in approximate rows, built in a huddle close to the sea and close to each other. Then the roads widened outwards into the radials of town planning; suburban streets, villas taking the sun, cul-de-sacs approached through high stone walls where grand hotels sheltered from the wind and the gaze of passers-by. The shape reflected the evolution of the town. It was a fishing village until the middle of the last century when its nearness to Edinburgh turned it into a seaside resort, one of half a dozen on both sides of the Forth, Crail, Kinghorn and Gullane among them, that grew up to meet the annual exodus from the capital in the summer months.

The town fanned out behind two crescents of sand, the east and west bays which were technically called Milsey and North Berwick Bay but were referred to locally by their geographical position. These two flanks were divided from each other by an outcrop of rock and inside this natural spur the harbour was constructed. The sandstone of the sea wall, the red-brown wharves and warehouses which towered over the layout, the dipped steps to the water and causeways between rocks made up

15

a visual set piece popular with artists. It wasn't delicate or quaint like Crail, it wasn't sedate like Gullane. It had its own rough-and-ready quality, born of its origins, so that it was not possible to divorce the town from its activating nub of fishing. In his time, the off-shore industry had declined. Once a substantial fleet had trawled from the harbour. The remaining smacks were a straggling representative of it, preserved against the economic trend but even so, fish were landed here, lay stacked in boxes on the jetty, were sold to local mongers or sent to market at Newhaven. Seagulls still took their chance on trimmings and the constant dredging of the sea brought up the pungent smell of barnacle and whelk.

To the eye, the town had other natural advantages. On the landward side, the volcanic cone of North Berwick Law which was topped by the jawbone of a whale, dominated every view while to seaward, Bass and Fidra which were large enough to support lighthouses stood like sentinels, one to each bay. These were the three points of a triangle which described the inner core of the town. Wherever you turned, you saw one or other of them. They were the landmarks a sailor navigated by, rock forms that were distinct and famous in local topography, dangerous perhaps, a hazard to shipping but a marker too – bastions of unchange in the middle of a fluctuating universe.

The harbour was busy with traffic and he felt a sluggard having been daunted by climatic adversity. Up and doing. Others were. Men he knew went up and down the steps to the yacht club and nodded as he passed. By an accepted code, the members did not speak to each other unless they slowed to a halt, and so merely by walking on, Innes could dispense with the formalities of greeting.

There was a high tide before ten which those who were already afloat rushed to catch. Looking down into the swell of waters, he found a dozen craft assembled in various stages of preparation, like butterflies emerging from ugly chrysalis, ready for trans-formation into movement, the land-locked becoming airborne. The sails, hoisted to catch the slightest breath in the static air, were crumpled, newly unfolded, and the heavy bodywork of each vessel, cramped inside the harbour wall, gave back no images of intended flight. They were as cumbersome as grubs.

Still, the preparations thrilled him. Stores passed down from hand to hand, indicative of voyage, paintwork renewed for the incipient season, names fondly inscribed year after year like anniversaries that had only personal significance. *Marie Stuart. The Flight of the Heron. Gladstone Lands. Treasure Island.* Such boasts! Such ludicrous inflation, making an epic from the everyday! He had to smile at a sentimentality which did not afflict him, as men said their wives were beautiful when they were not, but reiteration seemed to renew belief. Belief. Yes. It was that. Belief in one's own adventure and the minute preparations were an insurance against hazard, and a guarantee of it – hope and fear in balance.

One vessel in the harbour ousted the others in his regard, a newcomer. Looking down at her, an ocean-going motor cruiser, six-berth he guessed, thirty foot and fitted like a palace, he experienced again the yearning he had felt when the statue emerged from the old man's carrier. Proprietorial greed. He wanted it, wanted it with a sharp and exclusive envy. And then almost at once said, No. It was unsuitable for the way he sailed, single-handed, and in any case was just a rich man's toy, not a serious craft at all but powered by engine and not sail, emasculated, a eunuch of a boat. The only point in having a yacht was to control it yourself, by skill, to make it do what it must under your hands. A motor diffused that by taking away the power of human muscles.

"Welcome aboard," said a voice and in a moment was accompanied by a body, mounting the steps from the water level to his side.

Innes paused before he made a reply. His words were commensurate with his opinion. The less he said, the less he thought of you. If he could have said nothing at all to Jack Shaw, that would have been appropriate, though common civility demanded something.

"Fine boat," he conceded, glad that the sentence had no verb and therefore seemed an imperfect statement of his regard.

"Traded the old tub in. Have a look round," he offered. Innes hesitated between his outrageous curiosity to see below and his unwillingness to do it in the company of the owner, gloating over acquisition. He glanced at his watch, and the other, quicker than his own reflex, said, "We've all day. I'm not catching any tide and you've not hit the water yet."

His excuses dissolved and so he followed the man back down

17

the steps and jumped aboard.

They traded tonnage and draught, power and construction so that the terminology of salesmen thickened the air. Behind this factual parrying, neither man was deceived about the true aim of their dialogue. Innes Hamilton was fraught with curiosity about how much money had actually passed hands and Jack Shaw was equally anxious to tell him. They knew it was indelicate to arrive at a figure, boldly stated, and so they led up to it and retreated by a devious form of question and answer, a guessing game complicated by the fact that the owner wanted to bolster the price artificially and the onlooker deflate it.

Innes arrived at an approximate valuation, give or take a thousand, and let the bidding rest. But almost immediately, a second question formulated itself out of the first to torment him with futile enquiry. How on earth did Jack Shaw afford it? The man's origins were masked in secrecy. Up to twenty-five, he had boasted about them – local lad makes good. At double the age he was more canny and the stray facts that filtered out from behind a self-made legend, had been passed on from prehistory, the ballad of success enhanced with telling. It was breathed he was from gypsy stock but that his family made its money from the shows and travelling fairs round Edinburgh. But whether they manned rifle targets or dodgem cars or hoop-la stalls, Innes did not know and did not ask. Some hints remained. Robust good looks that defied all weathers and all hardship. A swarthiness about the skin. The droop of his moustache that grew lower than other men's, almost to the chin. Grizzling in the hair from an early age so that he had the appearance of a sage. Perhaps that helped towards success. He looked not trustworthy exactly, but unshakeable.

In a moment they were interrupted by two arrivals on deck, Jack's teenage son Barry and his confederate companion. Innes barely acknowledged them, finding in their breezy "Good morning, Mr Hamilton," something impudent. He sensed they talked about him behind his back because they could not make him out. The Mister was a slur, a false title, when everyone else in the club would have been given his personal name, warm and familiar. He did not resent the distinction, only that it was done in mockery.

"Well, I must be going and let your deckhands work."

"Here," said Jack, calling him back into the cabin for a

moment. "I hoped I'd catch you with this." He scrabbled among a pile of envelopes in a box and pulled one out already addressed to Mr Innes Hamilton, West Bay Lodge, Seaforth Road, North Berwick. "Saves postage."

Innes looked at it with thinly disguised disdain. What was the man thinking of, acting as his own postman to save the price of a stamp?

"RSVP and all that. Big do. Black tie."

Répondez s'il vous plaît. If only he could! He struggled towards an expression of gratitude, giving a considered "Thank you" as if he knew all along what the invitation was actually for. Presumably among more social members of the yacht club, this was a much heralded event. He did not dare to open it in the presence of the host in case it was too ludicrous, a champagne party held in the middle of the Forth to launch the cruiser. To open it would initiate the process of acceptance, and he wanted time to mull on that.

"Hope you can come along."

"Thank you," he said again, using a surface courtesy as self-defence.

He put it in his back pocket, still unopened, and headed back through the town. The pavements were crowded now as the frenzy of weekend shopping reached its height. More than once he was forced off the kerb and stepped into the road. He had to queue longer than usual for the two or three additional items he wanted to buy for his own table. He remembered an era of gentility along the High Street, small businesses boasting local fare, the greengrocer arranging his displays of the exotic vegetables in baskets with artistic precision, a form of floral decoration made up of artichokes and asparagus and watercress in bunches, the way that some men grew these plants in among their flower-beds with pride. A supermarket took its place, neither super nor a market but predictive of all change, even linguistic. Too many people in places that were too small for them. The town in season was bursting at the seams, losing under the weight of influx the qualities it had out of it, smallness, intimacy, character.

Evidence of the decline in standards was legion. Litter collected insidiously in corners, overflowing from wastebins that coped adequately over the winter. Coaches disgorged day-trippers, taking tea en route for somewhere else. The *Bed and Breakfast* signs, a flag flown in several gardens, were obtrusive,

19

stuck on posts and in some cases were abbreviated to an illiterate *B & B*, a hideous truncation. Even his favourite hotel, which under a previous management was a retreat from enforced camaraderie, had gone down a star and provided a buffet lunch instead of silver service. It signalled a lamentable change, refinement and exclusivity being filtered down to suit the masses, among the lost arts of gracious living.

In the decline, he too was implicated, an invader bringing strange mores and attitudes to hybridise the native. There had been a moment of optimum balance between the indigenous and the imported, but he thought the moment had passed and the scale tipped towards the newcomer, people like himself who worked in one spot and chose to live away from it, making the place into a suburb of the city.

He reached the house intact and over lunch undid the seal of the envelope in his back pocket.

It was an invitation after all, formally done. Printed. It aimed high. Mr and Mrs Jack Shaw request the pleasure of the company of Mr Innes Hamilton and partner at their house-warming party.

House-warming then! Not boat-launching. One event or the other, it hardly mattered what as long as it was an excuse for a party, for spending money on the transient and making a show of one's own festivities. So Jack had changed house as well as boat. Must be doing well. And then he remembered some snippet about a place that he was having built, high up on the Dunbar road, towards the easterly golf club. A links man too, he chose his spot for convenience to all his entertainments.

He looked back at the printed card and his eye focused more clearly on its handwritten inscription. Mr Innes Hamilton and partner. Done out of kindness probably. Your friend is my friend. Whoever you elect to come is welcome, but he felt, perhaps as a result of the previous day's encounter, that the phrase was somehow lacking and half finished, a form of etcetera, trailing endless combinations after it, like himself. Mr and Mrs Innes Hamilton seemed a neater phraseology. Who could he take? He thought of half a dozen likely women but in the narrowness of his own community, knew they would be gauged as potential wives. Other attendant difficulties presented themselves. Having one or other of these women, whom he met on neutral ground, stay in his house, casting an eye over the effects with a view to purchase, was repellant. He did not think he would submit to such perusal. If a partner were a necessary adjunct to this function, he thought he'd rather not attend.

The afternoon broke free of cloud. His own mood lightened with it and he made up his mind to carry out the function of the day.

His boat, a Mapleleaf of some antiquity, was kept in a double garage which he rented on the far side of the High Street. It was already mounted in its trailer and he hitched it to his car so that he could pull it into the sun and work on the rigging. The sails had been repaired by a sailmaker he trusted in Dunbar, laundered and lay furled ready for the opening of the season. The rigging was kept supple with linseed oil in a cupboard that now reeked with an impregnation of the stuff. And having dismantled this equipment and stored it, he set about reassembling it again, a jigsaw puzzle where he knew the bits by heart but got some thrill from putting them together faster, year by year.

The hull was sound. He'd spent a dozen weekends really stripping back the wood, scraping off encrusted barnacles, and then started the laborious job of rubbing down, filling, priming, rubbing down again until he was thoroughly sick of the process of maintaining the boat in prime condition and wondered if the summer compensated for the winter. She was a bit ancient now and, prompted by Shaw's example, he thought it was maybe time to trade her in for a sleeker model in glass-reinforced plastic to save himself weeks of this back-breaking, tiresome work. There were better things to do than painting hulls.

The launching point was adjacent to the harbour where a ramp ran from the main road into deepish water. Other yachtsmen congregated to a launch because whatever Hamilton was doing would be a textbook exercise on how it should be done. Half a dozen men came without asking, or expecting to be thanked. They helped him float the yacht and step the mast because there would be payment in kind. He would do the same for them, or had done so already.

Any one of these half-dozen men would have said Innes Hamilton was the best yachtsman in the club, although there was no obvious measure by which to judge him. He didn't keep the most up-to-date boat, though he maintained his craft in nearly new condition and they knew what that involved. He didn't race. He didn't pitch himself against anyone. He sailed in his own way and in his own time. So his reputation was based on abstruse qualities, knowledge of the tides and depths which he remembered with a meticulous eye to detail. He had a kind of neatness under sail, was very seldom caught up in a mess, which implied first-class handling of the rig. They admired the fact that he sailed single-handed and was quick about the deck, with the combination of tenacity and strength which that entailed. He was fit, adhering to standards in the personal that were as high as for his boat. Prime. At peak. He did it in style, was the sum of it. So, when he manoeuvred into harbour, the eyes from the yacht club looked over with interest to see what he was doing and felt that if Innes Hamilton was out the season had opened in earnest.

Chapter Three

He woke very early on Sunday morning to strange sounds.

Feet on the pavement. Scraping and banging. Raw, clipped voices matching the hour and the state of his nerves at being roused prematurely.

He got up to investigate but couldn't see anything useful from the bedroom window. So he put on his dressing gown and, confident that no one could act as a witness to his curiosity at that time, he opened the glazed doors of the balcony and walked out on it to get a better view of the street.

Below him there appeared the roof of a large white van. A removal van he would have said, except that the side panels bore no name, no insignia to declare it was a removal van exempt from other categories of haulage. But certainly furniture was emerging from it, carried along between two men who puffed and heaved with the strain. It was ugly furniture. Some of the ugliest furniture he had ever seen was bumped across the pavement and he realised his new neighbours, whoever they were, were not persons of taste or discrimination.

He retreated and shut up the doors again.

The previous owner, he remembered almost with a pang of wistfulness, had been a widow in her seventies. They asked each other in for a drink before Christmas dinner and occasionally he took a sherry at her invitation on a wet Sunday. He did not know which was bleaker, a wet Sunday when it was too stormy on the Forth to go sailing, or her sherry.

Such libations were not probable now. Whoever owned that furniture was not a sherry drinker. Then it struck him with appalling likelihood that the van was a rented one, accounting for its presence on a Sunday, and that the new occupants carried out the move themselves to save the cost of hiring a professional firm.

Throughout the early morning, he felt unsettled. His routine had been disturbed and the upheaval in the adjoining household acted like an irritant in his own. There was no point in staying indoors. The communal wall throbbed like a sounding board to trampling feet, interrupting his reading of the newspaper. He put it down, distracted also by the thought that he ought, by the terms of good neighbourliness, to go and make some gesture of welcome. But as nothing practical suggested itself, he decided to escape.

Going through the front gate, however, he passed the removal men who by now had worked their way down to hand-size objects, and over the top of a cardboard box, the larger man said, "Good day to you."

Innes gave back a perfunctory greeting, thinking he was a workman, but the man did not adhere to the standard etiquette of the club. Although Innes kept on walking, the man put down his box and dusting off his hand, offered it with the words, "Jim Stewart. I think you live next door."

Cornered, Innes gave out his hand and his name, and then went through the same concessions when he was introduced to "My brother Alec. He's come down from Grangemouth to help me with the flitting."

His suspicion was confirmed. The specialisms were blurred. All men did all things nowadays, like primitives, a do-it-yourself mentality prevailing over the apprenticed skills. "Have you come far?" he asked.

"Only Edinburgh," he said as if it were a joke. "Hardly seems worth it. But it's a good big house here and lower rates. And the seaside's better for the kids."

Kids? In the plural. Oh bring back the widow. And then as a manifestation of what he feared, two children did appear from over the putting green, a boy and a girl. Six or seven years old, he judged them to be. They did not speak and that perhaps ingratiated them into his better opinion. They each carried a plastic bag with small pieces of driftwood and corks inside which they had combed from the beach for kindling, bags so big and heavy they could hardly carry them but dragged them along the ground like sacks.

"This is Mr Hamilton," said their father and they stopped and stared at him saucer-eyed. The girl let go of her sack and backed into her father, holding up her hands behind her in a gesture she knew would be reciprocated. Jim caught them, and the child

24

looked out unsmilingly from the protective space he made. "Off you go then. Take the bag with you."

They obeyed mutely and Innes followed them with his eye towards the door which stood open, revealing the makeshift landscape of their rooms. He heard voices rise and fall indoors, muffled, not unpleasing, and then down the long length of a corridor saw the outline of a woman, Mrs Stewart herself no doubt. Untidily pregnant. He averted his eyes. Another one. Was there going to be crying at nights to put up with as well?

Innes did not know what to say, lost among children and domestic upheaval. "Will you be working in North Berwick?" he asked.

"Oh no. I'm a joiner. I'll keep on working for my firm up in Edinburgh. A lot more trade. I'd not get enough work down here. We're fitting out a big bank in Princes Street just now." Innes nodded. The man said "joiner" with such a curious intonation that it took a second for him to work out what he meant. Djina. Could have been Arabic. The vernacular he recognised. It was his own, and there was nothing to make him cringe quite as much as the vernacular of home. He had distanced himself from that with some rapidity for he was educated at Fettes and had been taught to speak the Queen's English and drop the Lallans. The thick accent was an unwelcome reminder of their common heritage.

Just as he was about to terminate the interview, crisply, the man said, "We'll press on. The van's got to be back by six o'clock. Nice to meet you." He nodded dismissively and Innes, dismissed, turned to head across the shore as a short route to the harbour.

As he went, he saw the Stewart children come out of the house and walk in the opposite direction. Not two but many. A whole troupe of children heading over the green like ducklings in a row. They followed the eldest, a girl, but really there were so many of them he lost count, heads bobbing past him up and down, up and down. What were their parents trying to do? Aiming at a good round dozen. He recoiled, remembering a phrase he had over-heard somewhere about a family being half a football team. If the Stewarts went on like this, they'd be fielding a full side.

As he watched them, mesmerised by their plurality, a mass rather than identifiable units, he acknowledged reluctantly that they were particularly beautiful children. They were tow-

25

headed, each and every one of them. Hair blond and bleached by the sun. The offspring of his friends were sickly, spindly things that whined. These children were strong and silent, marching like a regiment in each other's hand-me-down shorts over the beach to where the girl had been instructed to occupy the brood among the dunes till it was time for lunch.

He watched, amazed and fascinated by their silent drill, following their leader wordlessly. A tribe. A whole clan. Like the children of Israel, they were fruitful, and increased abundantly, and multiplied, and waxed exceeding mighty; and the land was filled with them.

Behind him, Jim relayed the encounter to his wife and to her question, "What was he like?" answered a neutral. "Seems a decent bloke." The terms of this commendation would have struck its subject as strange, and set him wondering who the joiner was to decide if he were decent or not, and what the epithet implied.

Peace. Silence: but it was a silence made up of a hundred different noises. The sheering of the bows through the water made a note in the background so continuous that he discounted it after a while, though it held all the rest in tension; whole sound and whole experience. Slapping rig. The creak of wood and metal under pressure, chords of anxiety. Sometimes his own footsteps patterned out a rhythm on the deck in a burst of energy as he responded to a gusting wind, cut back, trimmed, adjusted. There was a tide which he activated himself as well as the running tide, two sets of waves cutting across each other and where they met, heading up the main drift, there was a peak made by the concourse, crests and troughs of sound as well as experience. Birds from the sanctuary of Bass made their own discord, descending near him hopefully then wheeling off again in disappointment. He carried no spare cargo.

The sounds held him in suspension, making him buoyant. He did not press too hard against the walls of space or the deep echo chamber of the sea, but kept himself light and minimal. Absolute economy of movement was what he aimed at, to be a poet under sail, nothing wasted. He strove towards a reduction rather than an expansion of himself. No floundering or threshing, but each action clean and considered, honed to its essential. Other men ran round the deck in circles, clumsily busy, as they did in life,

26

convinced that activity was somehow self-fulfilling. Mere bustle. Time-serving. He found that by suppression of the ego, by stillness, silence, inactivity, a kind of voluntary death, the ultimate moment was achieved. Stasis. Frozen life. Perfection.

The motor cruiser, which was named *Rosemary* after Shaw's wife, plied the firth effortlessly. Its variation in angle to the level of the water was created by its own dynamism, not by the natural force of wind or wave. So it hung on rather than in the sea, a surface craft. It churned out a heavy wake the way a poor swimmer makes a disproportionate amount of turbulence, which others avoided crossing till it was well past.

On board, while Barry took the wheel, manoeuvring negligently, Jack sat at a bolted table and dealt another hand. His cronies looked on their cards with caution, seeing them blurred through whisky and several antecedent hands.

Noticing the pile of money on the table had run low, Jack unpeeled another handful of banknotes from the wad he kept rolled in his back pocket. It was a long time since some of these notes had seen the inside of a teller's drawer. They bypassed official counting. Sod banks. They had the Revenue down on you in no time wanting a cut.

They staked on their dealt hand, doubling as they went.

"One."

"Two."

"Double up. Four," in code.

Those remaining in the game exchanged their cards and Jack, in the lull of concentration that followed this, got up and poured himself another glass of whisky from the cocktail cabinet, one of the fixtures he'd insisted on. He topped up the other glasses round the table, set in recesses at each corner.

"Ease off," he called to Barry. "We're slopping about."

"You've overfilled them," came the reply. "Nowhere near top speed." He swaggered with borrowed power.

"Ease off," his father said again, clearing a spot of condensation from their amassed breath on the glass to check against the moving horizon whether they were really going at speed.

They were, sending out a deep ripple of wash. Five hundred yards away, Innes Hamilton sailed past, going east against their direction. He watched him rise and fall on the current of the motorised boat, buffeted by a power he couldn't resist. On deck

27

Jack might have raised a hand in apology or greeting, but nothing could be transmitted through the porthole. The reflex gesture was cancelled out by the nature of their different craft, but also by a surge of feeling brought on by Hamilton's glimpsed figure on his deck. A profile by the jib, legs braced to take the swell. A simple outline like a child's cartoon. Man on boat, but it had a graceful curve about it, like an Egyptian king duck-hunting in the reeds, an image faded into the rock of tombs. Jack Shaw was confused by the impact of this one shot, a still flashed up from darkness, blinding the retina before it disappeared again. There's Innes Hamilton, was all he thought, doing it properly. He did not know what this properly consisted of, but looking down into the whisky streaked with a prism of light from the lead of his glass, he was sure it did not consist of that. Hamilton had no paunchy attitudes. Slim as an athlete. Taut. Every angle taut. Oh God, the man had . . . class.

"Come on, Jack. The cards are getting cold."

He'd forgotten what his hand was and turning it over again, card by card, saw what a poor deal it was. Bluff, that was what it would come down to. Bluffing his way out of it. A slow smile stole over his face, like something he tried to suppress. "Where were we up to? Sixteen? Easy. Double again." Time to act out the part of confidence. A con game, nothing more.

But underneath his steady gaze, the slow and mannered gestures smoothing an eyelid, draping his moustache, other thoughts pulsed more disquietingly. He wondered if that was the done thing, the way that Hamilton had responded to his invitation. No gush. Almost surprised to be asked along. Slightly offputting, as if stressing that he'd have to go and check his engagement diary to make sure the date didn't clash with a prior claim, and that he was much in demand. Maybe that was true. Jack's own social calendar was quite blank, planned a week ahead and usually round summer sailing or winter golf, an easy enough schedule to carry in your head. Maybe men like Hamilton lived more complex lives, or pretended that they did. But he could have opened it, said "Thanks very much" instead of being such a supercilious bastard. He recognised that if he had ever met Hamilton when they were boys, he would have catcalled at him in the street, Lord Snooty, toffee-nosed, stuck-up, the language rich in class abuse, and tried to knock his cap off in a puddle for he was an enemy on sight.

28

So why on earth ask him? Why give him the time of day? The idea crept in, through a maudlin crack, that the only person he really wanted there was the connoisseur, partly to impress him, to show off what he was worth, but also to gain his patronage. Like asking a minor member of royalty to a charity ball, or the Lord Lieutenant of the county, it ensured success. He emerged so seldom in their milieu that an attendance of his was a freak event, a high-water mark for comment, and conferred at least the status of the unusual on whatever he graced with his presence.

The opposition crumbled under his dogged persistence as he upped the bidding by twenties. They knew these decoys of old, the hooded eyes giving nothing away, the impassive flicking up of cards to assure himself he really did have an insuperable combination, the pendulous slowness of his movements, out-staring them. An eye-wrestle. Or maybe they were impressed by the size of the wad which did not seem to dwindle however many layers he peeled from it. His last opponent faltered. A pair of Kings and tens were nothing if Jack was sitting on full house. He capitulated, and Jack Shaw smirked as he started to shuffle the deck over the single pair of Aces his hand concealed. Winning was only thinking that you could.

When Innes returned at nightfall, the van had gone and the *Sold* sign was removed. A new habitation had begun, but only as far as externals went. The curtains were not hung, the lamps lacked shades and he could not help noticing the turbulence indoors, a disarray which was part aesthetic but more deeply social. The widow had been a compatible neighbour, all the better for reinforcing polite distance. He did not think the joiner was. He could not foresee any form of interaction with the man or with his family, and was puzzled at the chance that threw them together. The town took a downward turn, mixing trade and profession, them and him, in heterogeneous disorder.

His own house, as he went about his affairs, was not restful. It was disturbed by analogy. Sitting quietly as he had done on previous evenings, he could feel their power somehow pounding out of the walls at him. The children were not noisy. Though he couldn't know it, the house rules allowed them infinite mess but no noise, so he wasn't troubled by raised voices; but he could still hear feet at play, jumping, scampering like mice behind a wainscot.

Every so often when he caught a muffled bang or thud in the middle of his reading or note-taking, he thought, Really this will have to stop. He wondered if he had redress in law, disturbance of the peace, unreasonable behaviour, invasion of privacy. Surely they were doing it deliberately to annoy him. Sometimes the fire seemed to leap in surprise at the goings-on, or the enclosing curtains shake, and he had every sympathy with them. He could not recapture the blissful solitude of normal evenings at home. His senses were alarmed, assaulted. He looked round from time to time to make sure they weren't bringing plaster down from the ceiling or making soot fall from the chimney. But the shepherdess slept on.

Gradually, the house grew quieter as beds were put up in the middle of disorder, made and filled with occupants. And he too was lulled and put in several good hours' work before eleven, when he retired.

He lay and read a novel for a time, relaxed under the cone of the bedside lamp until, turning over the pages passively, he was made aware of another sound, another thudding which seemed to come not from the adjacent house but from outside. Curious. There were long pauses of maybe a minute between each thud but when it came, preceded by a scurrying, the effect was identical, a soft thud.

He got up and went to investigate. He could see nothing in the dark and so, just as he had done early in the morning, he put on his dressing gown and went out onto the balcony.

The oldest of his neighbour's children was playing outside. Still. Towards midnight. This struck him as such a wanton piece of negligence on their part, allowing a teenage girl outside so late without supervision that he was for the first time during the day, actually angry rather than irritated.

She was dressed in shorts and a windcheater, the fleece-lined variety with pockets at the front, a zip and a hood which gave her an odd pixie look. He became intrigued by what she was doing. She seemed to be jumping off the end of the barricade that separated the green verge from the sand, a height of about three feet, and launching herself out in a makeshift attempt at long jump. He was impressed by her application, to detail as much as anything. She was a stickler, patient, persistent. Repeatedly she fell forward, actually out of his sight and he agonised on each occasion, thinking she had hurt herself. Then she picked herself up, made a line with a stick against the back marker of her heel to gauge her own progress, and swept the sand to give herself a clean jump next time. That accounted for the pause, and her scampering was the run-up over the grass, swiftly and professionally executed.

He began to admire her perseverance, her legs rotating in the air as she flung herself out with wilder and wilder gestures over the edge. Why was she doing it? Who was she beating, or what was the point of beating herself?

He turned round and went inside again, but from the comfort of his bed he heard the sounds continue as she went on pursuing whatever self-imposed goal it was she strove towards.

Chapter Four

The summer built to its height.

His correspondents answered. His name was recorded as the owner of a new find, the valuer gave his estimate which was fifty pounds above his own and he duly paid the difference. The *Burlington Magazine* printed his article in the June issue. He took a weekend away on Loch Lomond before it was invaded for the Glasgow trades holiday but was, among all these minor satisfactions, greatly relieved that the Stewarts put down carpet to deaden the sound and governed their children with more appreciable system.

Or rather, the oldest girl was made their governess and that appeared to be somewhat more effective. Discreetly, when he was passing or from behind the screen of his balcony or window, he watched the group when they were playing. He saw them in among the rock pools sifting the rarities of low tide, and coming up with crabs' claws to use as pincers, or the empty cases of sea-urchins and starfish. They went in lines retrieving seaweed and shells from the high-water mark to decorate their sandcastles. These sandcastles were spectacular affairs, quite unlike the motte-and-bailey heaps turned out by other children. Pat-a-cake wasn't good enough for them.

The girl arranged the exercise so that everyone was occupied. She seemed to have the master plan to which the others conformed. Her brother did the heavy digging to prepare the ground on damp and workable sand. Working in unison, they raised the walls topped by battlements and turrets at each corner. Innes thought they had a fine eye for architecture and period. Their castles were of mediaeval complexity and imitated polygons rather than predictable squares and circles, evolving round rock forms like natural fortresses. Crusader castles, a set piece for *Ivanhoe* or one of the Douglas towers in Border country, looped with water.

They made flags from the paper wrappers of lollipops and ice-cream, impaled on sticks, not their own but scavenged from the beach. Even their tools seemed to be rescued from the tide and the neglect of other children. Their bucket was a throwaway that had lost its handle, a metal spade went rusty lying in the dunes over the winter but retained the essentials for digging. They had the capacity to live off jetsam and driftwood. Beachcombing was more than a habit with them. It was an instinct and they were not ashamed of it.

He admired their cohesion. The six- and seven-year-olds were worn out making journeys to the sea to bring back buckets of water to fill the moat, which was never more than temporarily moist. Even the youngest was so well trained that he did not threaten the massed efforts with his patting. If bored, he would curl up and go to sleep. They became browner and blonder week by week and whatever the change of air was doing for Jim the joiner and his wife, it was gilding their children.

They were the most uncrying children he had come across. He heard them murmur to each other in easy voices, not sharp, not loud. Once or twice when they fell or cut a foot on glass, there would be a spasm of pain or a single cry as even the toddler crumpled in a ball and nursed the wound. Quickly, the older girl would descend, rubbing the spot, clamping the sufferer to her own body and rocking, saying all the time, "Shoosh, shoosh". He didn't know if this was a consolation or to prevent others from hearing.

The remedy was invariably effective. The smaller children burrowed into her. She had such power and such control over them that her volition made their pain cease. She flooded them with a massive antidote of love so that in a moment or two, calmed and soothed, they got up and walked away to carry on with the game, miraculously healed.

He watched her intensively. Nothing out of the ordinary. She did the things other girls playing on the beach did. She drew with a stick on the damp sand, outlines of Picasso-like simplicity, then when she wasn't pleased with the effect, she smoothed it out and began again, perfecting with strange application something that the tide would wash away in a few hours. Or she would lie on her stomach, legs bent behind her in the air, drawing on a pad of paper with some crayons and pastels. He thought that she was probably scribbling inside the preset lines of a colouring book but he was wrong. When he walked back from the harbour, he saw that she had attempted to capture the outline of the bay, and had achieved it so that it was recognisable even to his sceptical eye.

He found himself worrying that she had so little time to herself but was always consigned to the role of guardian to her minors. The only time she had alone was when she went swimming, usually at the end of the day when the smaller children went indoors. He saw her once from the old jetty wall behind the harbour, going too far out, he thought. She wore the funny green bathing costume she usually wore, with bloomers and a zip. It was boned in front in a way which her own superstructure hardly justified. It would be a reject of her mother's, naturally, and he tutted at such improvision, to give birth to children you could not dress in what was new.

In it she performed a lazy breaststroke, arms and legs making those peculiar triangles out of unison with each other, in out, in out, pushing herself along. She looked exactly like a frog from above. He burst out laughing at the sight of her straggling limbs.

She must have heard. She accelerated into a fast, efficient crawl and in less time than he would have taken, was out of sight.

Oh dear, he thought. I've given offence. And she was such a good swimmer too. He wondered how, without going out of his way, he could explain the laugh was meant as kindly.

One Sunday at the end of the summer he took the boat out, meaning to sail down to St Abb's Head. It was bright with a fickle wind from the south-east putting a slight chop on the water. He cleared the harbour without difficulty, and set an easterly course, hoping to make the southern point and Col-dingham by lunch-time. Under full sail, he cracked along, enjoying the eagerness of the stemhead cutting into the waves and the repeated cresting and fall of the surge under him. The shore was quieter now that the height of the season had passed and the schools reopened. The town began to revert to its normal pace. He had the pavement to himself again, and the sea it seemed. One or two early-morning walkers struck out along the shore and golfers on the east links took up their tee positions. From a mile out, they were diminutive and engaging specimens of humanity.

He settled down over the tiller and watched the clean lines of the boom pointing ahead. Anchor. Lunch at St Abb's Head. A return saunter in the afternoon, provided he was careful to catch the return tide.

Then in the middle of quite predictable normality, he was astonished – he couldn't have been more amazed to see a shark fin looming out of the water – when an arm and a head suddenly cut the wave no more than six feet from where he was passing. A swimmer drifting out from shore, he immediately thought, and hurriedly luffed up, backing the wind in the sails, an action like slamming on the brakes in a motor car. He slowed and then halted, pushed out by wave power only.

He stood up and looked out over the water thinking he might have to dive in and carry out a rescue, and didn't relish it much.

"Are you managing?" he called to the figure.

But the swimmer couldn't pick up the words though he seemed to alter course, swimming powerfully until he was under the bows of the craft.

Innes Hamilton put out his hand to retrieve the body, which didn't resist being hoisted up in this way. When he stepped back to pull the swimmer out he found it was his neighbour's daughter, the oldest Stewart unsupervised again.

"What are you doing away out here? You're out of your depth, aren't you?"

Before she answered him, she made a sweeping gesture of her face, using her two hands to clear it of water and pushing back her hair at the same time. Not a frog at all. A mermaiden.

"I wasn't in danger. I thought you called me, and I came."

"Well so I did. I thought you were drowning."

"Oh no, Mr Hamilton. I'll never drown."

The confident assurance of this statement would have sounded foolhardy on most tongues but standing in the reflected glare of the sun, with her green costume she did actually look like a water nymph. He was rather amused at the idea of infinite buoyancy, of some people being like corks and invariably floating upwards. He was taken aback that she knew his name, knew him out of context, but was surprised most out of these sudden and confusing impressions of her personality – up till then he had simply thought her one of a number, the leader of a pack – by the voice she used. It was not the voice of her father. It was not the subdued murmur he heard in play with her younger siblings on the shore. It was a new and unexpected voice. It went with her appearance.

36

She had grown over the summer and the costume no longer fitted. The lower rim of her buttocks protruded, which in a gesture of naive modesty she covered by stretching down the elastic.

"You should be careful of these tides. They're stronger than they look. The Forth can be quite dangerous, you know. I've lost more than one friend in a sailing accident."

"Yes," she said, "I know," but on what she knew she was not specific.

She seemed a little embarrassed as he went to tend the sails and take up the direction he had abandoned for her benefit.

"Shall I just swim back then?"

"I don't like to dump you overboard. I'd like to see you safely onto dry land."

"Well why don't I leave near the headland and then I won't have so far to swim."

"But that's at least a two-mile walk back home, with just a bathing costume on."

She looked down and did feel scantily clad, viewing through his eyes how she would appear walking through town on a Sunday.

"It's none too warm either." He was aware of the fact that he was carrying her further and further from her destination and said, after a moment's thought, "I suppose I'd better take you back to the west bay."

"But that would spoil your day, whatever it is you're doing." She seemed concerned that their accidental meeting was taking both of them off course. "I'll jump out near the cliffs."

"Why don't you . . ." he gave himself a chance to check the impulse, "why don't you come along? What are you doing for the rest of the day?"

"I'm meant to be doing my history essay. They've all gone up to see my uncle in Grangemouth but I said I had to do my essay."

"So they won't worry?"

"No, they won't worry."

She said this with complete lack of concern, and he realised that the cautious protectiveness he felt on seeing her out late, heaped with duties or swimming out of sight of land, was misplaced. He came up against the thing that had struck him about the group of children all the time he'd watched them playing, and hadn't named. It was maybe independence. They were equipped with a kind of survival kit at the outset. They knew not to waste time whimpering for attention or to squander their energies in crying and self-pity. Sheer numbers gave them a swift appreciation of what mattered, fuel dragged along the beach in sacks, food and each other. That was why she thought she was unsinkable. She had an in-built sense of where the bottom was.

"Come on then. You can't hang about in that wet costume. Aren't you cold?"

But though her skin rose in gooseflesh, she willed herself not to shiver.

He showed her below and found some things he kept as spares in case he was ever washed overboard or became soaked in heavy spray. She came back up from the cabin after a few minutes, shy in his clothes, and tied her bathing costume to the starboard rail where it fluttered like a green pennant in the breeze.

"Well, don't stand about. Make yourself useful. You must earn your keep."

She knew what this meant at once and fell to. Pay your way. Lend a hand. "Yes, what can I do?" She looked round vaguely at the mysteries of the boat he seemed to be controlling quite well single-handed.

"Go and make some tea. It's all down there." She was relieved it was nothing more onerous, manning the tiller or finding magnetic north.

The cabin delighted her. She was not so far removed from childhood that she had forgotten the fun of playing houses. Here were benches and a folding table which she suspected, yes, they made into a bed. And underneath, blankets and pillows. A cooker too, and a clean one, with tinned and dried stores kept at the ready. She marvelled at the order and the neatness of it, poking about while she waited for the whistling kettle to boil, and looked out of the portholes to the passing scenery.

He was impressed when she came up on deck again that she hadn't come to ask him anything. Fresh-water cooler, the direction of the cooker taps, matches; she'd found them all by herself. Not such a bad kid, he thought. Not bad considering.

Round the headland, steering was simple. He found the channel he always took, knowing the rocks and currents from years of practice and that on a day like this with a good wind running, there was no unforeseen hazard. He let the boat shift for herself and settled back to work on his companion.

"I don't often see you out by yourself. You usually have the family in tow."

"Yes," she said without resentment.

"How many brothers and sisters have you got? I keep trying to count them but they move too fast for me."

She sat a few feet away, wedged between the rail and the ridge of the cabin housing where she knew she would not be too much in the way if he went backwards and forwards to the mast or foredeck. She shifted a little uncomfortably, looking at her mug of tea and carefully dropping the crumbs of a biscuit over the side. "There are five."

"Five including you?"

She knew there was something inelegant in fecundity. At school she never told her classmates the truth about numbers in the home team and of course never dared to ask anyone back to witness the truth and broadcast it. Afternoon tea, chums to stay, birthday parties round a piano – not for her. His teasing question pointed to a terrible social stigma of proliferation, of not being unique that she kept trying to cover up. She was ashamed of the lies she told in answer to how many. One brother who was five years younger and one sister. The truth but not the whole truth. However, if he knew the tally, even approximately, there was no point in falsifying.

"Six including me. There are six of us."

"You sound like Wordsworth's Maid. One short. And what are they all, boys or girls? They're a remarkably homogeneous bunch. I can't tell them apart."

"I've only one sister. The new baby is another boy," he dragged from her.

"And what are they called, all your brothers and your sister?"

She hesitated. Did he really want to know or did he want to laugh at her ineptitude again? "Malcolm," she supplied, "and Alexander, though we call him Sandy, and Mary and Bruce. The baby is James."

"Ah," he said lightly, "all the kings and queens of Scotland."

Oh well, let him mock her if he enjoyed it. She could hate him in her heart even if she did like his boat and his wee cooker.

"They are, I think . . ." and as he spoke, she braced herself against the rail. He hesitated, searching for words she felt must be hostile, but in the end he said, "They are the most attractive and sensibly behaved children I have ever seen. Rather above the level of most of Scotia's royalty. And what," he wondered as she scrunched herself up in a coil, pleasure manifest that he should praise the children she loved to passion and had unwillingly to deny in front of other people, her arms round her knees and her chin resting on them, "what do they call you?"

"They call me Iona."

"Now that's a good name," he considered. "Don't you think? A name to be proud of. The home of Scotland's Christianity. Have you ever been to the island?"

"No. I've not been."

"Go to the churchyard at St Oran's. It's the burial place of dozens of ancient kings and chieftains. A birthplace and a burial place in one. There's nowhere like it." He fell into a kind of musing, his hand unconsciously taking up the rhythm of the tiller. "Listen," he said suddenly, "you must put on a life jacket."

"You're not wearing one."

He liked her cheek and smiled. "No. But I know what I'm going to do and you don't. Besides, I'm the captain and so I get to decide. And it doesn't matter all that much if I go down."

She went obediently and found one in the cabin's lockers, then came and stood on deck to fit it. Her planted legs did not prevent him from noticing that they were shapely.

"Tell me," he began again when she settled back into place, a snugger fit in her body vest, "how do you know my name?"

"You spoke to my Dad the day we arrived."

"I didn't know you knew."

"And I've seen you on the train every morning but you don't notice me."

"Oh? I didn't know you took the train. You go to school in Edinburgh?"

"Yes. I go to Mary Erskine. I started at eleven and just kept on when we moved down here."

One of the Merchant Company schools? She was no dunce then.

And as though she were reading his thoughts and the secret imputation he had made about her background and the probability that she was mediocre, she added, "I won a bursary."

He measured the matter-of-factness in her tone. He was sure she said this not as the boast of a prize-winning scholarship pupil, but to explain in practical terms how her parents afforded the fees. To test her, he asked, "And are you proud of that?"

"A bursary? No. It doesn't count for much. I'm not the cleverest there. Nowhere near it. It doesn't really matter."

"No," he confided. "I wasn't the cleverest either. But I made up for it with work."

They grew silent. The wind battered on the sails, smothering speech as they turned southerly and moved out of the lee of the firth. He had to work harder to keep the craft from following the current and she was happy to sit and watch him handling the sheets, adjusting course to take advantage of a sea channel or a burst of wind which would carry them sooner to their destination.

Yes, she was happy. This inertia, this freedom from responsibility was heady stuff. She felt released, skimming over the sea without her own propulsion. Swimming in air it was, where there was no resistance from the water. Another girl might have thought, I'll tell everyone about this on Monday. They won't believe me. A stranger pulled me out of the sea, took me along with him. Swoon. But she was not the telling kind. She would keep it close and secret, an experience to take out and unfold again when she was alone, a love letter that was unshareable, so private and intense were its emotions.

Her hair, blown out and dried by the sun, flapped noisily round her ears and her cheeks burned with the wind. She was buffeted by a hundred feelings. She was aware of the power he supplied to the experience, the craft under them speeding them along. He was rich. She did not know what rich was, other than a word, until she saw how it could be converted into belongings that were the adjuncts of experience. He lived larger because of them. He moved at a different pace. Her classmates had boats, some of them, and bigger cars than their rusty old shooting brake that had to do double service, transporting children at weekends and wood to jobs on site during the week. She hadn't flattered them with envy. For all her unassumed modesty, she knew she had more talent than most of them, and what was more important, better legs. Yes, she saw him looking at them and he wasn't the first. She had her own power and could handle it as well as he did his.

She glanced across at him once or twice while he concentrated on the rigging noticing his compactness of physique. His body

41

seemed an extension of the boat, the two suffused by the same intelligence, lean, driven, understated – the antithesis of clumsy. This unity between man and craft excluded her. She could not help thinking, it matters to me that I am here, but not to him. He would do exactly the same without me. He's not bothered. He'll come out next Sunday by himself and not notice the difference. So she brought herself down severely from the heights of romantic indulgence by repeating over and over again, He's not bothered. He's not bothered. This provided a very effective little stab of pain, until she remembered that her presence there was not altogether the outcome of casuistry. He had invited her along. He had the options of pushing her out again or dropping her off at the headland, and turned them down.

Moving on to explore this new potential presented by his actually seeking her as a companion, she found it was nevertheless a bittersweet comfort. He did it out of gentlemanliness and nothing more, natural good manners which extended even to a bedraggled sea urchin. She saw herself as she really was, fifteen, unsophisticated and a perfect nuisance. Brains and legs didn't go very far to reduce those limitations and would not for a dozen years.

He watched her drift away, blown and tossed about. Sometimes her head rotated like an astrolabe scanning the horizon looking for direction, uncertain, waiting for stars to give her pointers. This disquieting state as she turned on the pivot of her thoughts was not unproductive even from his point of view as bystander. She fell into poses of unconscious beauty, the body immobile but the head at variance with it as she searched out whatever answers were eluding her. It was the paradox he struck at times under sail, a kind of stationary flight, the moment when power seemed to be suspended as the energising machine reached the stability of perfection, giving expression to the mood that overtook it.

"Lunch soon. Are you hungry now?"

She travelled back from eternity to answer him. "Yes, famished."

"But what," he wondered looking down, "what are we going to do about your bare feet, my little wader?"

"Oh yes. I'd forgotten about that. Were you going somewhere very posh?"

Posh. Port out, starboard home. It was a long time since he

42

had heard the phrase. He found it naive, the preservation of an outdated vogue. The colonial mores of Edwardian England, officers and their wives travelling first class to India and choosing the coolest berth, sat strangely on her. He gave her a long look, wondering if he should explore the etymology of the phrase but said gently in the end, "Not so posh that you can't grace the garden. I was worried about you walking all that way. It's a stiff climb to the hotel." He looked upwards from the bottom of a cliff face where the jetty ran out to sea. "Can you make it? I have some espadrilles but they won't fit."

"Of course I'll make it."

He was perhaps excessively kind to her, made things too easy by courtesy, the charm of good breeding he had in reserve, and by anticipation. It was a kind of neutral gear he moved into as the easiest way for him to behave. He chose lunch, bought cider, found a corner out of the wind. People he knew came up to them and he introduced her each time as Iona Stewart, his neighbour's daughter. It seemed the truth. He tried very hard to wipe out the assumption she had made that because she was bare-footed, he would be ashamed of her. He wondered how obviously he had implied that she was not good enough. Was he so vile, so snobbish? He loathed the word – sine nobilitate – since he felt the natural aristocrat, or his near relative the gentleman, embodied the best of courtesy. To display snobbery was impolite.

On the homeward journey, she went below to make sure everything was left tidy, rinsed out their mugs from the morning sail, dried and put them away. She was gone a long time and he was puzzled what she could find to do. Lashing the tiller, he put his head below. She had obviously sat down on one of the benches, then put her legs up and fallen asleep with her head on her arm, artlessly.

He sat down on the opposite one, a little guilty at violating the sanctity of her sleep. The position she fell into was so innocent that he was put in the role of guardian and wouldn't have disturbed her in any circumstance. She was made drowsy by the wind on deck and the climb and the cider so that she slipped effortlessly into sleep. Her bare limbs, slightly parted, in the drill shorts and the ridiculous volume of his sweatshirt made her look more fragile and more bony than she was. Yes, she had a lovely head. There was a kind of clarity about the skin and the sun-bleached hair that made her ephemeral, only incipiently human or fleshly.

He left her to sleep on.

When she got home in the early evening, fortunately before the family and so no explanations were asked for or volunteered, she got out her books at once.

But it wasn't the Union of the Crowns that held her interest. She went and looked up Wordsworth's poem to see if he had been insulting her or not when he made the reference. On balance, she didn't think so.

> She had a rustic, woodland air
> And she was wildly clad:
> Her eyes were fair, and very fair;
> – Her beauty made me glad.

While the book was open, she read the poems on either side, "Lucy Gray" and "The idle shepherd boys", then in wider and wider circles, rippling out from the first poem he had led her to. Though she couldn't understand what they meant, some lines stayed with her and she determined that when she had more time she would come back and puzzle at them again.

She looked up Iona, her island namesake, and read about the settling of St Columba, driven out from Ireland by his great sin and the pledge to redeem himself by missionary work among the heathen Scots and Picts. She read of the cemetery he had spoken of, and the sixty-two kings buried there, the ancient, famous dead. The Abbey on the island was Scotland's Westminster, its first Christian burial place and still a shrine for pilgrimage.

A beginning and an end in one. Iona. She re-examined the structure of the vowels. Alpha and Omega together. Strange. Why had he made these comments about her name and about her character?

Was she this?

Was she so?

Dams burst in her mind and brought down huge cataracts of new thought together with the restraining masonry of conventional study. The landscape would not lie the same again.

Chapter Five

Innes Hamilton avoided the mirror as evidence of his personal vanity. He was content to read his qualities in other people's gaze. Women forgave him for having the finest eyes north of the border, where they would not have forgiven such an unfair advantage in other women. They were apparently dark blue, these eyes, the blue made famous by Royal Worcester and not one he particularly favoured himself. Unlike Colette's Chéri, however, he didn't examine why they were fine, in approximating to the nearly perfect outline of a tapering fish, or debate what fractional alteration would have destroyed their symmetry, making them ordinary eyes, mere instruments of seeing. Though he had been known to spend more than five minutes choosing a pullover, speculating whether light or dark would highlight the white of the eye or the unfathomable irises.

No. Not the mirror. He put away the looking glass at twenty when he found the first white hair and saw the beginning of those marks people referred to as expression lines. They were expressive, as far as he could see, of nothing but decay and the fall from the ideal. Nowadays he disliked catching a glimpse of his own face reflected in a shop window or a flat sea. Distinguished? Elegant? What recompense was that for visible ageing?

No. His face he let go its own way. But his body, that was different. That he could work on and keep young almost indefinitely. He was fit, an athlete by temperament more than by dedication, careful and rigid in his disciplines so that he had not stumbled into an excess from which it was necessary to extricate himself by self-correction. He had never been unfit, and at thirty-five he had the physique of a man half his age. To his body he extended attention which he denied to his face and was secretly proud that the measurements on record in the order book of Mr Anderson, the head cutter at his tailor in George Street, had not changed by an inch in twenty years. So in his structured leanness he could take risks and dress for formal occasions like an Edwardian in pale three-piece suits which declared from half a mile away that he was an eccentric as well as a gentleman. He was his own art form and took the aesthete's pleasure in it.

He took this body and this face to Jack Shaw's after all. He would not belittle himself to give a false excuse and ultimately thought it petty and undignified not to go. So he accepted out of an excessive arrogance and held enjoyment at arm's length.

He went alone. That too was easier.

He was late, hoping to side-step introductions. He followed the sound of music filtering down the driveway, light indeterminate music that set feet dancing. He joined the edges of a party that spilled on to the lawn where a marquee held supper and the foxtrotting band. Two hundred guests were easily accommodated. Jack was lucky with the evening. It was after sunset, but the sky was still luminously lit. The dresses of women settled on the air like dipped feathers, white curling into grey shadows, a particular shade of peony, one of watered silk that turned from blue to green as he watched. They drifted, brushing past him in the arms of other men, soothing creatures. He was content to look; he felt no desire to speak, knowing in what accents they would answer him.

Wide glass doors to the house were pulled back, and curious about Jack's interiors, he crossed the boarding from the marquee over an acreage of coloured patio and went inside. While women predominated near the music, men did near the bar. He tried the cocktail of the evening, served by a hired bartender and a dozen waitresses, steering their way through knots of people. He knew a good many of these and nodded in their direction, residents, yachtsmen, but drew a blank on the faces he thought belonged to his host's business friends.

He circled the room, and was impressed. Not by objects, but how much they cost for that was their most significant declaration. It had cost a lot to put together. A biggish plot. Prime building land, tucked into a corner of the golf course. Views to the sea, as in hotel brochures. He reckoned the footage and knew the local builder was top book. Hideous all the same, all this new plaster. Little bits of cornice moulding stuck in the angle, made of cardboard and filled with dust. It came in strips like quadrant ready for sawing.

The Shaws had had the rooms emulsioned, a colour to a room like women's dresses to try and distinguish between the indistinguishable. They were uniformly a shade too loud. Just one. A shade too strong, straight out of the tin, and there was no connective rhythm between the rooms where he wandered, unheeded, because there was no connective personality behind them, regulating choice. A study he poked his head into. Jack's study! What a laugh; and yet he would have liked it, could have imported the mahogany and brass fittings and the executive desk into his own life. If it were simplified, it would do quite well, but they had heaped detail on detail, destroying the simple shell-like quality they might have achieved by judicious neutrals.

Surely Rosemary Shaw had bought up Jenners' furnishing department in the sales. There was too much print material of a certain kind, designs that the nineteenth century had laboured over in block-printing so that the sheer cost in labour terms made them exclusive. Now they rolled off the machines in bale-loads, accessible to all. There would be no markers where the blocks touched, which was the giveaway of hand-crafting. Too many peacocks and parrots stylised in arboreal fantasy.

The pictures, as he went in search of the blue bathroom, or the yellow, were wrong. There were too many of them and they were hung too high because they were not meant for looking at but were a definable ornament, cash in frames. Two to a room, prescribed. They had come off another production line in yet another factory, dyes sprayed on without the touch of a hand. He looked in vain for signatures.

Jack pounced on him coming round a corner and shook him affably by the hand. "Good you could come. Now who do you know, or who do you want to meet?"

"No one really."

This was taken as an answer to the first question, not the second, lost under the host's determination to be dutiful. Innes was introduced compulsorily to half a dozen of the men he hadn't recognised, the men who lost at poker most weekends. They also viewed Jack's assets objectively, wondering how much they'd contributed. Two extended Masonic handshakes to him, and he put the rest down as Rotarians, or members of the Lions Club or the Round Table. Joiners and participators. Busy men.

"Yes I sail, but I'm thinking of changing to something lighter than the boat I have."

47

"Are you? Fred here's the one to get you discount. Motor?"

"Additionally."

Fred was a dealer, not in yachts, but knew a man who was. With expert casting, he threw out a bait or two, how big, how much being his game. Having established this, he went on to detail what was available in the price range, trying to pin him down. The others listened in and Innes, in spite of being used to monetary negotiation, found himself acutely embarrassed. His choices were wholly private so that he found discussion on what he might or might not buy too intimate for public airing. It was like being fitted for a pair of trousers in the open, and trousers off the peg as well.

"I bought a new sloop in the spring," said one man. "Cramond's my base. She's a bit temperamental, over-canvassed really. I'll have to change the rig."

Innes would have died rather than admit he couldn't manage and looked abashed for him.

Fred passed his business card over but to extricate himself from any commitment to using it, Innes said, "I may go for some designs of my own I've been working on."

They fell silent, knowing that there were no discounts to be had on a craft that was custom-built.

Innes was relieved when someone tapped him on the shoulder, forcing him out of the group, and turning round he found a man whose face he knew but could not put a name to. Then as soon as he spoke, the slightly falsetto voice reminded him of the schoolboy he knew better than the man, evoking his name at once.

"Come over here," said Andrew Mathieson. "It's quieter." He rolled his eyes a little, immediately conspiratorial. "Rowdy shower. What are you doing in this backwater? Oops. Beg your pardon. Maybe you live here."

"Yes I do." Relief forced him into a kind of amity. "It has its quieter side."

"You work in Edinburgh, though, don't you? Didn't someone say you had an antiques business up in town?"

"Yes, porcelain." Innes wondered who this someone was, fascinated by a bush telegraphy in which he did not transmit.

"I'm property. Jack Shaw's in property too, in a way." He hung a fraction of a second, then said, casting a baleful eye around, "Not quite like this. Anyway. Come and meet my new assistant, Judith. Been with me six months. One sharp lady."

Judith was the woman in watered silk, tall, cool and more

aloof than he had guessed, approximating to the style known as statuesque. Nor did she answer him in the accents he had projected, being English. He wondered two things about her. In what sense she had been with Andrew for six months, and wherein lay the acuity he ascribed to her. Sharp was one of Jack's words, sharp lad, sharp-witted only meaning quick and so a term of commendation. That inference stayed with sharp practice and sharp words, not hostile acts to those who could employ them.

She was gravely silent, speaking only when spoken to. Without explanation, the threesome gravitated towards supper in the marquee, eating ham and chicken to the accompaniment of easy melody and the ruffling of the pleated linings. The tent strained a little at the stay ropes, giving him the most unsettling feeling that they were out at sea.

"Porcelain," she said, pulling her head to one side. Her hair was shingled and the movement was incisive and considered in effect, rather than seductive. Possibly a trick of light, but her eyes changed too from blue to green as he watched their mood. "How very frangible."

"I warn against touching. But it often goes unheeded."

"It's insurable?"

"Oh yes."

"Well then," she breathed, "it's not like a contract for virtue."

She turned to the other people at their table easily, discussing the golf Open – held that year at Muirfield – the value of the pound against the dollar and the indigenous architecture of Scotland with equal interest. He was bemused by this social facility in women, talking to anyone about anything whereas men tended to talk about themselves and what they knew. Women did not particularise and had less talent in being themselves than in helping others to express what they were.

When the hostess came to check that they had everything they wanted, Judith succeeded in finding compliments without descending to the obsequious. Rosemary Shaw was well known. She was a local beauty queen at one time, Miss North Berwick graduating to Miss East of Scotland. She was a bonny woman still and listening to their voices rise and fall, he thought if he were inclined to covet any one of Jack's possessions, it might be his wife. Twenty years married to the same woman, kindly, companionable. Imagine that. He asked himself again however Jack Shaw managed it.

★　　　★　　　★

Midnight came and went, bringing a change of tide. It carried a warmer air inland and under its influence, restraint melted away. Men changed their partners, looking for what they had not had till then.

"Shall we dance?" he asked of Judith, feeling that was progress.

They circled at arm's length, talking rather than touching.

Her conversation was easy, like familiar music, placing no stress on his capacity for listening. She talked of Cowes and Henley and he of the regatta in North Berwick that weekend, so that he was not unconscious of the approximation in their interests. But what, he asked himself, did she know that he did not? What was her speciality? The word she used earlier in the evening, "frangible", teased him, carrying a hint of mockery. Frangible virtue. He puzzled again at what she was to Andrew, coming up against the ubiquitous assistant he described her as, but found himself dissatisfied with that maieutic precept.

Over her shoulder, he saw three heads together in a group with Jack's. It was warm now inside the tent for there was no ventilation. The sides billowed gently between hot and cooling draughts. One man mopped his face continually on a handkerchief as though he were exerted. There was some strenuous bargaining going on. They were closing on a deal and Innes was moved to wonder what Jack's affairs consisted of. Under what legend did these men carry on their business? Scrap-metal dealers offering to take job lots off each other's hands; so many thousand feet of copper tubing, uncut headstones, which were the stock of an undertaker who had died himself, the stuff of junkyards. He was appalled by the subcurrents of the black economy with money like the product of illicit stills, laundered assets. He feared the system of accounts that shifted income ahead of reckoning, elusive and undeclared, as well as the mentality that would not pay a bill until it was accompanied by the threat of legal action. Men who would rather pay a parking fine than put their coins into the meter and play safe. Chancers, chiselling a margin for themselves. It smacked of the haggling of market tradesmen, men holding a Dutch auction with their wares, not far removed from the hand-slapping of horse traders, a kind of fringe economy of barter in which he did not know the rules. Discount for cash demanded. No paper statements. Kiddology.

50

So the question hung in the air, charging it with excitement: Shall we trade? Shall we exchange commodities? It seemed the only form of social interchange that counted.

He remembered the security of knowledge as he acquired it piece by piece. Knowledge seemed important long ago, a credential which it was possible to present when all else failed. It did not always reside in facts but could be a knowledge of procedure, rules, etiquette, all social marshalling. It was a drill he went through every day as a boy, unconsciously, although he could remember when he was seven or eight years old being given a list of male and female nouns to learn. Fox, vixen and so on. Count, countess stayed with him as did marquis, marchioness, a distinction he had not once been required to use in nearly thirty years. So why on earth had someone thought it important enough to teach, or was it evidence of residual gender in English, a coccyx of language minimised by disuse, the tail end? Titles were eroded, like class and lineage of which they were a spurious reminder. Empty knowledge and empty honoraria. He could not recall the equivalent of earl and fretted at his ignorance. Countess surely, serving both masculines – even more absurd. He, the repository of antique formalisms, seemed as redundant as they. The niceties had gone for everything was buyable. Men boasted not of their father's or their own achievement in valour or skill, but of the size of their holdings. "Where is the newspaper? I haven't seen my shares today." Even men who should know better said it.

The marchioness and her consort seemed a century away. War had been added to the rift of generations, so that the strata which had lain predictably folded since he was a boy, started to break up. Another Ice Age covered the earth, creating fissures as the upward and downward layers grated past each other. Or a sea change. The fractional processes of continental drift suddenly speeded up so that in one man's lifetime, sea and land fused or broke out of their conventional form. He did not recognise the landscape any more.

He was tired. People on the floor slowed down to walking pace and he realised they had been dancing for an hour. Was his partner Andrew's mistress and if so, did Andrew care how long she spent in the arms of other men? He did not know, and even wanted to be free of the responsibility of knowing one way or the other. All he wanted was to lay his head on some breast, seeking an assurance of something non-tidal in the universe.

When he went outside, he saw that the dawn was starting to break. The light was fluid, blue and watery, heavily diluted, so that daylight rose by capillary attraction up the sky. He walked, breathing in the early morning, to the edge of the path where he could see down from the top of the cliff to the beach below. He stood for some time watching the tide come in, casting its flotsam on the shore, objects and people.

Chapter Six

Iona watched her father whittling wood. He took a length of dowelling, an offcut of four inches, and first with a gouge and then a chisel, pared out the innards like scooping the flesh from the inside of a grapefruit with a serrated spoon. The wood peeled away softly, curling onto the floor. When she picked the shavings up, they broke across the short and weakened grain, crumbling as easily as a dry leaf or the remains of a biscuit. They had a better smell, fresh rather than stale, reminding her of green and growing wood as though a residue of sap clung to the pulp whenever it was newly worked. Itself indelibly. To the last grain. The fragment did not break under her father's hands. He held the hollow tube delicately, as a surgeon would hold an artery. No pressure, only strength. With an incisor, he shaved a fold of wood between the upper and the lower chambers he had made.

Then passing it to her, he said, "Blow."

She put the funnel to her lips and blew. It made a noise. Her outgoing breath caught against the reed and vibrated it. A simple sound, but music. Seven made the pipes of Pan. "A whistle," she said, enchanted.

"Go and give it to Bruce. He'll like that."

They shared a workshop, one of the outhouses that had been a coalshed and so windowless. He dusted it and sealed the brickwork and put in a light and wall fire so that he could carry on with smaller pieces of work in his spare hours. A work bench, almost as worn and dented as a butcher's wooden slab, took up one corner. On the walls he put up racks to hold his tools, which were ancient but sharp as razor blades, so that there was a visual conflict between the handles, sweated from the palm of his hand, and the savage edge. Usage stained them; usefulness kept them sharp. Saws, hacksaws, adze, mitre cutter, claw-head and pin hammer, chisels by the dozen, hand drill and plane – the list was as endless as their function, each specialised to one task. He kept the small items in screw-top jars along his shelf, labelled carefully in infinite gradations. *Brass $\frac{1}{2}''$. Ovals. $\frac{3}{4}''$ tacks.*

She often handled these jars, turning them over and over, the way a child will roll a jar of sweets, watching the contents tumble. It enhanced the appetite, gladdened the eye. She thought of all the things he'd make. How many joints would this pot of Scotch glue strengthen? How many thousand blows could this hammer deliver before its head came loose? And even then, he'd go and buy another hickory shaft and fit it, driving it into place with cleats, tools constantly renewing themselves. What was ever thrown out, finally broken or wasted? Nothing. A piece of dowelling made a whistle. A handful of shavings started the fire.

She tried to imitate him, whittling wood with a knife like a boy's penknife or a worn Stanley blade he passed her. He wouldn't let her touch the working tools. But she found that it was disappointing stuff to carve. If she tried to make a shape out of it, any shape, the grain deflected the knife from where she wanted it to go. It sheered off at an angle so that she ended up with chippings and an object like a totem pole, faceted with cuts and somehow clumsy, inelegant. She wondered what skill it was that made her father's blunt-ended fingers so nimble round wood as she watched him do the impossible, bend pieces in a vice, joint them so they never came apart in angles that were as strong as growth, or made the warped straight again.

She did not have it anyway, that skill, finding carpentry too slow and too precise. Meaningful only if you knew what you wanted to make but not expressive in itself. A craft and not an art.

The granular feel of sandcastles came to mind, reminiscent of plasticity. The ability to build up rather than the breaking down implied by woodwork, appealed to her. She kneaded putty till she extracted the smell of linseed on her fingers, rolled soft candlewax into a ball and fashioned it round melted drops of wax crayon. Preparatory play. She moulded plasticine and modelling clay and papier mâché with the younger children, and a flour-and-water paste her mother made up. But this went smelly after a time and grew fungus. Besides, it was too glutinous in handling and made her feel she was making pastry for the oven instead of objects.

So she dabbled, rolling and stamping out, painting colours on sun-hard artefacts but was not satisfied, longing still to dig and build large structures that would stand.

He watched out for Iona at the station.

No wonder he hadn't recognised her before. She was wearing uniform, the extraordinary regulation that put girls into shirt and tie and blazer, pseudo-men. The features which in normal circumstances he might have known her by were hidden, the streaked hair went under a hat and the feet were encased in sensible brogues that would have made short work of the Matterhorn.

They smiled, Monday-morning strange.

"How are you?"

"I'm fine."

The interchange could not do them justice, snatched as it was between arrivals and departures.

When her friends came up, the half dozen from her own and other schools who travelled up each day to the city, they moved apart on the platform, unconsciously, and he went to sit in the first-class compartment by himself.

The train which he regularly joined came up from Berwick and most mornings was quiet, so he had developed the habit of reading his letters and making notes for a reply that evening. He had a large volume of correspondence for a private individual. A dozen letters a day were not uncommon. The magazines he wrote for and other specialists kept up a cross-current of notes about new finds, new facts, losses and damages so that there was a body of privately held information about the state of the market or the likely effect of the sale of a major collection, which took a couple of years to find its way into print. Catalogues were always out of date and that was why he supplemented his own with notes. "Destroyed by fire." "Later than previously supposed." "Part of the theft from the house – unrecovered." And then in time, even the notes were updated.

Some mornings the train would be unaccountably full and he would find he had to share a compartment with some busy stranger, or worse, a busy acquaintance who stopped him from getting on with what he was doing. Talking. Asking. Passing the time of day. Dreadful imposition it was, thinking other people wanted to chat or hear you chat over the aisle about the weather or the timetable or whatever else obsessed the British mind, delighting in the attempt to change the unchangeable.

One morning he was thoroughly put out to discover there was an invasion on the 8.13, heading towards the Ideal Home Exhibition at the Waverley. He tried to imagine how much would be ideal there. The latest plastics. Resins and bonding agents fused to look like every other substance, superb in ersatz. Wipe-clean. Scratch-resistant. Wears and wears. And looks shoddy all the time it's trying to be everlasting. Longevity was more important. They'd even be making plastic figurines soon, turning them out by the million so that every home in the land could have a collection in a glass cabinet. He saw his shepherdess pressed out in moulds, just like the original.

Well, the train was packed with these enthusiasts for the unbreakable and the new and the altogether ideal, so that the only seat he could see in the first-class carriage was beside a rather heavy-jowled and heavy-drinking man from the yacht club, the pleasure of whose company he normally avoided. He walked on and found no other place by the end of the carriage.

He stood by the connecting door and chose the lesser evil, electing, much against his principles when he had paid for a first-class season ticket, to rub shoulders with the commoners.

He found a seat just inside the door and buried himself in paperwork. But it was noisy. Laughter, albeit suppressed, kept interrupting the sentences and after a while he looked up to find who was making such a din. There was a group of schoolchildren, boys and girls, in the next section of the open carriage and they were involved in the sort of hearty horseplay that was thoroughly irritating to anyone adult, without being offensive.

He stood up to deliver a reproof but the second he got to his feet, he realised that Iona Stewart was one of the group, sitting on the opposite side of the corridor but attached, if somewhat loosely, to her contemporaries across the way. He compressed his lips. He didn't want to embarrass her or put her in a difficult position, so he responded with a nod to the smile she gave him and made his standing up logical by taking off his jacket and folding it into the luggage rack overhead.

Sitting down again, he found himself listening to the bursts of dialogue that came over the backs of the seats, waiting to hear what she said in amongst it all.

They seemed to be playing some sort of game with questions and answers and then gradually, he remembered the rules. Each person in the group was asked "Truth, dare or promise" and was free to elect his own undertaking. The individual who had previously performed or answered, sometimes nothing more outrageous than going to open and shut the carriage door, had the task of selecting a suitable challenge.

"What did you really do with Barry Shaw on the top of North Berwick Law on Sunday afternoon?"

The questions often drew more hilarity than the answers, even if Barry Shaw were present to protest about the allegations made indirectly against him. One of the girls replied simply, with a number, and Innes guessed that there was a scale of demarkation of physical intimacy known within the group and, judging by the shout of laughter, that the girl had indicated a point fairly far along it.

He glanced at Iona.

She was looking sideways out of the window to her right. It was a look of dissociation from them and their goings-on, their silly boasting about things they either hadn't done or, if they had, were much too personal to air. He thought she flushed a little.

He dropped his eyes back to the letter, but he could tell that she was watching him in the reflection of the windowpane at her side. He had a kind of double focus which enabled him ostensibly to read by looking down, but at the same time he could spread his sight and glimpse in the outer cone of vision, her face leaning on her hand to contemplate him.

She was in a state of high anxiety as her turn drew near. What if someone had seen them together that weekend, and a daredevil asked, "What did you really do with Innes Hamilton on his boat one Sunday afternoon?" There were a dozen slighting inferences her peers could make about the encounter and she knew they were unscrupulous enough to make them.

He listened to the raw young voices and noticed how quiet she was. Not a syllable since he sat down, for she was tense and nervous waiting for her friends to shame her.

He saw her move, shadowed in the cornea.

She leaned down and opened up her bag of books.

"What are you doing, Iona?" a companion asked.

"I've got a test on these French verbs."

"But it's your turn next."

"Well, I can't help it. I wasn't really playing, only listening. I haven't done my homework."

It was a lie, he knew.

"You've always got your nose in a book," someone complained.

"Come on, Iona. You're a real spoilsport. You never play the game."

But in spite of the abuse, Iona stuck doggedly to her text and did not look up at him or them.

The town banked up in layers for exploration. The beach she knew already and left behind with childhood and the turn-around in the weather. The streets were more diverse, a sample of geological rock split open so that she could trace the history of its evolution. Not decay. She sensed the earth did not decay substantially, but renewed itself by tidal and organic interaction. The disasters of earthquake or volcanic movement weren't simple, primitive concepts like stars falling from the sky, herald-ing the end of the world, but a revitalising mechanism of change. Green shoots sprouted after a bush fire, fed by its ash; floods carried a fertile silt across the fields; rainbows followed storms, optimistic of more than good weather. How could the universe be static when its elements, earth, air, fire and water were the stuff of mobility?

Cooled, like old lava, the houses lay along the water's edge. She wandered round the stones noting the strata of their form, boulders making a rubblework, slates, proud quoins, or dressed sandstone from a quarry. Their colours were the fabric of the earth, ochre, pinkish red, grey, with a dusting of limestone like a wash. At its best, paint imitated the natural so that the town flowed out of its setting to the sea, tuff, sill and laccolite in sediment, the whole harmonious.

She walked, picking up ideas like pebbles, feeling and admir-ing and putting back again though a knowledge of them stayed with her, for it was acquired first-hand.

The faces of the people that she passed projected from their houses like human gargoyles, but less grotesquely caricatured. True, they carried their vices on display, sharp-featured, prim, ogle-eyed like buildings, but they wore their virtues equally. Wandering alone among them, she was not short of company. She was almost blind to manners or status in the populace, ignoring types in favour of individuals. The old or the careworn or the eccentric embodied more vitality than the self-consciously good, and certainly than the good-looking. She looked for some upheaval in the face that left a cragging, visible weather, people hewn out of their lives and surviving it. Sometimes she thought it would be good to photograph or paint them, but knew they deserved more than the two dimensions. Substance! But what was it?

The winter wore away. He saw her occasionally on the station platform in the morning but never of course in the evening, for she came back two or three hours before he did. The chance meetings which had been almost daily in the summer, on the beach, round the harbour in the long evenings, disappeared with it. He did not have to join her carriage again and was relieved at that.

Normally, he walked to the station and back but after Christmas the weather turned very wet and having been soaked from the knee down three times in one week, for gales made an umbrella superfluous if not an added impediment, he decided he would have to use the car and leave it parked in the station forecourt during the day. If he happened to pass Iona en route, and she were unaccompanied, he gave her a lift but it was such a short distance that hello and goodbye were consequent upon each other.

One morning he leaned over the passenger seat to open the door for her.

"I'm going into Edinburgh," he said.

She had sat down, glad to be out of the rain, before she took in what this meant. "You mean driving all the way?"

"Yes. That's right." He started the engine up again. "I'll need the car this evening."

"I see."

"Would you rather go by train? I'll drop you off if you like or you can come with me. Whichever you prefer."

"Do you mind if I stay?"

"No, of course not. But I like listening to the news headlines at this time." He switched on the radio and found the wave band. "It puts me in a bad mood for the rest of the day."

When the news items finished, he kept it tuned to that frequency and whatever it was seemed to alleviate the bad mood. It was classical music, though she had no idea what. Orchestral music, "horrible scraping" as her brother called it. Whenever it

59

came out of their radio at home, it was immediately switched off. Words with music were acceptable, made sense. Music alone was meaningless.

Again she had the agonising proof of her own irrelevance. He was lost in something she couldn't share. A bit of her did think it was horrible scraping, though she was wise enough not to say so. If her seat were vacant, he would be driving on through the rain past Gullane and Longniddry and Prestonpans absorbed in his music, immune to human emptiness.

She was tormented by another thought. He was staying up for the evening. The instant he said it, she wanted to ask, Oh where are you going? But the boundaries between wanting to ask and being in a position to ask were very clearly defined. She was a child he was doing a favour by giving a lift out of a damp and dreary morning. He was an adult pursuing his own life. Interrogations, questions of equality were out of place.

So where was he going, she asked herself instead.

Somewhere which meant he needed the car. There was a dove-grey suit on a hanger draped over the back seat and a shirt likewise. A small case. She read them correctly. He was going out to dinner and she presumed he wasn't going alone. She saw the kind of woman who would put her hand in the crook of his elbow and felt the hopeless impotence of the young. The woman would be smart and expensive, somehow. She didn't quite know in what this expensiveness lay, but her bag and shoes would match and she would have been to the hairdresser's that day in preparation, and the perfume she wore had a French name and came in a bottle with a ground stopper, too dear to waste a drop. Everything about her would be perfect, like a model, and he might well be tempted to stay overnight.

Her eyes filled with unaccountable tears.

Why shouldn't he have girlfriends, lovers? Why shouldn't he spend the weekend with them? It was absolutely none of her business what he did with himself.

But she railed silently against her uniform and her youth and her poverty – all the things which disguised what she might be.

At the end of the piece, he switched the radio off and turned round, surprised to see her eyes swimming with emotion.

"Do you know the Bach?" Perhaps it had some special significance for her that moved her more than other pieces.

"No. I don't know this music. I've never heard it before. Do

60

you often listen to it?"

"Yes, I listen a good deal. In the evening. In the car."

"They're all different, are they? I mean, you know these tunes?"

"Well, I wouldn't call them tunes, but yes I know them."

She measured the enormity of her own ignorance. "What makes them different then?"

He smiled. A crash course in harmonics? "The way the notes fall."

"But I can't hear it. They all sound the same to me."

"You just need to keep listening, that's all. If you like it. You're not compelled to like it if you don't want to. Do you like it, a little?"

"A little."

"Well, that's enough to build on."

"Can you tell who wrote them?"

"One composer from another? Broadly, yes, among the better-known composers. I'm not an expert but I can tell Mozart from Bach."

"And recognise a few bars on their own?"

"Yes, I expect I could."

"But how?"

"Because I know."

"But how do you know? Can't you tell me that?"

"No, I can't tell you that. You will have to learn it for yourself. But I can tell you where to find good music. Play your own radio. Do you have a radio of your own?"

"No." She felt that if he thought she should have one, automatically, then it was a serious omission. "There's one downstairs. It's a bit ancient."

"None the worse for that. It probably has very fine tuning. But it's better to have one of your own. Make a note of what you like. Listen seriously. Go to the Usher Hall when they're playing a classical repertoire. Beethoven."

"Beethoven. That's the best, is it?"

"A good many people think so. But you don't have to. You can listen and make up your own mind."

She sat taking all this in with an avidness he couldn't possibly appreciate. It was true it only began to matter to her because it mattered to him and so the first impulse was in effect towards acquisition. Give me what you have. Though she could see the truth of what he implied. She was going to have to work at it, put in years of experience if she was to understand what was happening behind the notes and that was a frustrating proposition to the young. She wanted it now, ready-packaged for her. So she was slightly disgruntled that he was already in possession of this valuable knowledge, this expertise which seemed important because so many people thought so, because a whole radio channel was devoted to sending it down the air waves seventeen hours a day, and which she couldn't for the life of her grasp the significance of.

She enrolled for an evening class in pottery. More advanced students were already engaged on working at the half-dozen wheels and so to keep her busy and out of the way, the teacher showed her the principles of Stone Age pottery, in coil and slab construction.

She rolled out pieces of clay in graduated lengths and placed them on top of each other. Then she smoothed the joins she made, inside and out, by vigorous pressure with her fingers and finally, with a flattened tool, tried to repair the knobbly effect left by her fingermarks. What she turned out was indescribably ugly, a lump with a hole inside. A kind of hollow, faceless totem pole with even less function, and no magical properties whatever. She fired and glazed it and pretended it was an umbrella stand. It was all too reminiscent of the plasticine, but it did inculcate a new respect for the Etruscans, the Beaker people, the tribes in Africa who could dig their own clay out of the ground and fashion pots with it that were not only symmetrical, but strong and functional and handsome. Museum pieces took on a new life she could not have imbued them with.

She fared better on the wheel.

Instinctively, she was able to centre the ball of clay so that she was spared the frustration of chasing it back into position time after time. The moment she perceived her hands as shaping tools, capable of notation as delicate as pianists', her skill was born and the excitement at the medium's range mounted with her ability to realise it. The clay which in the prehistoric coil had remained lumpen, became fluid and articulate. It rose and widened and narrowed again like chords of music, swelling under her impulse. The most fragmentary pressure of a thumb produced a radical alteration in the outline and she played for hours reducing and expanding the mass, feeling the element between her fingers.

It was pleasing to decorate, rippling a line up the side like sand bars on the shore. She liked to fettle the base with a tool, peeling off shreds of excess clay and perhaps best of all, to carve it when it was leather-hard and obedient, in a definitive stage between soft and hard, gouging out patterns in a surface she had worked on so long to make smooth.

She came closer and closer to creation. Not pots, no. She was not interested in pots. She enjoyed the process but gave nothing for the end product. She was inspired by the substance that came out of the kiln and had survived its shocks. Shrunken, tough, engraved with patterns by exposure to the heat which no one could have foreseen before the firing: blisters, bloating, cracks, colours magnified out of all recognition from the dull powders dusted on it. It was a wonder. She rushed to be present at each week's unpacking of the furnace, and was desolate if something had exploded. She rolled the pieces over and over in her hands, hers or anybody's, it didn't matter. The format of uniqueness was the same. The processes were mimetic of creation. By the application of fire in the kiln, water and air were driven out of the clay so that the residue was a ball of rock, reshaped in an artistic mould. A vase, a ewer, a pot or statue was only decorative earth and she rotated each, marvelling as she would have done at a new planet, a fresh universe washed with its idiomatic colourings.

The clay once it was fired was breakable, but indestructible. It would not burn, or dissolve, or oxidise to rust or verdigris. A fragment would not deteriorate however long it stayed in the ground. Roman pottery could be picked out of the nearby fields every day, its terra cotta as fresh as when it was broken. It could be ground down to a grog, a silver sand, but it never ceased to be, even in powder, its own element. It was the earth from which it came.

63

Chapter Seven

Judith wrote in confidence to her sister who was on a year's sabbatical to Berkeley, University of California.

Yes, you're right. There is a new man in my life and yes, I've been pretty mum about him. But don't get carried away. I haven't. The reason I've kept quiet is that there isn't much to tell and what there is, isn't very definite.

Innes Hamilton, mid-thirties, antique dealer who specialises in figurines (not my sort of thing, but there you are). Goes sailing. Probably good at it, just because he doesn't push it. The kind of man you could know for ten years before someone else told you he had an Olympic Gold for single-handed racing. Fancy him? Well hands off. So do I.

I met him when I'd been up here about six months and was frankly dying of boredom and manlessness. Decamping to get away from one man is all very well in theory, but leaves a vacuum in practice. Andrew Mathieson, the local boss and very good – if anyone can sell time-sharing to the Scots, it's him – took me to a deathly party held by some distant business contact. You've met the type. Passes out a card accompanied by an invitation to keep numbers up the very first time he meets you. Goes for quantity over quality. Anyway, Innes was there. Andrew was at school with him. Everyone went to school with everyone else up here. It's quite weird. I thought the old school tie was an exclusively English phenomenon. Don't you believe it. There are about half a dozen Scottish schools which "count" and you just need to say "Fettes 1967" and you're away. The names come rolling out. I have never been anywhere socially where this hasn't happened.

So Andrew knew him but doesn't like him, though he's too restrained to say so. Innes is not the sort of man men like. They admire him. They envy him. But they don't make pals with him.

He isn't easy company because he turns to women on instinct, photokinetic. A week later we met by accident at an auction in the Assembly Rooms, with Innes as the expert in residence. Keeping an eye open for anything tempting. A group of us went on to dinner and back to Andrew's. (You should see that. His lounge is literally a ballroom, tacked on to a small house because someone took a notion to it. You get some very strange aesthetic surprises up here.) It turned into one of those disarmingly easy encounters when you talk and drift apart and talk again and think nothing of it until you realise he's been working away at everything you said, putting things together and making pretty clever deductions. That always knocks me out.

We did a lot of theatre-going during the Festival, some cinema, a bit of concert attendance at the Usher Hall – he varies it nicely so to speak – but to be frank, there's less going on than in an average week in London's West End, so it's difficult to get carried away on a cultural high. I kept searching for something Scottish, but found the vernacular is an acquired taste. There's some good film-making I'll head you towards when you get back. He's also got a very good line in restaurants, one up on London for sheer quality I think.

At first I had my doubts about him.

How does a man get to that age without being married to someone somewhere along the way? Only if he's downright peculiar.

He must be queer. Relax. I disproved that one fairly rapidly.

Or he's divorced or separated and so recently he can't talk about it. He does have that disconcerting air of having someone on his mind and I thought any evening now I'm going to have the whole lot dumped on me. How he still loves his ex-wife. Why it went sour. What a bore, as though you can possibly be interested in someone else's sexual travelogues. I mean the most you can say is "I climbed Mount Etna too." Swapping snapshots of bare bodies. Nothing is as dull as celluloid sex.

Then gradually, when this didn't happen and it became clear he never has been married and if he once came close, wouldn't talk about it, I began to realise he was in a worse condition, and so was I. He is just ultra ultra choosy. He is maybe in love with that she-devil that haunts us all, the perfect woman. Have you met more than ten men who aren't? All those books and plays and paintings that are devoted to her. "Age cannot wither her

66

nor custom stale her infinite variety." Lucky old Shakespeare, not to mention Antony. But put in "him" instead of "her" and it's suddenly laughable. A real sexist giveaway. He can grow old and wither and usually does, but she mustn't. Women can come to terms with reality and real ageing, but men can't. I'd like to think that perfect woman gives back a grain of comfort in return for all the attention lavished on her. But I don't think so. She simply taunts and disappears.

Anyway, I keep these hard-nosed feminist opinions to myself in front of him. I'm too glad to have found him. He is utterly couth and there are not so many of them knocking about spare.

I suppose I find him rather enigmatic. He walks around like a king in exile. You feel he's just lost a throne, Edward Windsor or Charles Edward Stuart, but you're not going to get him to admit he made a mistake or that he's sorry for anything. Part of this is that he's moved into my life – we use this flat, dot about Edinburgh doing touristy things but in an offbeat way, he knows everything there is to know about my office and the trials of being a property agent for people who're canny with their cash – but I am kept firmly out of his.

One day I suggested picking him up at his shop in the Grassmarket before we went on to lunch but that was given a very sharp frost. Out of interest, I went down after closing time to see if it really was such a dump. Well it wasn't. It was pure Mayfair in style, but stone-built and solid, if you can reconcile the two. But I was definitely to keep out of that scene. He goes yachting each weekend and though my sea legs aren't all that shaky I haven't been asked along. That is private territory. The lone yachtsman. And the house he has in North Berwick sounds most unusual from the snippets I hang on to, the way you do to rock ledges trying to get a foothold, and he keeps promising to invite me down to see it – and never does.

So I don't know what to make of him.

He's the only man I know who makes love by willpower. He doesn't go in for much touching. A lot of looking, as though the eye were his most erogenous zone. And if ever I touch him, he very gently moves me on. Noli me tangere. I feel somehow compelled, seduced by hypnosis. Talking about it would be off limits. Not that there's much need to talk about it. Easily Olympic Gold. But I feel so many of the areas of people contact are missing. He's the kind of person who would get up in the middle of the night and drive the twenty-five miles home, rather than see you in the raw the following morning. He doesn't want to see me, and certainly doesn't want to be seen himself at less-than-best. It might give sympathetic access to his body or his state of mind. That's what I mean about being choosy.

I never make him laugh and hardly ever make him smile and think I'm a bloody fool for wanting to. And sometimes I do get generally disgruntled at the way things are done nowadays. The inevitable assumptions. Sex as a nightcap and you're the odd one out if you're teetotal.

Oh I don't know what I'm complaining about. He's smooth. Old malt. Distilled. What better to go to bed on.

Chapter Eight

One evening, about a year after the Stewarts had moved in, Innes Hamilton sat under a lamp with the books and catalogues spread out around him, balanced on the seats of chairs and armrests so that he didn't have too far to stretch to reach them. The corners of used envelopes, cut into quadrants, marked the pages he wanted to consult and on his notepad was a growing list of references he had confirmed.

The door bell rang. He cursed the interruption, making him lose his place. Some charity worker coming to shake her poor box at him. He dug into his trouser pocket for change on the way down the corridor and had the coins at the ready when he opened the door.

But it wasn't Alexandra Rose Day or the RNLI that had come to lift him out of his chair. Iona Stewart stood on the doorstep, fearful, ready to take off if he looked forbidding.

The heavier frown was on her forehead, however, so he opened the door wide and let her come inside to deliver her message.

"I'm so sorry, Mr Hamilton. I shouldn't bother you, but I've forgotten to bring my atlas home and I wondered if you had one I could borrow. The library's shut, otherwise I'd have gone there."

Good God, her mother would be coming to borrow cups of sugar next.

"I suppose so." He gave in with ill grace. "I think it's through here." She followed him into the sitting room where he was working and glancing round at the open books, realised what a disturbance she had made.

"Oh I'm sorry. I interrupted you."

"That's all right," he said grudgingly. "They'll still be here when you've gone." He searched along the bookcases and found an atlas, found three in fact, and gave her the most up to date.

"What a very peculiar room," she blurted out. "I mean peculiar interesting," she modified it. "I've never seen a room quite like this."

The room did tend to have this effect on visitors. He had thought it rather splendid and uncompromising until the minister's wife considered, over afternoon tea, that it would make a good Eventide Home. He had a certain degree of humour prepared for her reaction. "Oh? And why is it peculiar interesting?" He sat down to enjoy her discomfiture as she wriggled her way out of the thoughtlessly expressed opinion. "I'm very fond of it, so be careful you don't offend me."

"Well, yes it is."

"Is what?"

"The sort of room you get fond of. It's these pillars. I didn't know you could have pillars inside a house."

"What's wrong with them?"

"Nothing. I just didn't expect to see them."

"Pink Carrara marble. Considered very fine."

"And the panelling." It ran up the walls to within a foot of the ceiling, and from there the stuccowork was covered in medallions.

"That's dingy and forbidding, is it?"

"No, I don't dislike it, but it takes a bit of getting used to." She walked round the room, gingerly, careful not to disturb or knock anything. It amused him to watch her, like putting an animal into a new cage, seeing the way it nosed out the corners, measured the floor, ran backwards and forwards until it felt comfortable in the place. She settled eventually by one of the windows. "That's your dining room over there, is it?" She looked over the room, through glazed panels that illuminated the flanks of the central corridor and across the other side to his second public room.

"Yes."

"What a very funny house you have."

"So I've been told."

And then to his complete surprise she said, "It isn't a Scottish house at all. It's the least Scottish house I've ever seen."

"No? Well what is it then?"

"It's Italianate, isn't it? The wrought-iron work outside, and the pillars and all the glass. I mean that balcony is a bit optimistic in this climate, don't you think? And," she measured the distance with her eye, "isn't that a terrazzo outside the dining room?"

He was so absolutely staggered by this précis of his residence that he got up from his cynical detachment and opened the glass door for her. "Shall we?" Everyone who had visited the house called it a courtyard, or a patio if that was their inclination. But it was indeed a terrazzo, intended as a cool spot out of the sun, a descendant of the Roman atrium and he had furnished it as such. Urns with winter-flowering evergreens, a marble bust that took kindly to weathering while a bronze frieze – a modern replica he had picked up in a junkyard, not the real thing at all – was hung along one side.

"What a shame you have no fountain."

"What a shame," he reiterated. "You're quite right. The house is a misnomer. It's a miniature Duke's palace. I suppose some Victorian went on his Grand Tour to Milan and Florence and Venice, and came back fired with enthusiasm for the ornamental way of life. But as you say, rather optimistic in the Scottish climate."

"The panelling is odd. It doesn't fit. I wonder if it was added later, when he found out how chill the east wind blew."

He laughed out loud at this view of the traveller disillusioned. "Yes. I never thought of that. Do you want to see the rest of it?"

Going through the dining room again, she paused by the two alcoves on the far wall. They stood empty, although if he were dining formally he would decorate them with wine bottles and a stand of fruit. At the moment they were a void her eye filled. "Two figures. White," she said, "so high." And between her hands she defined eighteen inches.

"What do you suggest?"

"Apollo and Daphne," she answered at once.

"Apollo and Daphne it shall be."

He took her into the kitchen and then up the back stairs, explaining, "These were the servants' quarters. It's an incredibly wasteful house. Two public rooms, two family bedrooms and the rest is for the servants. So much space isn't being used. Half of the floor area is taken up with corridors and the terrace and the long passage to the High Street. Two staircases in a house this size. I ask you. He certainly had inflated ideas, whoever he was." They came back along the top corridor and she looked out onto the flagged yard from above. "Isn't this landing crazy. You could fit another suite of rooms in here."

"Yes, but it's rather gracious," she considered, sitting down beside a Davenport desk.

She landed on the right word and he was pleased with it. He found a chair against the opposite wall and sat down too. "How did you know it was Italian? Have you been to Italy?"

"No. I haven't been to Italy. I haven't been to anywhere. We've been studying the Renaissance in art. I've got to take a paper in architecture and I happened to be looking at something like this the other day."

"I see. How fortuitous."

The evening grew darker, enclosing them, but their books and separate occupations were forgotten.

"You live here all by yourself," she said as a statement, and one that puzzled her.

"Yes, I live here all by myself."

"But you've so many rooms, don't you get lost?"

"I've generally found myself by the morning again."

Looking up to smile, she caught sight of the statue of the shepherdess which he'd moved upstairs to the landing so that he could see it from all angles, on top of a torchère, every time he passed. He waited almost tensely to hear what she would say about it. Hers were the first eyes that had lighted on it during a year's habitation in his house.

She put her hand out instinctively, but knew better than to touch it. She said nothing. She got up and walked round it, emitting just one note. "Aaah." It was a raw sound, admiration converted into energy. It was the sigh of aesthetic gratification. It had a lust in it.

"You won't sell this?"

"No. She's not for sale."

She paused, appreciating his terms of value. "I wish that I were you."

"To have the things I have? They're not so difficult to come by."

"No. To be – you," she said with emphasis.

"Why? Why would you want to change places with anyone? You only want to be me in some ways. Not in all ways."

She could not disagree but listening to the silence of the house as night fell, specified one of his advantages. "How quiet it is here."

"Yes, it's quiet. I live the life of the mind."

The phrase exploded in her brain. A door flew open and showed her landscapes that paled into a distance of unattainability. That was it. He'd said it. The life of the mind. How admirable. How impossible for her. No peace. No solitude. No power of uninterrupted reflection. No radio for companionship. Just noisy layers of people.

"What were you writing downstairs?" She came and sat down again, though the corner was so shaded she was almost in the dark. Whether she sat or stood should have been immaterial, but her presence radiated in the gloom and he turned towards her.

"An introduction for a book on porcelain someone wants me to put together."

"Oh. And are you enjoying it?"

This was such a direct and unusual question that he floundered for a moment trying to answer it, and yet it was perhaps the only question that mattered. "It's different from my normal writing. Very general. It's not for a specialist book at all but more the coffee-table variety." There was no coffee table in the Stewart household and no coffee, so the phrase was lost on her. "I enjoy finding out. I don't know if I enjoy putting it down very much. I'm not a true scholar. He wants to impart. I just want to learn."

"And what are you finding out?"

"Nothing I didn't know already, or know by inference. I'm trying to sort out the various attempts to discover the secret of porcelain. Very interesting stuff, porcelain. It was first brought back to Europe by Marco Polo when he returned from China. It was he who called it 'porcelaine' which means 'seashell' or 'mother-of-pearl'. The Chinese bowls he brought with him were so highly prized they were set in gold mounts and studded with jewels, more precious than the gemstones used to embellish them. But when they tried to imitate the substance themselves, the Venetians and potters in Tuscany couldn't come up with the formula. It took nearly two hundred years of experiment in France and Germany and England before anyone landed on something close."

"Why did it matter so much?"

"They thought so highly of it that whoever discovered the secret had immediate power, and wealth. They searched for the secret of true porcelain as avidly as those mediaeval alchemists who believed in the philosopher's stone. It would transmute base metal into gold. Patents taken out, formulae guarded. All sorts

73

of industrial espionage going on as one factory tried to prevent its workers leaving for another. Secrets dying out with men who wouldn't pass them on or write them down. Quite unbelievable."

"And who found it in the end?"

"Maybe the Dresden factory about 1710. It's hard to tell because there were so many experiments. Porcelain is made up of two substances. A kind of clay and a stone, called kaolin and petuntse. You have to have them in the correct proportion and then they have to be fired at the right temperature. The kaolin is the more refractory of the two and it holds the vessel in shape during the firing, while the fusion of the petuntse takes place. Too cool it doesn't fuse. Too hot and it melts. Then you're left with a vitreous pool on the floor of the kiln. There were hundreds of near misses. Imitations. Soft-paste, majolica, faience – things that came close but didn't have the translucency."

"And is that what makes it special, being translucent?"

"Yes. The balance of lightness and strength. It's a substance that never ages, never wears out. Designs date. Bad glazes crack but porcelain, if it is well fired, is immortal."

He had come to the end, that is to the real point, and she respected the fact that he could go no further. She listened to his version of events, his formula for perfection, with some awe. It was an alternative gospel to her own, in which the distinctions confirmed her personal belief. He was interested in the origin of the substance, its scholarly history and the end product, resident in his sleeping shepherdess. She was involved with the inter-mediary making. But she did not dare to confess to him the clay, earthenware pots she threw, far less the umbrella stand, in case he found it laughable. Whatever she turned out was clumsy and inept compared with the objects he revered. Timeless and priceless were concepts that existed out of her sphere, and so she was silently inhibited by the grandeur he threw over their commonalities.

"Can I read it when it's finished?"

"That'll be never at this rate." He stretched out his hands over his knees. "Yes, of course you may."

They got to their feet to go downstairs.

As she went past the statue on its pedestal, she asked, "Who do you think the little boy is?"

74

"I don't know. I never thought about him. A young shepherd?"

"Oh, he's too small to be any use," she answered in the practical terms he overlooked. "Her brother maybe?"

"What about their son?"

"Oh, do you think they're married? She doesn't have a ring."

"You don't need to be married to have a child."

She faltered at his gravity. "The child of the imagination? I think it's Cupid."

"In the middle of the pastoral?" he ridiculed.

"Why not? It's all make-believe, or allegory if you like. Why can't you mix allegories?"

She found the atlas again, very nearly forgotten, and he saw her out. She clutched the book over her chest, arms doubled. "Thank you so much, Mr Hamilton."

"Call me Innes. Mr Hamilton makes me feel like a head-master." He followed her out a step or two over the paving stones, as if pressing for a change in his status with her.

"Innes, then," she obeyed.

He sat down again in the position from which she had roused him two hours before. It was quite dark and he had to put more lights on to see by, and pulled the curtains. But though the books lay in exactly the same position, he found the thread of concentration was lost and he glanced at the pages distantly. He felt distracted and looked about him for the reason why. A perfume hung in the air, assailing his senses. Not manufactured perfume in a bottle. Skin perfume. It was the smell of verbena or lemon-scented soap. Clean. Fresh. It reminded him of the daily washing of the tide, coming up and receding over the shore.

Chapter Nine

Borrowing the book was a pretext, albeit a genuine one. She had yearned to see the inside of his house, as curious as Innes was himself about Jack Shaw, convinced that seeing how someone lived exposed how he thought as well. She was rewarded by the spectacle. The strange layout of the rooms was the pattern of himself, not to be guessed at from exteriors. Beautiful, secretive, they haunted her because they were so close, through the partition of a ten-inch wall, but were at the same time the inverse of her own setting. Cameo and intaglio. All they had in common was oppositeness.

It was not that the house she returned to was ugly. She would have been mightily offended to hear the epithet Innes had applied to their furniture as it emerged from the removal van. Jim was too knowledgeable about his craft to put money into badly jointed wood; it was not shoddy, only unfashionable. The carpet in their hall was Chinese – at one time – but worn almost to its backing. Maggie was a natural magpie and delighted to tell how she had scavenged things from other people's rubbish bins. An antique typewriter on a wooden base, an oak side table, oddments scoured from jumble sales. She was proud to say it cost a few pence and better still if it cost nothing. Innes did not admit the terrazzo frieze came from a junkyard, but inflated its value with discretion.

Because there was no mystery and no pretence, her own home held no glamour for Iona. She was repeatedly disappointed by its shabbiness, its worn familiarity. She despaired about the fingermarks that appeared round door handles, indeed along any exposed wall two feet from the wainscot, as children patted their way around. Maggie, blind to niceties, let them accumulate between her twin purges which fell not at other people's spring-cleaning or autumn clearance, but at midsummer and before New Year when she exorcised the demon dirt from her household, for she was superstitious about new beginnings.

Iona did not criticise the lapses. There was no point.

She watched her mother with a new intensity, both fond and distant. The bearer of six children, she retained the features of a child herself with an unblemished skin and a clear eye. This was her face at forty. It would be the same at seventy, flawless like her nature. Recreating many childhoods, she had not had the opportunity to mature herself. Iona often felt the senior. She was a simple woman. A century before she would have been called a peasant, her family crofters on the Western Isles, nor was she ashamed of her own stock. She spoke of the Clearances as though they'd happened yesterday and the Duke of Argyll a personal enemy for investing in sheep instead of people, but for whom she would nevertheless intercede on Sundays.

The house was the work of the woman. As soon as you walked in the door, you felt her, and indeed Iona could not remember a time when she was absent. They were even born at home. Every object had passed through her hands and was the product of her effort. Watching her work, Iona was reminded of the clay that moulded to her pressure and saw how her mother shaped them up, daily, daily, with infinite labour.

She saw her mother in snatches, in vignettes. She was incapable of constants of perception when she was in a state of change herself. The child in her loved the unaffected woman and the unhurried routines of which she was a product; the adult was exasperated by them. Sometimes she wanted to sit down with a piece of paper and draw up a schedule. This is how it should be done. This is how to organise them. Maggie complained about the trails of sawdust that followed Jim around the house. The solution was easy. Make him take his outdoor shoes off and change from his workclothes. To the suggestion, Maggie would smile and say, "But he's comfortable as he is." Logic was not enforceable.

She laboured to excess over some things, leaving no time for others. She imposed a system in one corner of the room, oblivious of the fact that chaos maintained in the other three.

A pile of washing accumulated by the machine every morning, swamping her. It claimed some part of every day, wash, dry and iron in a cycle of renewal, the clothes arriving only briefly at their destination before they started on the journey once again. All the same, she liked the job of sorting. Washing as art, and indeed the piles of clothes when she had finished with them were beautiful. It was no proprietary, branded whiteness she achieved. She relied on old remedies, long soaking, hard rubbing, suds as high as the tub. It renewed her as well. She enjoyed the homely task which contained a small perfection. A pile of line-dry garments into which she could bury her face, breathing up the ozone of fresh air, as other women would with bouquets. No starch. No bleach. No artifice. The things themselves evoked a kind of affection borrowed from their wearers. It didn't harm them in her eyes that they'd been passed down from one to the other, that the youngest wore the oldest's romper suits. They were a kind of living memory, and when she straightened and cared for them, she regenerated her own past.

Seeing this, Iona gave up trying to change her, accepting a circuitous slowness as inevitable.

She went into the kitchen after she came in from school, and sat over a cup of tea. The kitchen was seldom without a pot of tea, drawing tannic acid from strong leaves. It was the quiet time of the day, a lull between meals.

The Rayburn fire was becoming temperamental, refusing to draw properly, or maybe it was the latest delivery of coal. The stove kept going out and Maggie had had to relight it in the afternoon. Iona missed its warmth radiating through the back of the house, and shivered. To get up some heat while it caught, Maggie turned on all the taps of the gas cooker and there was an acrid smell of gas hanging in the air, making her eyes smart.

Maggie put a pan of water on one of the burners and started to peel the potatoes for the evening meal. She lopped at them largely with a knife, producing squares of vegetables. Iona had tried to implement thin paring, or scrubbing only to preserve the vitamins under the skin, but abandoned it.

The table where she sat was a utility model, which Jim had stripped of varnish, only to discover that underneath, the constituent woods were different, the centre planks beech, the frame oak. These discrepancies grated on her eye and she wished he had not improved it.

"Do you see what came this morning?"

"No. What?"

Maggie nodded in the direction of a brown envelope and, undoing it, Iona had a shock almost as great as her mother's. A bill, but a bill of such alarming size it blotted out common sense among reactions. Iona automatically checked the figures and their tally, a standing charge plus metered units, and found the two agreed. The man who came to read the meter must have made a mistake, misread a figure, bumping up the total.

"No. I checked it myself. It's right enough." Maggie precluded the objection.

"But how?"

"I don't know how," she said defiantly, as though a false accusation had been laid at her door, and working up her feelings against it was a form of vindication. She was innocent, was all she thought. They had not consumed as much electricity as was charged against them.

"Has the price per unit gone up?"

"I don't know about that. Does it say so on that leaflet?"

Iona scanned the accompanying piece of paper and confirmed it did. "It's correct then."

"We'll just have to cut back somehow."

Iona thought of the electrical appliances they used, wondering how they could use them less. The iron. The fridge. The light. How could they ration light? They used the minimum of each commodity as it was. "How can we do that?"

"We'll have to try."

Trying was the limit of Maggie's effort, seldom sustained as far as achievement. She offered up only passive resistance to life, carried along by currents because she lacked real self-determination. Upheaval was the mishaps that befell her and as she had no real foresight, she couldn't anticipate or minimise their effect. Every bill threatened economic ruin; every accident, even a tear in someone's coat, was an impediment to tomorrow's happiness. The children were familiar with these sporadic crises and hung on precipices waiting for a wage packet at the end of the week to deliver them from prescriptive poverty. Like their mother, what they hoped for was release from the immediate need. What happened beyond that was anyone's guess.

Iona had a better understanding of home management, even if it went with less experience. She already envied the salaried, the men with monthly rather than weekly incomes, who paid it into bank accounts against which they could draw a cheque. The Stewarts did not use cheques or bank accounts. There was no give in the system, and so no margin for error. Paying their way meant paying it on a daily basis, and in cash. Without discount. She came up against the dead limit of their resources. Income versus expenditure. She knew the quotient of happiness was sixpence in the pound, but also knew how hard it was to adhere to Micawberish principles of economics when there were a thousand demands on the extra sixpence.

"It's not as though I'm throwing the money about. I'm doing my best with it." Putting the knife and the potato down, she went over to the dresser and found her purse. Dramatically, she emptied it onto the discoloured bands of table, and stopped the rolling coins before they reached the edge. "I went out this morning with eight pounds and that's all that I've got left."

Without telling, Iona knew her mother did her best. She performed weekly miracles, loaves and fishes embodying not faith but ingenuity. She made everything. The baker made no profit from her whatsoever. The yeast rested between provings in the tin. The pancakes dropped from her spoon onto the griddle iron in their hundreds, rose, bubbled and were turned. A bone was picked clean, a butter paper scraped. There was no economy she did not effect.

Iona averted her eyes from the pitiful remains, leftovers from thrift. She hated this revelation of the empty purse which brought with it images she greatly feared. Eviction. Bankruptcy. The dole. They were the dread words because they carried such humiliation. The physical threat they contained was less powerful than the loss of respectability, not far removed from the terms of history books, poor relief, the workhouse and being on the parish. The needy! Oh God, what shame to be termed the needy. Not even the real poor, the dossed out, homeless, vagrant, beggarly and unfortunate poor. They were only indigent, struggling to stay decent and above debt. She knew these were not real possibilities as long as her father stayed in work, but the net between them and safety was desperately stretched.

She wanted to utter some consolation. The bill would be paid. It would be a thin week that week, one without meat, a held breath till Friday but Friday would come and they would go on squeezing by. It was life honed to its basics, the next meal. Iona reflected that in the nineteenth century the standard measure of a working man's wage was against the cost of a loaf of bread. Governments had foundered attempting to protect the price of wheat. The simplicity of that concept was almost reassuring, diagrammatically pure compared with the price of electricity per thermal unit, the local authority rating level or the interest set by banks and building societies, forcing up the cost of their home by artificial means that were not reflected correspondingly in their weekly income.

A budget, she wanted to say. You need a budget, but realised at once her mother was no Chancellor of the Exchequer. She would not balance her accounts no matter what her income was because she lived perennially up to it, incapable of either saving or apportioning which were mental habits.

The square potatoes went on being dropped in the pan.

"I sometimes think, you know, that Jim could do better on his own." She produced this lightly, a precious dream she did not want to be destroyed because in dream-form it was happiness.

"On his own?"

"I mean working on his own, without the firm."

"You mean self-employed?"

"Yes. Working for himself instead of them."

Iona was arrested by this novel idea. Her father self-employed. It had its attractions. It made him into his own business, an independent instead of a hired man. "Why do you think we'd be better off?"

"Well, he'd keep all the profits. He's the best workman in the firm. He's the only apprenticed craftsman. The rest are just hands."

"That doesn't mean anyone would give him work. He'd have to find a clientèle. Advertise, and have premises."

"He doesn't need premises if he works from home. There'd be no overheads. And he has the shooting brake. He could drive to jobs all round." She cast out her arms expansively, like her hopes. "The folk he works for are pleased with him. They'd recommend him to each other. There's plenty of work going."

Iona dwelt for a while on the surface of the reverie. She knew vaguely there were advantages in running your own business, and hazy thoughts of registered address and tax deductions floated through her mind. But after a moment she realised that an income was necessary before these concessions came into play, and pinpointed this weakness. "Customers can get awkward about paying their bills. Sometimes they take months to pay them, and then what do you live on? Sometimes they don't pay at all, and you've lost everything unless you take them to court.

There's not much sense in that." She measured hazard and decided it was too great. "At least if you're working for a firm, they take the knocks."

Maggie agreed. "Just a thought," she answered, as though her hopes had not been demolished. She put the lid back on the pan and adjusted it back to simmer.

"You've forgotten the salt," said Iona.

"Are you sure? I don't want them too salty."

"I've been watching."

Her mother took the lid off again and tasted the water from a spoon, grimacing. She wiped the spoon on her cloth and used it to add two spoonfuls.

The steam rose from the pan, creating condensation on the windows. And Iona, watching it gather and run down in pools, fell into despair.

One year to go. Just one year of dependence, then she could leave. Although it was never specified, Iona carried a burden of guilt. Her education had cost her parents a great deal, not in fees, but in other provisions; travel, clothes, books. She was anxious about every pound she took from them, and anxious most of all that the sacrifice they made on her behalf estranged them from each other, pushing her out into a wider context. They laboured: she benefited. The shaming thing was that as she rose through their agency, she saw them in a reduced perspective. She didn't disparage them, was shocked when other girls spoke slightingly of their parents. Sometimes even stole from them. Unbelievable, an excess from which it was possible to steal. But she saw them dispassionately, as if it were possible to do so.

As a small child she accepted the domestic mores, like the folklore her mother clung to. Superstitiously, Maggie avoided everything that could be a harbinger of bad luck, a broken mirror, an open umbrella indoors or shoes on a table. In vain Iona tried to combat the inhibiting effect of these precepts with logic or with science. They were golden rules. Her parents read, but only partially, unable to connect Dickens with social history, Tolstoy with the rise of communism, but were mesmerised by the power of fame. Household names were household gods.

Seeing this in them felt like a great deceit. She stole all right. She stole their effort and rewarded them with callous objectivity. She was tormented by the disloyalty of an imperfect love, a love

83

without delusions, for she adored and denied them simultaneously, and was forked by her own complexity.

Maggie went out once a week in the evening to a singing practice of the church choir. She was a fine soprano and the organist, who doubled as choirmaster, placed her in the middle of the group so that her voice could swell out and cancel some of the lesser euphonies nearby. He gave her as many solo verses as he could without arousing the envy of other members. Her phrasing was natural, following the sense of the words rather than the structure of the rhythm, and her stance and movement were unaffected. He thought that if she had been caught early enough, she could have made an operatic singer, able to act her parts effortlessly but with great stamina. He tried to persuade her to go on with training her voice but giving way under the argument of expense, asked if he might enter her in local festivals and competitions. The medals and certificates she won at these were her only vanity, and she read the commendation of the judges with a smile, unable to believe they wrote of her.

She sang about the house when it was empty, thinking it was an imposition on others for them to have to listen to songs they had not chosen. She had an ill-assorted repertoire, comprised of church anthems, "Hosanna, loud Hosanna the little children cry", and "O God of Bethel, by whose hand thy people still are led", and "The Lord's my shepherd" which she sang to the tune of Crimond. She liked the simple ballads, like "I'll take you home again, Kathleen", which suited the harmonic pattern of her voice.

There was an audience, though she didn't know it. Occasionally Innes Hamilton picked up the notes like off-shore signals, through the walls, across the rooftops if she happened to be out of doors. He put his book down and listened, attentive to a more vital beauty than the printed word; a living note, the human voice embellishing sound. He could hardly believe it was the woman who made it. She sang in English for a start, without a hint of accent, and he was much struck by the superimposition of another form on her voice, as if music brought about a double change in her, a double elevation. One song in particular he noticed because she seemed to have difficulty with the timing and went over it again and again to get it right, stopping and starting so that he too became impatient, waiting for it to come right, for practice to cease and turn into performance.

> Where'er you walk, cool gales shall fan the glade,
> Trees, where you sit, shall crowd into a shade.

Nonsense. Pure nonsense. Grotesque romancing. Alexander Pope in atypical mood, surely translating from a more passionate Roman master, on summertime and Pastorals. And yet, when her voice dwelt on the final protracted note of shade, extending it to ten, twelve, fourteen syllables so that sense and sound were fused, the word becoming its own protective cover over the beloved woman, he was profoundly moved. Emotion sprang up, hot and painful, like an artesian well breaking through the soil – and was capped. How could this perfectly ordinary woman with half a dozen children, no elegance, no knowledge to speak of, produce such an enchanting sound? He did not know, but all the same she did it. The notes soared upwards like her aspirations, escaping into the free air. He began to listen for them, strain after them like music carried from distant hamlets, the way a non-believer can enjoy the chimes of campanology, calling worshippers to church on Sunday. He did not have the faith, but still it was a gladsome noise.

Chapter Ten

Innes drove Iona up to town more than once during the summer term. He often stayed away two nights, driving back early on Sunday mornings in time to go sailing. She noticed all his movements with a sharpened eye. She was in despair about it, and couldn't understand the reason. Did she have a crush on him? She didn't know the meaning of this word until she went to school, and wasn't sure if she did now. A hopeless and unreciprocated interest. A one-sided love affair. Adoration from afar. The practical side of her didn't think such feelings were real or sensible, and she was quite irritated with herself for giving in to the pangs of hurt and neglect and longing that afflicted her. Every now and then she stopped and asked herself what it was she wanted. But she didn't know what she wanted, couldn't focus on what she expected him to do, pay attention to her, notice her, but how more than he did already?

She gave it up and started to live her own life, instead of waiting attendance compulsorily on his.

There was a group that hung around the café at the front, mostly the teenagers who travelled up on the train with her, swollen by a few younger members of the yacht club. For want of anything better in the first week of the summer holiday, she hung around with them too.

On wet days they met in the public shelter opposite the swimming pool. It had tables and chairs and the boys often played cards for money, poker or pontoon, winning or losing small sums but it heightened the game if they risked their pocket money or their entrance to the cinema. One afternoon, the girls were daring too and took on a game of strip poker.

"Aren't you playing?" asked Barry Shaw unexpectedly, turning to her as he dealt the cards.

"No." She shook her head. "I won't play." But she went on

watching, walking round the misted-up windows of the shelter which encased them in a thin privacy.

In every game dealt, the one with the losing hand had to remove an article of clothing. After a few hands, she began to think that Barry Shaw was losing deliberately, taking off his socks and shoes with negligence though the others made catcalls. Then others lost, but gradually, his outer clothes came off one at a time, down to his sweater. He sat in his trousers and shirt and, everyone else swore, nothing else.

Iona looked away. He was the most wicked of the boys, and the best looking. There was hardly a girl in the town who wouldn't like to take a turn round the Law with him but he'd been going steady with the girl who had made the pert answer on the train, until very recently. For some reason she had been cast off and he was on the look-out once again. Iona thought of going steady as the prime state; it implied constant male attendance on all the occasions when they were useful, dances, trips to the cinema, hours spent in Victoria Café. It was a fixed relationship, achieved without the frenzied striving to find someone, which she couldn't understand and couldn't be bothered to put into practice. All that dressing up and making up and fussing about the hang of your skirt – it baffled her. She hankered after the end product, everything settled, and sometimes envied the young people who seemed pleased with each other, not for themselves but for the equipoise they achieved so early and so effortlessly, without being personally moved to go out and find the balance to herself.

She turned round from the steamed-up windows when she heard a shout. At the central table, Barry lost again. He must be keeping a weak hand. He couldn't lose this often. His shirt came off. She looked aside. He went out sailing as often as Innes Hamilton did and his torso was a chestnut polished brown, the skin looking oily with a gleam to it. He was a showman all right. She remembered what she'd heard about his family, that they were Romany long ago, part of the Egyptian legacy of travellers. They were respectable now, or respected because they had the biggest and the best. They were flash. Jack Shaw was famous for his socks with silver lurex thread through them and his clothes were garish enough, with a strong drift towards mauve and burgundy, to earn him the nickname Multi-coloured Jack. Barry was slicker, a generation up.

So he sat there, leaning back, a grin on his face, knowing every youth in the place wanted to hit him for looking like an aspiring Mr Universe, and every girl wanted to touch him to find out if it felt as good as it looked.

The other stages of undress were not marked. One girl, though she'd lost several hands, had cunningly removed her earrings and other pieces of jewellery, one at a time and as far as clothes went, was quite normal. Barry's henchman, though he couldn't compete in impudent style, outdid him in eccentricity. He was working from the bottom up and sat in his underpants, leather jacket and a yachting hat which occasionally was snatched off by someone in the game and thrown across the room, so that he would have to go and retrieve it, thereby giving rise to more laughter at his strange, top-heavy outfit.

Eventually, three people sat in crucial stages of undress; Barry, his sidekick and a girl who'd come ill-prepared and was already down to her bikini. Someone whispered it didn't matter if she lost. Every boy there had already had a sight of what was underneath. Iona shuddered at the loss of reputation. How could she face life, knowing what was said about her.

The hand was played. Barry went for a Royal Flush and ended up with nothing. Ten, Jack, Queen, Ace and a rogue seven went down on the table. It was his trousers now.

He stood up, hand on zip.

"Must I?" he pleaded.

"Get them off," came back the chorus.

Iona blushed for him and for herself, unaccountably. She had seen the naked male body every day of her life. Why should it make a difference that it was his? But it did, and he knew it. Almost brazenly, with the indifference of the male stripper used to getting it off night after night, he slid the zip down and loosening the waistband behind, dropped his trousers.

Howls of derision greeted him. He had on a pair of admittedly very small and admittedly flesh-coloured swimming trunks but was, in fact, utterly decent.

"You bloody cheat. You told us you'd got nothing on."

"Tough. It's still poker, isn't it? You shouldn't have believed me."

The girl in the bikini started to get dressed. Whatever she'd got to offer, she couldn't follow Barry Shaw.

They broke up, drifting home for tea or dinner as they variously called it, according to refinement. They straggled back, a dozen of them, in front of the cottages that were let now in the season as holiday homes while the owners aestivated in a back room, or went to bother their relatives.

Iona hung back, in no hurry to lay the table or change somebody ready for bed.

Barry hung back too.

"What are you doing this evening?"

"I don't know," she replied truthfully.

"Do you fancy going to the pictures?"

She looked up, surprised at the question. "No, I can't do that."

"Why not? Won't your Mum and Dad let you out?"

"No." She was ashamed of the imputation that at sixteen she had no freedom but was maybe more embarrassed at the real reason which she was forced into offering. "I've no money."

"Is that all? I've got plenty."

The assertion confirmed the purpose of the original question. It was a date then. He was asking her out. He was paying for her.

"I don't know," she prevaricated.

"Come on." He saw he would have to make up her mind for her. "I'll meet you outside at seven o'clock."

Two hours. Two hours! Her mind took leave of her body. Two hours and she would be, what, sitting in the dark with a boy who'd asked her out. What did he expect? What would they do afterwards? She realised that she would have to give Maggie an explanation when she got back, and skilfully rolled it into what she had been doing to keep her out of the house all afternoon. She outlined the group, highlighting its more respectable members, said they'd played cards in the shelter and were going on to the pictures in the evening.

"You'll need money for that," her mother said on reflex.

"No. I saved a bit of my dinner money in the last week."

"You're getting too thin, Iona. Shooting up so fast. You'll outgrow your strength if you're not careful."

This much-repeated phrase infuriated Iona, mostly because she had no idea what it meant. Wasn't growth evidence of strength? But she didn't stop to ask for an explanation. "I didn't like the look of lunch that day."

"It's not like you to be so picky."

Iona wished the lie would stop rebounding. Whatever was the

matter with saying Barry Shaw had asked her out and was going to pay for her ticket? It involved the admission of a different growth, and of a change that was too hard to state.

After tea, she went upstairs to wash her face. There wasn't much else she could do by way of preparation. She looked quizzically in the mirror at herself. Lipstick, powder, the blandishments of woman were all missing. She brushed her hair out, freeing it from tangles. At least that was by itself the things that cosmetics aimed at, long and blonde and silky. The pale streaks began at the root again now that she was in the sun all day, the winter dark behind. With her finger, she rubbed two highspots on her cheek and pressing her lips with her teeth in alternation, produced a deeper red.

Her toilet done, she slipped out of the back gate and went to her assignation.

He had changed his clothes completely. She felt dismayed by the evidence of so much variety, and so much affluence. She thought her routine appearance disappointed him. The same blouse and the same skirt implied she couldn't have made less effort, that she didn't care how she looked or what he thought about her. She was in a state of excruciating discomfort because she had nothing different to offer him. He was just so much smarter than she was, had all the latest gear while she looked like an urchin in comparison, a stray.

He noticed. "It was a bit of a rush, wasn't it?" he said to cover her dismay and she nodded in agreement. It had been for her, but she knew quite well he'd had a meal put in front of him, bathed, changed and left the dishes and the towels for someone else to clear away.

He still liked her. He liked the way she didn't munch popcorn, kept a straight face through the jokes of the silly film they sat through and when he took her hand, that it was cool and small and sat tidily inside his own. But her profile did not alter in turning towards him and the angle of her eyelashes was steadfast, straight ahead.

They sauntered back along the High Street afterwards and when they passed the back gate to her house, he said, "You don't need to go in yet, do you?"

"No, not just yet."

They kept along the back road and cut down one that led to the sea. He took her hand in his again now that they were out of public view and when she shivered, though she said she did not feel the cold, he put his arm around her shoulder. They came to the links of Wester Dunes and passed the paying kiosk, deserted now of golfers or strollers heading for the beach. He stopped here. He put her neatly against the boarding of the kiosk and with both arms around her, kissed her purposefully.

Much discussion raged on the difficulty of kissing. She found it was not difficult at all. It was astonishingly easy and astonishingly pleasant. It started off connective thoughts here and there in her body which were not unpleasant either.

"You're nice to kiss," he admitted.

"Why?"

"Some girls swallow you whole. You're nice. Firm and warm."

She pondered on this. So there were different ways of kissing, were there? She found the words he gave her of greater interest than the deed.

He pressed more heavily to show her how and opened his lips wider, taking her completely by surprise when he slid his tongue along the line of hers.

She drew away.

"Don't you like that?"

"Not so much. Yet." The night was closing in fast. The clock on the church tower started to chime eleven. "I must go in. I mustn't be late."

He moved away and took her hand again, this time winding his fingers in between her own. He was somehow subtle and frightening close up, as well as comforting, because he was so assured.

"Can I see you tomorrow?"

"Sunday. Won't you go sailing?"

"No. My Dad's got friends with him this weekend. There won't be room for me. I'll meet you at about two at the harbour."

Two it was.

Iona was desperate that some chore would descend on her to keep her from the meeting, that she would be asked to mind the children, a task she shared these days with Malcolm who at eleven was old enough to take responsibility for watching the younger ones on the beach, and being nearly as big as she was, had power to carry out any correction. But he ruled with threats and not with love. They did not like his governance so well as hers, or fear his retribution half so much. They clung to her. Worse would be if Maggie had planned an outing for them all, something of such huge complexity that her withdrawal from it would require equally huge justification. And in the school holidays, homework was no pretext.

But it was all right. The baby slept. Maggie was going for a nap herself. Malcolm could cope on his own. Iona rummaged frantically in her mother's drawer before she went out, looking for something different to wear with her shorts, but all she could come up with was a ribbed cotton sweater that was fine except it made her look a bit bosomy. Well it would have to do. She rushed out, late.

He was there, waiting.

They walked along the east bay. He knew the boats that moored in the harbour and could recognise the class of other, visiting craft on sight. They reached the edge of the further golf course and took the hill path that led along the top of the cliff to the promontory of the headland, known as Rugged Knowes, which gave a view down over the Leithies and Leckmoran Ness. Iona knew these walks well. Every angle that the path gave onto the Bass Rock, Fidra, the Law behind and the rocks lying scattered down the steep slope at her feet, was familiar to her. In eighteen months she had explored every one of the footpaths round the town. She could tell the season and the state of the tide by the seawrack exposed on the rock, and would have noticed a shift in land formation on the instant.

He sat down on the top of the headland where the scrubby grass rolled onto the rough of the course, but was separated from it by a wire fence. She sat down too, circling her knees with her arms. She noticed the eyebright and wild thyme mixed among the grass, and Scottish lovage distinctive in the context of the miniature orchids and bellflowers of the herbage.

He kissed her once more the way she liked, and then with the slightest pressure on her shoulder, made her lie back and kissed her lying down. That was different again. Easier. So easy they kissed for maybe half an hour without moving particularly, but making long slow patterns like the run in of the tide. He was strange, Barry Shaw. He did not speak. So she thought perhaps they should not speak at all. He moved closer in on his elbow and put his free hand on her ribbed sweater. That was pleasant too, continuing the connections that broke out all over her. He kissed her more emphatically now and put the hand under the sweater. But all the time he said nothing and she began to be dismayed that he would never talk to her.

His hand inside the sweater made demands she did not understand. The kissing and the rubbing started to become irritating, leading to nowhere, or round a corner she hadn't turned. He leaned more heavily, almost on top of her, and when his hand moved away from the sweater to the waistband of her shorts, she was shocked – under the injunction of saying nothing.

She did not want him to be intimate with her body, did not know or like him that well and above all, did not trust him enough not to say about her what they said about the girl in the bikini. Anybody's. A right little goer. It was her doubt about what the slanders meant that caused her panic. She shook her head, not knowing what else to do to stop him. Shook it again and again until at last he desisted from trying to establish the geography of her buttons, and lay back on his elbow again, further off. She was lucky. Whatever his faults, he was not an oaf and he'd been with enough girls to realise that if they didn't want it, it was useless to press on regardless. He'd flipped a dud coin. Tough. Both sides came up heads. He knew he only had to wait. Generous time would bring him everything he wanted.

Innes Hamilton sailed past the headland about four in the afternoon. Iona saw his sails but did not recognise them. He carried round his neck the binoculars that gave him a close-up view of the birds nesting on the sanctuary of the Bass Rock. He was no ornithologist but knew a cormorant from a gull at fifty paces and used to go home and try to identify the rarer birds he'd seen passing up the Forth, from an illustrated handbook that he kept open and ready in the summer.

He was chasing one of these, a roseate tern, up the cliff face of the headland, when he went out of focus on a couple lying together at the top. He tutted to himself at such public display and then thought, surely there was something about the . . . and readjusted the focus of his lens.

It was.

It was Iona Stewart and that young no-good Shaw, fumbling her shorts.

He put the glasses down, disbelieving, and wished he had not looked. He was so angry at her being out unsupervised again, that he drifted too close in to shore and had to work hard to get himself out of the shallows. "Oh damn," he said, "oh damn," over and over again.

Wasn't anybody keeping an eye on the girl? Such irresponsible parenthood, he fumed.

But what were her parents to do, after all. Keep her under lock and key? How could they? The girl was over age and free to do whatever she wanted. But Gypsy Jack and all his tribe! Hawkers and pedlars every one of them. Fairgrounds and flashing lights and balloons and plaster statuettes for prizes. He couldn't stomach it. Cheap fairings were outside his scope. Cheap. Oh cheap was unendurable.

Iona walked along the promenade, not hurt but baffled by what intimacy showed her. She came back to what she felt when she was with Innes on his boat and in his car, that he was completely self-reliant and satisfied by his solitary occupations; that no company at all was preferable to hers. She simply didn't matter. The young man made her feel the same. He needed someone to kiss, yes, to feel, to project himself onto and eventually into, but it wasn't necessarily her. He had done it with a good many girls before, the girl in the train, the girl in the bikini probably, and she was forced into the conclusion that she simply didn't matter. She didn't add anything to the experience which was her own. Any company would have done as well as hers. He didn't talk to her. He didn't know anything about her. She was anonymous.

She wondered if what she had done was wrong, if she had suddenly become cheap. Cheap as dirt. She thought back to the numerical scale of chastity and felt she had not gone very far along it. Not very far at all but wished she had not started on its progressive chain which made the end inevitable. In any case, she knew she would be dropped. He would not bother to ask her out again because she hadn't . . . come up with the goods. Was not even fun or funny with it.

She left him at the café and walked along the western bay alone. The tide was pulling back, slowly, and she wandered in among the rock pools happily, revisiting the places of her childhood, revealed under the ebb. Barnacles and sea anemones left behind. Strange hiding, diving creatures darting out of sight. And on the sand, the flies hopped and worms, already at work, left conical casts she flattened as she passed.

Every receding wave of the sea said the same thing to her: "I live the life of the mind." She walked closer to hear it more intimately, a great assurance. "I live the life of the mind." It held such comfort in its breathing sigh that she was almost lulled by it. It took away the pain of the everyday.

She slipped off her shoes, and hanging them by their tied laces round her neck, went deeper in. The water curled and foamed round her ankles. She would have liked to take her clothes off and go swimming out between Bass and Fidra, out of the Forth altogether into the North Sea, out, out, out, feeling only the clean, cold water on her back and the buoyant sea underneath.

"That's far enough, Iona," a voice said. "You'll get soaked."

"Oh hello, Innes." She looked down. The spray was above her knees and had made her shorts wet. She waded back to the shore where he stood waiting for her. The duck shoes that he wore made a pattern of ridges on the damp stretch of sand while she left a trail of toe and heel prints, one shod, one naked foot in step. She came to a halt at the edge of the beach, sitting down on the bank to rub her soles dry and free of sand with a handful of grass before she went indoors. But neither of them moved when she had finished and she dug her feet back into the coarse, dry sand, dangling from the ledge from which she had performed the dramatic long jump into the dark the night that they had arrived.

He sat down beside her, wanting to say something about what he'd seen, words of advice or words of warning. But what could he offer her as a compensation for raw and inept youth, other than cynical and prescient age. Don't do it because I know where it will lead, making the assumption that he knew better than she did because he knew more. She didn't want such dismissiveness of her own judgement either. He looked slantingly into her face and wished he had some authority to speak.

"Wasn't there a coral reef in the North Sea at one time?" she asked him.

"So they say. Then it broke up, probably after a change in the climate, but it's left us these fine sands all along the east coast."

She picked up a handful and ran it from palm to palm like the sand in an hourglass. "Funny to think that was coral at one time."

96

"As well as bits of shell and rock ground up small."

She dug her feet in, holding grains between the toes. The grit was abrasive. She felt it sharp next to her skin. Pumice. Taking off a shred of skin at every touch.

"Funnier still to think it's sand like this that goes to make glass. They win sand all along this coast. Imagine – these grains actually have the capacity to become transparent. Or hard. Hardness itself is rather difficult to associate with sand."

She looked up. "Yes, that's strange. That it starts as solid rock, or reef, then becomes granular through the action of the tide but can turn solid again if you manufacture it as glass or porcelain." She shuffled her feet in circles, feeling the metamorphosis through her own body, in final knowledge. "Which would you choose if you could have just one? As it is raw or as it is manufactured?"

He took a long time to reply, and then with the digression which her question had prompted. "I do detest that word. Of all the words in English I detest that most."

"Why? Which one?" She thought she had given offence.

"Manufacture. It ought to mean 'made by hand', crafted. Instead it means turned out by the million, in the manufacturing industries. I don't know which is worse, the decay of craft or the decay of language."

"But which?" she insisted.

"The real world or the artistic one?" he clarified her original question for her.

"That's right."

"I don't know. You can't choose like that, can you? There's no answer to which is better. I can't say which is more real or more beautiful. I like the artefact, the thing that is made out of sand, glass or porcelain or pottery, whatever silica is used for. But I like the sand and the action of the tide in making it. They need each other. There's no glass and no statue without the raw ingredients but equally, there's no point in the element unless you do something with it. Lying there, it is just talent, a potential, unfused."

She very seldom understood what he was saying at once. She thought about it for days, weeks, went away and looked up the facts behind his opinions, evolving quite slowly her own response and whether she agreed with him or not. So she let this lie fallow and sat in silence, letting the hourglass sift through her fingers.

"Are you coming in now?" He stood to leave the almost empty beach.

"No. I don't feel like going inside yet."

When he had gone, she continued to sit swinging her legs over the sand, scuffling and shaping it about. He seemed to say, after all, that the life of the mind was not enough and she thought that in his place, John Keats would have said, "I live the life of the senses." Oh for a life of sensations! Other phrases leaped to mind spurred by this one. Kissing with the inner lip. Music arose with its voluptuous swell. Oh the Romantics, defying death with the immediate. She began, although there was no fulcrum point she could arrive at, to balance the unequal proposition contained in the factors round her. She sat on for a long time, till it was quite cool, though to the passing eye she was just a girl kicking sand about.

He hovered in the front room of the house until he saw her get up and go safely indoors. He found himself going over and over her strange declarations, just as she repeated his sentence to herself. Sand real or sand fired? What an odd and uncompromising way to put things. He reviewed the other oblique observations she made: did he enjoy writing, why did the notes fall with their particular distinctions, his house had anomalies where he had thought it pure. Disturbing. Disarming. How much of this stripping back to basics, diving below the surface of normal conversation, was attributable to femininity – something simpler and more direct – or to herself, youth, enquiry and the shape of her own mind?

The questions did unsettle him. He liked to find an answer in a book to pin the question down with, once and for all. Put question and answer together and have done. He wasn't comfortable with these strange reverberations she set up and found, to the end of every conclusion he hammered out about himself or his way of life or his work, she appended the words – Is it? And so he went back again and tested the validity of his ideas and was almost agreeably surprised when he had to modify some of them, discovering inside his preconceptions a more rounded form of truth, transparent inside opaque, fluid alternating with fixed.

He returned to the scene he had witnessed through his binoculars and regretted it. He compared her forcibly in his imagination with the girl who climbed on his deck the summer before. The moments of that day began to seem precious, more carefree and innocent than their moments now. He remembered the gestures she had made, sweeping back the water from her head, pulling down the elastic of her costume. They haunted him just for their lack of sophistry or guile. He searched back for the girl-child as opposed to the girl-woman and found her in those moments. But he knew it was a resurrection. She had really gone, the chaste, the virtuous, the perfect. He felt overwhelmed by regret as though someone had breathed on a windowpane, fingered a display and spoiled it. Touching removed the bloom, the way some Lalique glass never recovers from a fingerprint.

Chapter Eleven

Jim Stewart found the Shaw house off the Dunbar road but still wasn't sure from which angle to tackle it. He wandered about, rather like his neighbour before him, trying to find the way in and at length came across a gardener cutting a lawn as wide as a fairway behind the house.

"Tradesmen's entrance next to the garage," he called from a distance and Jim, designated tradesman, found it at last and rang.

He waited a very long time for an answer, but eventually Jack Shaw himself came to the door with the air of having interrupted something important he was in a hurry to get back to, a telephone call or a transaction.

"How do," he said. "Come in. I haven't got long so we'll get down to it straight away." His manner was briskly impatient with finesse. His reputation as a hard man to deal with had reached even Jim, who was not unduly daunted. He stood by what he could do and the fact that the other wanted him to do it, was out to hire his skill. That put them on an equal footing. The one thing that made him a little awkward as he followed the owner down a corridor and into a large and open hallway with a grandiose staircase spiralling up from it, was the lack of introductions. He liked a formal handshake and the exchange of names. Then he felt he knew who he was dealing with. In the vacuum of civilities, he could not decide how to address his would-be employer. He did not feel inclined to extend the terms of deference and call him Mr Shaw as he would one of the firm's customers, and was even less disposed to give him a matey Jack. He didn't like to be so nameless himself but felt it wasn't his place to stop and put matters right. So he walked on down the corridor, confused at the contradiction between the opulence of his setting and the poverty of manners.

"You are a skilled craftsman?" Jack asked over his shoulder.

"Yes I am that."

101

"The last one said he was too."

Jim wondered who this other man was that his failures should devolve on him, but soon discovered.

Jack led him to a section of the hall that was directly under the stairwell. A bookcase had been constructed to flank one side of the stairs, utilising dead space effectively. It was an awkward area, useless in fact for most purposes because no one voluntarily walked under an overhang. Normally this space would be blocked in with a cloakroom cupboard but here, Jack had elected to have a cocktail bar, finishing the bookcase in a curve.

"Handy, you see, from all the rooms."

Jim would not agree, taking measurements with his eye. "And this is what you want me to build in for you?"

"Finish off. It's almost complete already."

Jim looked round. A couple of battens had been plugged into the wall and a piece of hardboard curved round, forming a bow front. There were no uprights, stays or bracing.

"I wouldn't say that. This is a real lash-up job if you ask me. Whoever did that for you?"

"Highly recommended he was, by a friend."

Jim tried to square this with the allegation made earlier that the man had been unqualified. "You won't be taking that friend up on his commendation again."

"Pig in a poke, isn't it? With tradesmen you don't know what you're getting till you see the job finished. Anybody says he's a joiner who can hold a drill. I'm a better joiner than some of them."

"Oh aye," said Jim. "Just the way any Tom, Dick or Harry says he's a businessman or a consultant this and that. But you can't help wondering what he consults in. There's a grand profession of liars about nowadays."

Jack would not gainsay this, having met a few, and he did not altogether like the shaving answers the handyman gave back. "Well then. The job is what you see. Can you finish it off?"

"No indeed. There's no way I can finish this off. I'll have to start from scratch. There's nothing here I can use."

"But what about the wood he bought? I paid for that before he walked off the job."

"Wood. Is that what you call it? This isn't wood. See the knots in it. You lean on this batten and it'll be away from under you, drinks and all."

"It cost me plenty."

"You were done then. Look here at this." Jim found a plank of wood which had been intended for the surface of the bar. It was solid pine, not the plywood or the veneered chipboard he could hardly bring himself to use, but it was the worst quality. "It's not been seasoned right. It's away already." He held it lengthwise against the light and squinted along it. "It's out of true and if I use this for your top, you'll be complaining that it's buckled in no time. I can't take the responsibility for someone else's work. And he's not jointed a thing." He felt the butts of wood. "Just glued and pinned. It's not my kind of work he's done."

The other tutted with impatience. He'd had two years of this, contractors letting him down, subcontractors going bust on him, workmen late on site, out of synchronisation with each other so that the plumber swore at the supplier, and the electrician swore at the plumber. He'd had enough. Why couldn't he get a reasonable job done, without endless fuss and delay? They each made out their part was especially difficult, which meant he would have to dig especially deep to resolve the difficulty. He was utterly sick of living with sawdust and plaster and draughts.

"I can cut the pine up for struts if you like. I can't make a better of it."

The concession was timely and effective. "OK. How much?"

Jim was genuinely taken aback at the challenge of how much, so boldly stated. He was not used to bartering over his talents. The firm fixed the price and he took what was due to him. He found it hard to think of himself as worth so much an hour, a hireling or a journeyman engaged on piecework. "The whole job? Let me see." He tried to figure out how many hours it would actually take, how many weekends he would have to consign to finishing the job. Maybe four.

Before he could arrive at an estimate, however, Jack Shaw forestalled him. "Call it a hundred."

"A hundred altogether? Oh no. That's nothing like."

"How much then?"

"Three hundred pounds is more in the region," but even as he spoke, he thought he under-estimated.

"Three hundred? You must be joking."

"I want to give you a fair price for the job."

"A fair price is one I can afford."

Jim did a few more sums in his head. "I can't see my way to

103

cutting down on that."

Jack suddenly took on a wheedling tone. "What you've got to say to yourself is, What's the job worth to me? It's handy enough. Five minutes away. And it's a bit of a moonlight." He smiled knowingly. "No tax. Cash transaction. Call it a hundred and fifty."

"You drive a hard bargain," the workman conceded, not knowing this was praise. He did not like him, did not want to work for him, did not want to leave behind in this man's house the craft of his hands or the benefit of twenty years' experience. And yet, as the bills piled up, and the term started with new uniform to buy to keep his kids as good as other folks', he knew he'd got no option. "My time's worth more."

"So's mine." He shrugged with a take it or leave it air. He flicked a look at his wristwatch, a timepiece with a face as glaringly stated as Big Ben. "I can't hang about all day. Tell you what, we'll split the difference. Two-two-five."

"I can't do any kind of job at that. I'm not a shoddy worker and I don't turn out second-rate work. That's what you've got here. Rubbish. That's what you paid for and that's what you got. But that's not me."

"Oh God, you're breaking my heart." Jack waited only half a second to see the offence register on the other man's face, then amended his bid. "Fair dos. Two-fifty. All in. You supply the wood."

"There's no all in about it. A decent bit of wood will be another hundred. I can get trade discount on that and I'll show you all the bills. But I'm not putting my work into matchwood."

Jack thought he couldn't beat him down any further and so closed on, "Two-fifty, when you've finished and provided I'm satisfied, and up to a hundred for materials."

"As I go along so I'm not out of pocket."

"As you go along." Jack was well enough pleased. He'd already had three written estimates, including one from Jim's firm, and they were all for over five hundred. He turned more affable now that the bargaining was done. "Well, what do you think of the place then? I don't suppose you see many like this."

"No, I've not seen many like this."

"Architect-designed."

"As you say," drawled Jim, "there's architects and architects."

104

"It's been featured in a magazine, you know."

"Very fancy. But I'm not a great one for modern. A modern place always looks as though it would take off in a high wind." He couldn't say in so many words what was wrong with it and wouldn't have been enlightened by hearing Innes Hamilton's view of the same building. Taste or decoration was a frill to Jim, something stuck on like wallpaper or pictures, not deeply significant. "I go for a stone-built place myself. This brick now, it doesn't matter how good a brick it is, the frost gets in and then the water and breaks it up. What's in this wall? Breeze blocks? That's a good name for them, right enough. Clinker they're made of, the leftover from firings. Refuse, that's all."

"Structurally sound."

"I've no doubt. But it's what it's made of in the end, and the modern building has just no substance to it. I like your bookcase, though," he added as a consolation.

"Oh? That was my idea. Gives a nice feel. Quiet too. Good deadening."

Jim walked along the length of the stair which had been panelled with the bookcase up to the ceiling. But as he paced it, he realised something was amiss. The books didn't seem to be the right depth given the width of the stairs.

Jack answered his hesitation. "A full shelf would have taken up too much floor space so we cut them down."

"Cut what down?"

"The books."

Jim went to pick one of the volumes out to check what the other meant, but found they had been glued in place. About a thousand books had been sliced in half so that the spines and a little of the leather and tooled cover of each still showed in the shallow recess of the shelves.

"Neat."

"Very neat." He reflected that the books must have been cut on an electric saw, and imagined them being fed in one after the other. Used to careful putting-by, he wondered what had become of the pages severed from their binding. Had anyone kept the half-sheets to make spills, or even used the leathered boards to start a fire? They would burn well, old books, as dry as tinder.

"You can start straight away if you like," Jack conceded. "I'm going out but the gardener's keeping an eye on the place."

Jim felt this implied he was untrustworthy and might ransack the place in the owner's absence. "I'm well used to working in a house on my own."

"Maybe so. Please yourself when you start."

He walked away and Jim went back to the car to fetch his box of tools, hearing a door slam after a few minutes. As he undid what the previous carpenter had put up, he found himself asking why the other workman had walked out. Had Jack badgered him to the point where he couldn't stand him any longer? Poking and querying and interfering? He knew that type, and bleakly foresaw endless wrangles which in the normal course of events he referred to the foreman. Even when he'd done, Jack would be slow to pay up. No cash on me today and we agreed no cheques. Half a dozen visits he would have to make before he finally stumped up. And then he'd call him back to alter the height of the shelving behind the bar because he'd changed his glasses from Waterford to Edinburgh crystal, and they were taller; screwing the last turn out of him so that he could say to himself, I got the better of that deal.

Chapter Twelve

Innes did not go to Edinburgh the following weekend but stayed close to home with a newer entertainment.

He met Iona on the foreshore, surrounded by the bevy of children, and was relieved to see her in more tender company.

"I'm having a new boat delivered this afternoon, Iona. Do you want to come and sail her tomorrow?"

"A new boat?"

"Yes, a new boat."

"Brand spanking new? Not second-hand?"

He smiled. "She's new. I can hardly improve on that. The maiden voyage. Or is there another history essay to keep your nose down?"

She thought it strange he should refer to their first meeting, and wondered why its circumstances stayed with him. "No, I'm on holiday. I'd love to come."

"Well, you must tell your parents so they know where you are. Or would you like me to speak to them?"

She shot him a glance, curious about what lay behind this caution. "No. I can speak for myself."

"Can you be at the harbour early? About eight. I want to give her a long trial. And at least you won't have to swim out.'

She smiled wanly.

She was there before him, sitting hunched up on the sea wall with a duffel bag. She ran down the steps ahead of him, bursting with eagerness, and jumped on board. "It had to be this one. Isn't she beautiful! So smart and polished and shiny." *Obsidian* he called his new craft, hard and gleaming like volcanic glass. "How can you bear to take her out to sea and get her all salted up and rusty?"

"The fittings are made of stainless steel, so she won't rust. And anyway, you can't sail a boat in a bottle to keep it free of damage. I don't much care for inland sailing. It's dull stuff puffing round the same loch even if it is Lomond. Now watch out. I'm not too nifty with this yet. She whips round on me. I nearly made a fool of myself yesterday afternoon. Have you found a life jacket?"

She obeyed and sat for'ard out of his way until he negotiated the harbour entrance. He picked his way among the smaller boats, the pleasure craft bobbing on the high tide and two or three fishing boats, scarred by storms. The heat haze lifted a little in patches over the sea, but it created an effect of total suppression of colour on land so that the town, strung out before them like a narrow ribbon, was indistinguishable in its various bands, shore from houses from vegetation; they merged like fused slip glaze in a firing, potash, oxide, manganese and salts. The high tones of a white house or the embattlement of the church tower, tall enough to catch the sun, related less to light than texture. They seemed roughnesses on the surface of the day.

The yacht he had chosen was a three sail craft which was over thirty foot from stem to stern. It represented the limit of his capacity to sail single-handed, but still tested it. He'd bought a standard design after all. There was no point in proving abstruse theories of construction when he had no intention of racing. Races stultified his interest in putting to sea. The complexities of the handicapping system, with more variables than golf, which enabled craft from different classes to compete against one another, while fair in establishing a median, took away the simple visual pleasure of being first to the marker buoy. He liked that all right. He'd drive himself on for a visible reward. Having the prize taken away, however, because the ratio of sail to length was too high, prejudicing his rating was a double penalty. He'd rather not compete than sail under the assumption of holding an advantage. He wanted to win, pure and simple, against all comers and if refusing to submit to the test guaranteed him the ethos of a champion, then aloofness from the rules of racing was the method he would choose.

To Iona, the escape into the maritime layer was more a matter of wonder. Not uncritical or undemanding; she was under no illusion about a magical barque. The stiffness of the sail, bright chrome, the new rig taut in the freshening wind mid-channel were not unreal manifestations of a Flying Dutchman. They were hard converted currency. She knew what they cost, not in terms of cash for her range ended near her mother's, in weekly sums, but in terms of unattainability.

This didn't lead to resentment or its derivative, greed. Their cash value was of no interest to her whatever. Standing on the deck, she was impressed by another form of rarity, true uniqueness. She said to herself as the sails cracked round her ears, taking up the variable direction of the wind, I will never be able to do this again. I will never stand for the first time on the deck of a new boat. If she were mine, I'd be worrying about grounding her or letting her heel over or how soon the surface will start to scratch and show signs of wear. But that's his problem. I just don't care what happens.

So she took the best of what he had to offer, pleasure without responsibility or the ties of ownership. She let herself go down the slipway of experience, making the most of the moment. Not to boast, or recount it for waiting ears, a thrill which was attenuated by lesser thrills that tried to imitate or recapture it; but for the quality of the day alone. It was true, she could have been a sybarite, going from one sensation to another, but lack of opportunity prevented that. The high points remained high.

He was exultant too.

He'd spent the previous evening plotting a route, consulting nautical almanacs and the local pilotbook, opening out the charts wider than he usually did. To the uninitiated, these charts revealed a disconcerting inversion whereby the land surface was left vacant, or was denoted by the isolated symbol of a beacon or a headland, the interior landscape being of no advantage to the sailor. By contrast, the sea on which he rode was compact with information, reef and hazard and an occasional shipwreck accentuating the contours that marked depth. These charts put the globe in a different perspective, bringing to the surface what was otherwise invisible, the underwater world which was as varied in its structure as the one that emerged into the air. The addition of hydrogen to oxygen did create a striking difference, but not a radical one. The elements of rock and plant and animal remained constant, so he moved among the shifting currents with some certitude.

"Where shall we go then?"

"I don't know. What were you thinking of?"

"I thought I'd go further afield. Have you been to St Andrews?" He set a course north-east towards the Isle of May, emulating ancient pilgrimages.

"No. I haven't been there. I would like to see St Andrews."

"The Rome of Scotland."

"Why Rome?"

"The ecclesiastical centre at one time. Fifteenth century, I think. Before Knox and Calvinism. I don't know the harbour there or where I can berth but we'll take a chance. If the worst comes to the worst, we can drop anchor and use the tender."

"Do you swim? I've never seen you swim."

"Yes, I swim."

Before noon they rounded the north coast of the Forth, staying well away from the land but could still pick out the towns and harbours of Fife as the morning mist lifted, dotting the sea and the land with shafts of radial light that fell like columns from perforated clouds. He was preoccupied, noticing the land features as they passed and correlating his position on the chart, with depth, sand bar and rock to consider.

"I didn't know you kept a log book."

"I don't, for the south shore. But I haven't come along here too often." He flicked back several pages in the log. "Five years since I was here."

She sat down beside him and he let her hold the tiller steady while he jotted. "And has it changed?"

"No. It doesn't change. But it's interesting to see how differently the boat handles. My times were so much slower in the Mapleleaf."

It was almost the first reference he had made to the past, to anything past. She found she was dismayed by it. Five years. Nothing to him. A trice. To her it was the scope of adolescence that spanned her years at school in Edinburgh, incorporating so much it couldn't all be said. The point of comparison to him was speed. He went faster now. She looked for some comment on quality, value, the essential ingredient implied by his movement forward in time but there was nothing. He was not a retrospective animal, far less a sentimental one.

She picked up the log book and looked through it curiously. Even his handwriting hadn't changed in what, twelve, thirteen years of entries. Thirteen years ago she was hardly out of her pram and he was already inscribing these peculiar markings on the page, the characters of a Dickensian ledger clerk. Time. Direction. Speed. Comments on the weather, all in neat ruled columns. Written out it looked like the stages of a laboratory experiment, its own coded hieratic, to which he would append a conclusion when he reached the final stage which he was still in the process of working out. And what would his conclusion be? Not so many disparate journeys, haphazardly undertaken but getting faster and smoother. Surely more than that. She wanted the fragmentary pages of the log and their message to break into prose, to be logical and reasoned and lead her somewhere with conviction. "This was the sum of my experience and it was worth it." But it didn't say that. She ran her fingers over the empty pages to the back cover, assessing the time that had elapsed as against the time to come. It was a diary without thoughts, without character, and she didn't anticipate that it would change significantly now.

Then, as though he were following the track of her thinking and had to intercede to do himself justice, he said, "That's all false. Or it gives a false impression. Just data, facts. Sailing is practically timeless, you know. Times don't really matter at all, except for safety. If they tell you your position or the run of the tide. But trying to go faster is just putting a bet on a race or a card game to make it more exciting. Specious exercise when what is really exciting is the race or the game and even then it's not with anyone or against anyone. Beating the boat, beating the weather, beating myself for the most part. Going further and further out. I like that. I suppose that's why I do it. If I were more energetic, I could probably get the same thing from walking or swimming but I only do those for fitness. I find them a bit too simple to be interesting. Just motor activities. The special quality about sailing is that you are moving through two elements, water and air, and you have to harness both of them to stay afloat. I like knowing the boat is bigger than I am and is really much more powerful. It could easily drown me but I can use my wits to control it. I know I can make it obey me. A battle of wills if you like. The inanimate and the animate. And when I come back at the end of every day without having got myself in the drink or put a hole in the bows, I think, Today I won. Today I came out on top.

"But then sometimes I think I've got it completely wrong. That I haven't won at all. The boat's won when it got me back in one piece. I'm the inanimate, the cargo, and it's much more intelligent than I am. It's been crafted by someone who's made boats all his life. It's balanced to perfection and I'm just a clumsy recruit staggering about the deck pretending to myself that I'm in charge when really, the boat is sailing me."

She opened her mouth, and shut it. Perhaps in a decade she could answer him.

They passed the point of Buddo Ness and sailed into St Andrews bay. The harbour was crowded for it was the season of Lammastide, inaugurating a bank holiday weekend, and the town and beach areas were full of people. He was disappointed. He had thought he might have the place to himself and that the human race would obligingly clear off to suit him.

"I don't mind swimming ashore," she interpreted as he surveyed the masts and sails along the harbour wall where no immediate berth presented itself. He was acutely dismayed by the bunting and other signs of leisure as it was enjoyed by the populace at large. He anticipated transistors, jostling streets and restaurants, and blanched at the thought of making one more in the crowd.

"Are you sure you want to go ashore? All those people. We could push on, find somewhere quieter."

"Well, I'd like to see St Andrews now I'm here. I'm not wild to press on to Dundee."

"Put like that, neither am I."

He dropped anchor to oblige her.

"Actually," he admitted as she prepared to take her shoes off for the swim, "there's an inflatable dinghy below. We could take that inshore, I suppose."

"Well why not?" she asked, baffled that he sounded hesitant.

He stalled for a while, and frowned into the sun. "I don't really like to leave it unattended when the beach is so crowded." He looked over to the rim of bodies taking the sun.

"Oh really," she was exasperated. "I tell you what to do. Leave it with a couple of boys and tell them they can use it as long as they look after it and don't let anyone else mess about."

"But how do I know they won't pinch it themselves?"

She threw him a look of despair. "You mean you'd go another twenty miles because you can't find anyone to trust? I'll pick the right boys for you. It'll make their day for them."

And she did, cool, bossy, on their own terms to two shoulder-high lads who thought the gods descended. "Don't go far out," she warned. "The coast guard's got enough to do without chasing you over the North Sea. We'll be back at three o'clock so make sure you're right here, at this spot."

"Right-o. Ta."

She walked away with him. "You must give them some money when we get back. Not much. Enough to buy an ice-cream each."

She had longer shorts that day, and wore knee-hose with plimsolls so that she had a strangely American look, a sophomore in Bermudas and sneakers, or a lady golfer taking it seriously. He found he was delighted with her and risked her in Rusack's for lunch. He discovered other people spoke to her spontaneously. Now if this ever happened to him, he clammed up, determined to give nothing away. He was convinced strangers were trying to get something out of him, get him to admit something he didn't want to admit. Yes, that was his yacht in the bay, rather fine too. Yes, he had come from North Berwick that morning and his house was unattended in his absence. He was always sceptical about the interest of one human being in another. If nothing else, it was done to criticise.

She completely bypassed this. She fell into the most unaccountable dialogues with unaccountable people. This couple at the next table were visiting from Wyoming, and they loved it and the golf was so good and they had visited so many interesting places, Scone, the Falls of Lennie and the Soldier's Leap. They were going on to Paris but they wouldn't enjoy it half so much . . . . And the girl behind the buffet said it was the chef's own mayonnaise and he used walnut oil in the dressing. Not that she was Pippa, delighting in everything that passed. She spotted an unruly child she wanted to wallop, a quarrel brewing between lovers, and gave characters to the men and women teeing off outside the window. This one's nervous. That one's a show-off. The day became populous with her acquaintances.

Outside, in heat that was crushing and intense, she was awed by the quadrangles of the University where they strolled to cool themselves and lose the masses by the shore. And they succeeded in being largely alone. They took a meandering course along the flagstone passages that separate the library from the private courtyards and the academic halls which form a bank between the Scores and North Street. The haunts of students were deserted and so he felt himself to be multi-privileged, in finding a thoroughfare empty and with good weather to boot. The walk, contained within an hour and which at one time he would have regarded as scant entertainment for it was purposeless and impromptu, became what such entertainments can – priceless. She stopped and admired, noticing the inscription on a plaque or the unusual entablature above a doorway. Because she was so young and so unaffected, he felt he shed years and might have been a student himself again, hurrying to lecture theatres. The greatest privilege was sharing the day, and sharing it with her.

"Almost as old as Oxford," he said.

"And more beautiful."

"How do you know? You've never been to Oxford."

"It has to be. It's more mine. Everybody's been to Oxford, great armies tramping through it. This is more private."

In the deserted cloisters, he had to agree. The wrought-iron gates of the quadrangle were open, giving them a view without bars of the ivy climbing to mullioned windows while the rector's doves pirouetted, a command performance for them alone.

She sat down on the bench opposite, and considered, "Perhaps I should apply to St Andrews."

"Apply?"

"To the University. For next year."

"But you're not leaving school, are you? You're too young."

"I'm seventeen at Christmas," she said indignantly.

"Well," he tried to recover lost ground, "whereabouts are you in school?"

"I take my Highers in May."

"But you'll stay on for a sixth year?" He was suddenly alarmed at the prospect of her moving on.

"What's the point if I already have my Highers?"

That was inarguable. "And what are you thinking of doing?" He couldn't equate her with a fully matriculated student. She seemed embalmed in her school uniform and incapable of ageing to the point where she could shed it.

"Well, I could take History of Art at St Andrews but I'd like to go to Glasgow art college as well. Or there's the course in Fine Art at Edinburgh which combines the two. Practical and theoretical. I don't know what to do."

"I didn't know you were thinking of studying art."

"No, I don't suppose you did."

Then he remembered her drawings on the sand, as she sat poised over the imperfectible medium, and her coloured outlines in a sketch pad. Her father was a joiner. She probably had some

114

leaning towards a craft. "If you're not sure, why not leave it for another year?"

"Well," she admitted with a sigh, "it looks as though Malcolm will win a scholarship to Daniel Stewart's. They can't pay two sets of schooling. I've had my turn. I've got to get a move on now."

This severe practicality induced strange contradictions in his head, seeing her as perennially a child and then compulsorily mature. But it was something more oblique that was spoken. "So Malcolm's bright too, is he?"

She shot him a glance that was summary. "They're all bright. My Mum and Dad are bright. My Dad could beat you at mental arithmetic any day of the week and my Mum can spell every word in the dictionary. At least," she amended, "I've never caught her out. They've just not had the books, that's all."

He stood accused and had no real defence. "Is that why you wanted to come, to help you to make up your mind?"

"Partly. To know what I was working for. If I went to Edinburgh," she thought aloud, "they might be hurt if I didn't stay at home. But I need to . . . " a space formed into which her ideas grew. "I need to get a move on now."

She had seen all she wanted, or all that was useful to that end. "Come on," he said, "let's get back to the boat. We've been in town long enough."

The boys were there, punctilious. He gave them a pound for the good care they'd taken of his dinghy which they had been rowing round the bay for three hours. They were almost speechless with pleasure. Perhaps it would have been better if they had been. They larded their gratitude with so many "Tas" and "Misters" that Iona began to crease with laughter, not so much at the obsequies as at his acute discomfort in having to receive them.

"What are you laughing at?" he demanded, pulling at the oars.

"Oh you are so solemn. That's what's funny."

"You mean I am ridiculous?"

"Oh no," she straightened out her features. "I don't mean that at all."

The boat was hot when they reached it, lying becalmed on the enamelled bay. Everything throbbed with the reflections from the sun and when she put her foot on the deck, heat shot through her sole as though she were on lava.

115

"Oh this is unbearable. I'm going in. Leave the dinghy tied up for now. I'll help you aboard with it when it's cooler."

He agreed. It was too hot for easy movement. She stripped off in the cabin and he found when she came up on deck again that she had a new costume to replace the green one. She had made it herself from a yard of cloth with many hours of patient treadling on a machine. It was a bikini in triangles like sails held together, or apart, by yards of cord, crossed like rigging on her hips and back.

But then she was over the side, floating away from him, pulsing the way an anemone pulses with her hair streaming out behind. He watched her circle the boat.

"Won't you swim?" she called. "It's divine, the water. It's like silk."

He moved languidly round the deck, seeking a shady spot. "Tempt me."

"How?"

"With words."

"Well," she took up a mouthful of brine, trying to think of them, and spouted it out again. "I feel like one of those very expensive marzipan sweets in Jenners, dipped in toffee. Except the filling is hot and the toffee round it is cold, a lovely frosted wrapper. And gradually it cools the filling down and the marzipan feels much more comfortable."

"Hardly a lovely metaphor. Try again." But he laughed at the absurd picture she drew.

"Then I am a drop of molten glass." She swam on, suspended in the water.

"Go on."

"As I fall into the water, I take on a shape where before I was fluid and amorphous."

"You would crack."

"No. I am special glass and this is special water."

"How?"

"I don't know how. Hows don't matter." But for a moment she did look like special glass, a paperweight, showing the floral sprigs of her costume transparent through the vitreous sea. With a splash he joined her.

They swam in circles, made races with each other between incalculable points or measured the distance they covered with a hundred strokes while the sun descended over the bay and the

116

tide that had brought them in, swept out again.

"Oh tired," she admitted clambering up to the deck again.

"Are you? Well, rest a while."

"Shouldn't we catch the tide?"

"Oh, I'll cheat on the way home and use the engine. This time of day's too good to hurry. Let's go below and have some tea."

The cabin was roomier and better appointed than the old boat, with a separate area forward where she could change. Sitting down on the padded benches in her clothes again, she was suddenly acutely aware of his near nakedness which seemed natural outdoors and paradoxically exposed inside, like Barry Shaw's when he undressed to pay his forfeit in the poker game. This was not the young man's body, but a body deliberately built and tougher just because it was older.

Catching her unease at the disparity in their appearance, he said, "Ah, are you dressed. I'll change too. I don't suppose we'll be swimming again. Wet trunks are so . . . comprehensively wet."

"You know," she said when he came back, "it's marvellous on deck in the open air but somehow I like it better in here. It's so restful, like crawling down a burrow."

"You domestic creature."

"Am I? How dull."

"There's nothing like an old boat for the cabins. They were built higher, more headroom which meant they were slower under sail. But the wood and the brass fittings and the smell of an oil lamp after dark. That really was something. My first boat was like that. I had her for nearly ten years. But I seemed to spend all winter varnishing. Perhaps I should have hung on to her. She was a good boat."

"Don't you go on long trips, overnight? You could be quite snug here."

"No. I never have spent a night in a cabin. Stupid to have it, I suppose. But I'm really sailing boats that are too big for single-handed operation. I ought to have a crew if I'm away for longer than a day. This is nothing more than a private bathing hut, for stray mermaids."

The sun fell lower in the sky and warned him of the hour. Six weeks after midsummer, the evenings were appreciably shorter and he had no wish to navigate strange waters in the dark, even with the assistance of a motor.

"We must get that dinghy up and make tracks."

117

The sea was glassy, dark and heavy as the sun slanted across it filling the bay with depths and shadows which, with the light vertical, had seemed pellucid. The beach emptied. The professional at the Royal and Ancient considered that would be the last tee-off time of the day and put up his boards for the evening. The ice-cream kiosk shut.

They pulled the small craft aboard and she deflated it, packing it back flat in the locker while he went to raise the anchor. They stood for'ard, ready to move off as soon as the anchor was clear, but he was unused to the extra weight of the heavy Danforth and as it swung away unpredictably, it caught against his left hand and snagged one of the fingers.

"Oh bugger it."

She burst out laughing, and to his enquiring eyes explained, "I never thought I'd hear you say anything so uncouth."

"One of the advantages of sailing alone, you know. There's no one to hear what I come out with."

Then as he knelt to fix the anchor into the deck chocks, she caught sight of his finger which oozed a dark, purply blood around the nail and without thinking, she lifted the hand and put the finger in her mouth as though the cut were her own, the gesture of every animal to cleanse its wound. He was more shocked at this movement than if she had made a deliberately sexual gesture and much more shocked than she was by his expletive. He felt assaulted, his body made vulnerable not by its pain but by her impulsive attempt to relieve it.

"Kiss it better," she said, looking at the finger where the flow was staunched.

"I am too old to believe in the efficacy of kisses."

"Ah well." She let the hand go. "It is only believing that makes it work."

"What a statement of faith," he mocked a little to cover his awkwardness. "Unfortunately some of us are incapable of faith, blind or otherwise."

Kissing implied lips. She looked at his eyes then unconsciously dropped hers to his mouth, to the dark rim that in a man separated one flesh from another, the hard chin from the soft lip. She remembered how easy it was to kiss, to meet lips one on the other, and if he had made the slightest move towards her, she would have made it easier still.

But he didn't. "I think there are plasters in one of the cup-

118

boards below. A medicine chest.''

He started the engine while she went rummaging till she found the box and brought him a strip of plaster which he applied himself. They sat opposite each other huddled against the cold as the engine propelled them towards the open sea. He sent her below for extra sweaters.

After a while, when they were clear of the bay, he said, ''The wind is still favourable. It seems a shame to waste it. I'm going to hoist sail. Get us back all the sooner. Will you hold the tiller and keep her steady as she is. I won't be long.''

He went, raising sail and adjusting the sheets with care. She watched him moving about the deck ruefully. She suspected that he did it to abbreviate their contact, so that he didn't have to sit beside her or opposite her again, so that the day of their outing would be cut short. She bitterly regretted her unthinking act, and read its presumptuousness in his eyes. She didn't regret the gesture for itself but because it terminated their mood of relaxation and ease with each other. She felt like someone who has foundered on a sand bank, no harm done, only inconvenience and delay, but railed against the charts that misdirected her and the powerful tides that shifted her off course.

No matter what, they were self-conscious. Their eyes followed each other with new awareness, or avoided the other which was the same thing. It did not matter how many sweaters they put on. Like Adam and his spouse, whatever apron or breeches they wove themselves to cover their nudity, the garment was inadequate. They were transparently naked, perceptive of what lay below the surface, as treacherous as it was alluring.

They made good time, driving south-west across the open mouth of the Forth towards the twin lighthouses of Fidra and Bass.

They both knew, going into the moorings, that neither of them was likely to make a gratuitous comment about the pleasantness of the day or one another's company. They would part in genial but distant fashion, more removed from each other in spirit than when the day began.

An unforeseen circumstance saved them from such a cool farewell.

When they walked round the curve of the bay from the

harbour, Iona found the children had been allowed out late, anticipating her return. For once, their parents were in attendance, Jim Stewart finding curiosities of the tide while Maggie was content to sit on the ledge and be consulted or crawled over according to the age of the child who approached.

Innes had misgivings, seeing them en masse, but Maggie lifted a beaming face to him and said, "You've had a beautiful day. It couldn't have been better for you."

Maybe it was a trick of the light, mellow on her skin, but Innes felt the girl inherited more than a quickness with orthography from her mother. If careworn or neglected, it was at least a face without artifice. She had a kind of embracingness which it was hard to resist. He took her on the level and sitting down beside the woman, explained what they had done with the day.

Iona was pleased to see them all again and clung into a group with the younger ones. She held the baby who at fifteen months had reached the optimum age of babies, mobile and articulate but not excessively so. This James had the same head as all of them, covered with down, and it gave the outsider the strangest sensation to see the girl holding the child in the hammock of her crossed arms, leaning away from him at the hip to compensate for his weight. She rubbed her lips against his head and the boy often reciprocated with a kiss. This witnessed fondling affected him with the deepest pang.

He stood up, feeling a little unwanted in the middle of their kinship, ready to go and close his own solitary door behind him. The baby made a mistake common enough in infants who look straight across or down, not up into a face. He mistook Innes for his father, a male, a blue pullover, and leaned out his arms to be taken. The man obliged, lifting the child from Iona's grip.

He was not disagreeably surprised. The child was hot and solid, utterly pleasant to hold, look down on, feel braced against his own side. The boy was intent on a shell someone had given him and enquired inside its coils with his eye and his finger, and then inevitably felt it with his mouth.

"Ah no," Innes restrained him from getting a tongueful of grit and the child, alerted to the fact that he was being carried by a stranger, cowered shyly and leaned away again towards his sister with a whimper.

"I think he's eaten half the beach by now," she said as she received him. "That's why he weighs so much."

120

He smiled. The boy gave him covert looks from the safety of Iona's shoulder but in the direct gaze of the man's eye turned away abashed.

"Thank you," he said at last and, taking leave of them, went indoors.

For a long time afterwards, she hugged the words to herself like an embrace remembered. Thank you. That was everything.

Chapter Thirteen

Sometimes he imagined a companion pair of figures, seated for novelty.

There were many sets of figurines in genre poses, boys and girls holding trumpet-like shells, in bathing dress or acting out some narrative from life below stairs. He, a pageboy in breeches and waistcoat, carries a fish to table and drops it. It lies at his feet on the plinth. She, transporting lemons to accompany it, laughs behind her hand. Such stories went on being told for a century, seconds of agonising dismay and embarrassment caught for ever. Which was worse for the young server, he asked himself, to drop the fish or to be laughed at by the girl?

Or there were more sedate, rococo couples. A man with a handkerchief, a lady with a parasol, strolling perhaps through the Tuileries on a warmish afternoon while he complains a little of the heat, fanning himself. No wonder he is warm. Stockings complete with ribbon garters, knee breeches, shirt, crop, waistcoat and redingote all topped by a powdered wig. Excruciatingly hot for July. She smiles a little at his foppishness, at the frown and the dangle of his wrist as he wafts the handkerchief. She will improve that when she marries him. In the meantime while she serves out their engagement, she must humour him. And the smile which bedecks her face is full of humour. He will not mind being improved too much, by someone who is cool in muslin with bare neck and arms and lifts a parasol to shade her face, and the too-knowing smile.

Hundreds of couples walked this way.

Hundreds of couples he had sold to sit in china cabinets or grace the two ends of a mantelpiece or a sideboard which was little used in one of the sedate dining rooms of the capital.

He always felt vaguely sorry for these couples on their separate plinths, relegated to spend a lifetime away from each other at the extreme corners of a piece of furniture. And so uncomfortably,

123

standing all the while! The least the modeller could do was make them sit or lie.

So he imagined a companion pair of figures, seated for novelty as well as comfort.

He would put them on chintz perhaps, or the kind of Jacobean print he liked. An Edwardian couple, just pre-war, 1911 say, the last period when dress was elegant. He reads the paper. A dove-grey three-piece suit, plain against the patterned chairback. And the lady of the house, what should she do? It is hard to assign her a role. He does not want her to look bored, Hogarth's *Marriage à la Mode*, drifting to dissatisfaction and their separate ways. So perhaps he should put his paper down, he thought that might be a good idea, and pay her some attention. But what can they do that involves them both without being plainly narrative? What can they be saying to each other that will make itself manifest even without words?

He played the scene over and over again, working out parts and gestures for the woman as well as the man, trying to make them integrate so that they looked as though they belonged together. So that if ever they became separated, a connoisseur who had seen one or the other could with accuracy reconstruct what the role of the missing partner must have been. The compensatory movements must be inevitable.

But thinking of this reminded him of all the broken sets he came across, pieces that were attractive on their own but had less meaning and less value than when the pair survived intact. Perhaps breakages were inevitable with such a fragile medium and he did sometimes wonder what proportion survived. It would be safer then, to put his ideal couple on one plinth, like the knoll with the tree-stump that the shepherd and his sleeping shepherdess reclined on.

He would put them . . . on a bench, yes, on a garden bench. An outdoor scene. Not a rustic bench of wooden spars but a wrought-iron one, white. Delicate. Hard to mould but there need not be, if the figures were disposed along it carefully, too much exposed metalwork, a filigree that in porcelain would be vulnerable to damage.

Yes, wrought iron and they sedentary in light summer dress, or undress. He liked best the statuary where the painter had taken some care to match the clothes of man and woman, where the same colours were picked up and amplified, one to the other, so that there was a kind of reiteration going between the figures, unifying them and the design of the piece as a whole. The same turquoise on her bodice and his necktie. The same line decorating his waistcoat and her underskirt. Tiny insistencies.

The colours of the shore. Cream, biscuit and blue highlights. She would wear an outfit of sprigged lawn, florets to the hem which was a little lifted over the knee but cascaded downwards in a bouquet, cascaded from the gown onto the base, the two not separable, pediment and woman as if she had grown into place and fused there. The colour of the central flower echoed his waistcoat, the Worcester blue invasive to the end.

He turned the piece this way and that, making sure it had the requirements of perfection. He looked at her, while she looked to the side, abashed at ardour. There was a flowing rhythm between their arms. She chose from something that he offered her, a nosegay or a sweetmeat or a piece of fruit, and that might serve as a title for the group. "The Choice".

In such style he could immortalise her.

But then at night when he undid the flounces of her bodice and loosened the cummerbund at the waist, leaning over the bench, for though it was outdoors it was not cold on the terrazzo where the walls kept the heat of the day long after sunset, then when the corsage was opened, he discovered that the meticulous art of the creator extended far beyond the visual. He had taken care to paint her underneath. He mixed the skin tones in such gradations that they lived, breathed, were subtle, mobile flesh. He could trace the blue veins under the breast where the aureoles were moulded in like a gemstone circled with seed pearls. Or shells; they were the pale cones of the limpet with outer ridges that teased the thumbnail in its circular caress. He explored them with his eye and with his hand, and then inevitably felt them with his mouth.

And found she wasn't cold, cold alabaster or marble to the touch. She was warm. All his similes dissolved under her warmth for there was nothing like her. She was incomparable. He put his head back on her lap, feeling the texture of her skin, and thought the modelling was exceptional; rotund and delicate, the interplay of lightness and strength.

Then as he lay comfortably admiring the composition, she did a quite alarming thing. She moved.

She leaned forward over him and took him in her arms and murmured something. Words, words came breaking out of her, hardly recognisable as words because her lips were pressed against his face and his neck and his hands, stifling the sound, and him too with their weight. They seemed words of love, evoking a reply but he could give none because she suffocated him with her embrace.

Without preparation, she began to touch his clothes, undoing the blue waistcoat and the buttons of his shirt, feeling round and under him, appraising him as he appraised her. He did not think it seemly as she threatened to expose him and his body to a degree that was – unaesthetic, out of keeping with the tenor of the group. An open bodice, yes. Opened trousers, no. That was yet to be modelled in porcelain. He felt the grossness of demands that were whole and equal and involved the display of everything in their emotional and physical range as men and women, man and woman, one to one. Her gestures went on shocking him, real and raw, making him . . . making him react. Uncouth, by God she was uncouth and made him that way too, removing one at a time the layers of what was decorous, clothes, manners, inhibitions – the distancing that made intercourse between humans bearable. And the words, he made them out in the end, that she said over and over again with every inflexion in the register of pain and urgency. Be human. Be human. The cry of life, of the loving to the unloving.

He woke up, clammy with sweat.

A hot night, that was all. He opened the balcony window. The sea had withdrawn far out of sight. It was still but very close. He went to the bathroom for water to drink. He looked out of the window into the terrace as he passed. It was quiet, moonlit, empty. No bench had suddenly appeared. No couple disported themselves on it. Not even a ribbon or a garter lay undone. All imagination.

He went back to the bedroom having splashed himself with water and peeled away half the covers so that the bed wouldn't be so stifling. He sat for some time under the light at his side, reading, or attempting to read but the dream or the fantasy kept coming back, asserting itself in his mind, a nightmare he was relieved wasn't true.

Though, if he examined it without bias, it had enough honest elements to make it very nearly truth. He longed for the simplicity of Galatea, the capacity to fall in love with a statue and

126

breathe life into it, for it to come to life and love in return. His lot was more complex. He did not think he was capable of loving to the point of creation, when the thing he loved became alive and lived independently. The real point of the fable was that the sculptor believed in his power to bring the woman into being. Yes, she said, it's only believing that makes it work. Well he didn't have that belief, or held himself aloof from it. He dreaded animation and the ugliness he was capable of creating with his body, of setting into motion the sequences of mortality, decay and death, even the death of affection, following inevitably on the propulsion into life.

It was better to have a whole range of substitutes than to risk losing all by aiming at the real experience, and falling short.

For handling the statue, he found an ironical creator had inscribed in gold lettering on the base, *Et in Arcadia ego*. No escape. Even in the midst of pastoral idyll, the ego death was present.

Chapter Fourteen

When he was eventually paid by Jack Shaw, her father gave Iona a five-pound-note as a present. It was a lovely thing and she spent hours admiring it, smoothing and smoothing it, feeling the ribs of engraving underneath her fingers and holding it to the light to see the shadow of the watermark. Its serial number meant it was just hers, impossible to forge. It was a fortune and she could not bear to part with it because, unspent, it was amenable to fifty spendings.

But the joys of the miser palled on her. She needed to convert it before it had any meaning and at long last she decided to invest it, in a pack of clay.

She set up her table at the far end of the workshop and cut open her polythene pack carefully so that she could reseal it. A disused metal breadbin with a lid was its more permanent container, into which she could drop waste or over-dry scraps to be rehumidified. Every particle was precious.

She prepared it the way she had been taught in the evening class. She cut off half a pound or so and rolled it on the tabletop with the heel of her palm, a curving pressure that in a few minutes produced a coil with imprints, like the humped shell of an ammonite. Not fossil yet, dried and preserved, but living under her hands, mobile and yielding to inspiration. She beat it to extract the air, by throwing the block down on the table, and watched it find its own form as it fell in wedges, misshapen parcels. Then when it was dense and the air pockets were driven out, but more pliable through this continuous massaging, she set out to fashion something with the clay.

Not pots, no. She was not interested in pots, had not the potter's patience with symmetry which in any case was an artifice not found in nature any more than the straight or parallel line. She rolled the clay into a ball and put it on top of another like a col, a neck or spur. She pressed in sockets for the eyes, built up a

129

jaw and watched a face take shape. But the skull she moulded was the skull of anyone, man, woman, modern, ancient, as feature-less and sexless as the early human embryo. It waited for the stamp of growth and time. She looked at the bonework, daunted by the variety of its potential and the responsibility she had for clothing it with just one flesh, one statement of being.

Which? Which out of all the faces she had seen, alive or pictured, should she project onto the mobile clay?

She faltered and went to find a model, leaving the head covered in a sheet of plastic while she thought.

She started on the sculpture of the ancients, Praxiteles and Myron but found, disappointingly, that they concentrated on portraying the body at the expense of the face. Without their distinguishing anatomy, Milo and Discobolos were neuters, their features conforming to a hermaphrodite beauty rather than an individual one. They were not themselves, but standards. The eyes in particular disturbed her, the scooped-out, unseeing eyes which gave back no expression. Blank irises. She didn't want to imitate those paradigms of human form with their painless, unlined faces.

Turning the pages of a book, she was waylaid by the skill of Egyptian craftsmen who made ducks of alabaster, receptacles for unguents, easy on the hand. And Chinese horses which were miracles of balance with one single hoof skimming the ground. They were an exercise in logic as much as art. How many angels can stand on the head of a pin? How much weight can be balanced on the rim of a hoof? Answer – infinite, provided the creation is right.

She passed through the arid, artless centuries of flat crucifixes with figures in stylised woodenness, thinking all the time, This is not what I am looking for. Michelangelo bodied out more reality, a Pietà that evoked just that, Medici giants hacked out of blocks, grumblingly aroused, or Bernini's David biting his lip in defiant anti-classical pose.

But it was only when she came to Rodin that she felt moved and excited by the heads that were tense, and even tortured with emotion. The unfinished rawness of their plinths seemed to make them more immediate and more recent, an event still in process of happening rather than compactly done. Finish was staid. She liked Epstein's flying bronzes, marvelling at the

130

paradoxes between stability of medium and fluidity of design, a wilful contrast, land and sea locked into a moment of fusion, a unit.

Reading the account of how these artists worked, she was struck by the fact that for many sculptors, the shaping of the head in clay was only the beginning. From that they made a mould, again of clay, and then a bronze cast from the mould, pouring in molten metal like the blacksmith at the forge. Some complex works would take days to cast, each section being tackled separately. Wooden scaffolding would have to be built to support the weight of the moulds while the bronze cooled. Imagine, horses were cast like this, life-size, and composite statues with several different figures in a group. The scale of this foundry workshop staggered her, half a dozen men working on one project. Craftsmen were depicted doing just that on a Greek vase which was two and a half thousand years old. They already had the art and she was just beginning.

Examples were worthless and confusing. There were no examples; only part-solutions to problems that remained insoluble. She came back to the incipient face a little nervously, weighted by the impertinence of making man into clay, clay into man. She tried to overlook the finished product which would be rough, imperfect, childish possibly, and concentrate on the doing. She only learned by doing. It would not be wasted.

So she pressed on and formed, liking the person that built up on the board at the end of the table. She had long dialogues with this individual until the head became her closest familiar, most known because it was a projection of herself. It was there waiting every day, patient, tolerant and compatible, sometimes better and sometimes worse than it was the day before. They looked at each other quizzically, with lopsided humour, forgiving of each other's faults.

Her hands effected a powerful transference. Skin was shredded from her fingers in minute particles that mixed unobtrusively with the medium while grains of clay attached themselves round her nails, into the creasing of her joints, embedding themselves deeply so that while she worked on the sculpture, she was never completely free from them. There was a dusting on her hands even after she had washed them. It began to feel natural and proper, indispensable to reality.

Of course she wasn't satisfied with the roughcast when she had

131

finished it, but gave up trying to improve the thing. She left it to dry out over several weeks, watching the patchy effect of the various stages of dehydration. It paled in blocks, the nose first, lips, ears, all the external features turning to a dusty pink while the main part of the head stayed damp for a long time. It made a patchwork of light and dark. At length, when all the surface water had evaporated, she moved it indoors to a warm spot where the heat of the fire at room temperature would provide a mini-kiln and shrink it thoroughly. She examined it minutely each morning in case cracks appeared from over-drying.

Of all the people that she knew, it was perhaps most like Jack Shaw, although neither of them would have known to look at it. It had that ruggedness which he did not recognise in himself, a temperamental lack of smoothness. Emergent rather than accomplished. Certainly her benefactor would not have given five pounds for his portrait, would not have given house room to an original work. No power on earth would make him boast of having been the sitter for the unconventional.

Jim looked at the finished sculpture, appreciating the work that had gone into it, if not the workmanship. "Why don't you take some sandpaper and rub down these ledges?"

"The ledges are meant to be there."

"It doesn't look a lot like skin."

"No. It's meant to look like a landscape."

"Ah well. You can only get better."

Chapter Fifteen

As they grew, physically, space was put at a premium in the Stewart household. There were not enough bedrooms to go round. Babies who slept in cots needed beds of their own in time and beds took up more floor space. It became difficult for all of them to fit into one room comfortably. Meals were a daily marathon, with staggered starts when each of them was obeying a different schedule. The work of caring for so many people was never-ending, one meal flowing into another with hardly a break. Ironing became mountainous; washing a sea. Maggie coped marginally.

As they grew mentally, quarrels erupted which were not serious or acrimonious. They didn't come to blows with each other, but they did start to barge at the turns, fighting for place and privilege. Iona, working at her portfolio or school books, pottering about outside with her heads and her clay, had not observed the gradations of change. Sometimes she came back in from the workshop and found Malcolm holding sway in her absence. They seemed a more natural group without her, regent, queen, the jester Sandy and two underlings, and so bit by bit she resigned her tutelage over them, opting out of her position.

The mornings were the most difficult, school mornings any-way, because with three of them and her father struggling to assemble themselves and their thoughts to make an early exit, collisions were inevitable. That morning there had been no blouse for her to put on.

"I haven't had a minute to do the ironing," said Maggie, deep in porridge.

"Well, what am I supposed to do? I'll be late for the train."

"I'll tell you what you're supposed to do. You're supposed to get the iron out yourself and do your own. A grown girl like you, Iona. You should be giving me a hand instead of always complaining when things aren't just the way you'd like them. Mooning around upstairs all the time."

It was the rank injustice of this that hurt. After all the times she'd tried to do exactly that, played with the little ones, helped out. Iona went back over her teens which had been lost somewhere in minding other childhoods, in premature responsibility, to see if there was something else she should have done, and felt there must be if it was expected of her. The mooning around was with her studies, trying to prepare for the future. Between it and the busy past, there seemed no space to live the present.

So she got the iron out and did the thing herself, but noticed Malcolm's shirt was pressed for him. She was arriving at the point of independence, which meant doing things for herself because no one would do them for her. Childhood, the protected state, was passing.

She arrived at the platform heaving and ruffled, plumping down in the first carriage she came to without looking round to see who was nearby.

Barry Shaw and his new girlfriend were there. They were going steady. Iona wondered what commodities she traded in for the security of saying, "He's mine." Barry caught her eye and nodded. The group that used to travel on the train had broken up. Iona peeled off from them because she started to find them too noisy and too public in the mornings. The ticket inspector had been summoned to warn them for being obstreperous, and she said condescendingly to herself that they were immature.

Barry and his girl split away so that they could sit together all the way to Edinburgh, indulging in as much love-making as was permissible in public. Iona wished she'd looked before she sat down in that spot. She could hardly move now that they'd seen her. They were opposite but in the next bay up, alone, so that she could avoid seeing them if she didn't look but couldn't help it somehow. Noticing. Watching the way they kissed. It wasn't innocent kissing. It managed to suggest, in its primary approaches, all the other numbers of their intimacy. Those numbers haunted her. What did they mean? What did they actually involve? It had seemed so shocking once, men and women putting their bodies together in that way, but now she turned a corner and the shock was that she wanted the knowledge and the putting together herself.

134

So Barry, winding himself around the other girl, out of view, tormented her with glimpses of the body's possibilities. Calling her coward, juvenile, the virgin every time he made a gesture to the more compliant female. Knowing she wanted these things done to her but was too reticent, or hypocritical, to carry into deed the thoughts she harboured. She almost thought he did it on purpose, flaunting in front of her. No, he had not asked her out again but in his company there was a conscious tension as if he might, as if he bided his time. This sexual proclivity before her eyes was tantamount to flirting with her directly, the peacock on display for any number of impressionable females. They still had a relationship, if in suspense.

She looked away, resting on her hand, but the reflection in the carriage window gave back a deep and intense picture of the thing she averted her eyes from, just as it had done the day that Innes Hamilton came to sit in their carriage. Avoiding the act, she was confronted with a more vivid image of it.

Her portfolio was giving her endless problems too. Her presentation work had to conform to certain standards, set by the art colleges and the examination board. She had dozens of sketch pads filled with Bass and Law and Fidra, and more folders of paintings than she remembered. When she went through these to mount and label them, however, she found she was deeply dissatisfied with them, could hardly bear to put them on show. There were compulsory figure drawings, all the bodies being decently clad, and compositions on a set theme which were required to include at least two figures, together with a pile of sheets of abstract designs. These drove her wild; perfecting little repetitions in little squares, making out that half-block or whole-block repeats added any significance to the footling pages at the end of it. They looked like bad wallpaper. She knew she excelled at whatever was big, mobile, plastic. The three-dimensional, not crabbed little dots of colour. Applied art, not theoretical. She wanted to mould the thing with her fingers, even paint, get stuck in, not hold a brush at arm's length. Direct contact with the medium was what she aimed for. But to qualify to train in what she wanted, she had to perform in different areas, as though an explorer had to take a degree in geography before he set out.

She tried to hold herself stable through this mood. Tried to say she was developing so rapidly that of course the work she completed a year ago was full of faults. But that didn't really

135

help, admitting she was half a step forward on a road to infinity, that was, perfection.

Everything was pressuring her towards change, her family's edginess, Barry showing her what being adult was all about, in his terms, time making her older and her parents more distraught in the attempt to make ends meet, to provide for them all, so that the solution seemed to be in leaping ahead and away, to do the thing she didn't feel able to do yet. Compete. Create.

She listened to the rails drumming under her. I live the life of the mind, they said with haunting mockery, for they carried her further and further away from it in perpetual motion.

Where was he anyway?

That was the worst thing of all about the mornings, falling out of the house, being or not being with the group, bracing herself for another day's disappointment at the easel, that was all easy compared with the tantalising glimpses she caught of Innes Hamilton on the station platform.

He spared the odd word, made the odd smile. Sometimes she tried to corner him. She didn't look in his direction, or pretended not to see him. Then waited for him to draw her attention, by tapping on his window or lifting his paper. He always did. That was the thing. He always did, as though it mattered to him too.

It was unendurable for him to be on the same train and to be separated by the connecting doors between the first and second class. Connecting? They connected only in emergencies. She wanted to be with him. She wanted to be with *him*. She wanted to get up and pull back the compartment door and go and sit down beside him and turn round and say . . .

All to no avail. He was starting to stay up in town again. The winter pattern of their lives reasserted itself, a contradiction of the summer one which brought them into close contact, full of accidental open-air meetings. He went on seeing the woman he saw, or the women. The pictures which taunted her a year before of public appearances together, hand on arm, changed subtly with new knowledge and she was driven into imagining, with more invidious jealousy, the private ones, hand on breast. He would. He did. But not with her.

Sometimes she wondered if her father knew the way she felt. He would tease her mercilessly. "No boyfriends yet, Iona?"

Then she wished she'd confided in him about Barry, if only to keep him quiet, but he was more of a boy's father than a girl's, good at making models and rough and tumble. Not much good for talking to, certainly not about boyfriends. And in a sense, he did it to take a rise out of Maggie, seeing past the girl to the woman.

She always interrupted when she heard him say something like this. "There's more to life than men and marriage. Leave her be. Iona's got her certificate to get first. Time enough afterwards."

Iona did not know what this certificate was exactly, but it was often referred to, a zenith of achievement. The two-handedness of her mother's aim did strike her as contradictory. She should not spend too much time alone, studying, but she must accomplish none the less. She tried not to resent the ambiguities, reminding herself that bookishness was its own language not everyone was required to learn; but was exasperated all the same. It was hard to formulate her ambition in terms that they would grasp. Her father understood this gulf better than her mother but couldn't reconcile the desire to strive with ignorance of how it was to be done.

Iona would still be surprised when he came out with stray observations. Once, after this common interchange, when Maggie had gone out of the room saying Iona had no time for boyfriends, he advised, "Don't save yourself for older men. You can be sure they haven't saved themselves for you."

She couldn't disagree but countered, "And will a young man? Will he be any better?"

To which he did not reply.

He was right. Innes stopped and gave her a lift into Edinburgh, intent on staying overnight. She went, happy at the immediate implications of enjoying his company, dejected at the long-term ones of sharing it with someone else.

For once he did not turn the radio on but waited expectantly as if preferring to hear what it was she had to say.

"And how is work going? What have you decided?"

So he did remember! He put the facts of her existence together better than anyone she knew. She was immensely flattered, but at the same time realised that this application of his intelligence was another form of polished social behaviour, extended to anyone who was worth the trouble.

"I'm not getting on too well. I don't know that I'm doing the right thing. I've ruled out St Andrews. It's a two-way decision between Edinburgh and Glasgow, which ought to be easier. And

I'm finding it very hard to work at home."

"Why is that? Why is it hard? You have a room to yourself where you can study?"

"No. I share with Mary, and she still has to go to bed quite early. So then I have to move downstairs."

This possibility had never occurred to him. Every child had a room of its own. Full stop. He could not fully understand the logistics of a move into a house which was still too small for your family, and indeed where work and schooling were so distant. Perhaps the Stewarts had not thought about these practicalities.

"And how do you get on downstairs?"

"Well Malcolm's working down there too. And everyone else. It's busy."

He saw the alternatives mapped out. A warm but crowded kitchen. Maggie thumping the iron, washing up in slow circles. Jim wandering in and out with bits of wood. A cold sitting room with no work table. He reflected on his orderly preparations for thought, the only disturbance his own restlessness or change of mood. Outside interruptions like the removal or the ringing of the door bell had greatly annoyed him, impinging on his safe-guards to the whole expression of an idea. His house was an aide-mémoire, prompting an exact conclusion. He felt guilty at the surfeit he enjoyed when she had so little space or silence to herself, an unfair handicap.

"When do you take your Highers?"

"In May."

"Six months. Not long."

"No. Not long now." She sounded optimistic.

"What time do you usually get in from school?"

"About half past four if I really shift, and catch the early train."

He wasn't back till almost seven. More than two hours. He battled with himself, knowing that if he were to make the proposal that she should use his house and its suite of empty rooms, he ought to do it then and there. The repugnance he had felt on her behalf at having to share a room to work in or to sleep in, was itself the main deterrent to making the offer. He was impelled towards a form of generosity. It was only space he would be giving her, not time. He would not be there. But he couldn't easily overcome the habits of solitude which included free mental space. He would have to give her a key to the house and trust her with his property, assuming she would not violate the authority vested in her. Could he share it? Could he really bear to think of someone else roaming freely in his own establishment?

He swithered. A crisis of conscience while they sped on past Greywalls, through Gullane and the open spaces of the links towards Aberlady, the car lapping up the miles as if he were not driving and she were not noticing that his thoughts were elsewhere. He struggled to control the impetus to help her, saying he had no responsibility whatever in the matter for it was up to her parents to provide the essentials. Why should he play benefactor? Besides, he thought glancing across at her, they might have their own misgivings at such an arrangement. Then he remembered how negligent they were with her freedoms of movement and association. His shelter might be the only one she had.

"Have you tried the library?"

"Yes, but it's such a bind going out again in the evening when it's at the other end of town."

He anticipated the school holidays at Christmas and Easter when he would be at work and she would be able to study uninterrupted during the day. But that would give her almost rights of ownership, her possession being in excess of his. The more benefits to her that accrued in the arrangement, the greater were the detractions for himself. He found it impossible to be wholly altruistic, when even charity had to be levered from him by force. The poor were always the poor, and unimprovable. He could not bring himself to make a gesture which was the antithesis of all that he held dear, privacy, withdrawal, the sum of self.

He tried to find another yardstick which he could apply to resolve this dilemma in the conflict of interests, his and hers. It came to him suddenly what Jack Shaw would have done in these circumstances. Now Jack would be generous at party-time, with large and public gestures for all to see. He himself did not adhere to the Masonic motto, Do good in silence. But as for actually allowing somebody to use his house, no, that brought no return. Thinking that the offer was in concept and in practice the opposite of what Jack Shaw would consider worth while, he made it. Besides, it cost him nothing. He could afford liberality when it was free.

"Well, perhaps," he said, "it might work out if you were to

139

use my house each day till I get back. I am home at seven, sharp, but you could study up till then." He must make the conditions clear in drawing up a verbal contract. "Your parents will have to know, of course. I'll give you a key to the back of the house and you can let yourself in and out as you please."

The proposal seemed to Iona the solution to everything, a godsend. She did not quibble over conditions, and was careful not to over-enthuse, embarrassing him with thanks.

"That would be just fine," she said, but knew what it had cost him.

Chapter Sixteen

Jim made a box for his elder daughter's seventeenth birthday which fell between Christmas and New Year, an event that was often given less than its due or was elided into those larger celebrations by analogy. This year, he was determined to make a special effort. She grew up, but at what point she was grown up, he couldn't say. Adolescence was a state of mind Iona had not suffered from. She was much older than his other children in temperament as well as age, so that she was always a miniature adult, involved in decision-making. The stages of maturity which fell at puberty, the age of consent, the school-leaving age, or those that were still to come with the responsibility to drink, to vote or to drive, seemed irrelevant in Iona's case. Now that she was almost seventeen, an age to which he attached a sentimental rather than a logical importance, he regretted their haste in making her adult and was determined to make the day a landmark.

So he decided to make her a box for keeping jewellery in. He used a piece of wood left over from some fancy work of Jack Shaw's. Jack came back again and again with other work, some in the house, some in the boat. It pleased him to employ labourers and to say with amplitude, My man is seeing to it. Jim sometimes heard him cast his authority about but didn't object. They did not haggle now, or only in ritualised form. Jim was confident he would be offered more work and Jack was confident he would not be asked to pay over the odds for it. They suited each other.

All the same, Jim consistently over-estimated the timber on Jack's jobs. Not by much. He would not diddle the firm because he felt his future was bound up in it, but he felt Jack was fair game. Their official bartering did not take account of the small fiddles he could work on him, which were his own percentage; a catch-as-catch-can where the only viable rules were the ones he could get away with.

He went in and out at weekends in his own time. Barry did too. As the light faded, Jim heard someone drop him at the bottom of the drive and listened to his energetic footsteps as he went to leave his golf clubs in the lumber-room which had a shower in it. Jim went on fitting the shelves in the study, sending up the smell of wood resin as he drilled. Small piles of fibre fell to the ground like wormcasts. The shower played for maybe twenty minutes, to the accompaniment of Barry whistling. It was not entirely tuneless but the notes emerged too as spray, pushed through a small aperture rather than full-throated. It grated after a while, the sound of running water and the whistle which became, in its monotonous consistency, a kind of aggressiveness going on and on and on without inflection.

Eventually he came out, wrapped in a towel. The young man padded across the hall and catching sight of the joiner, changed direction and came to inspect his work.

He ran a judicial hand over the shelf which was only balanced on its housing. "Not bad, Jimmy, not bad." But then he thought this was too laudatory. "A bit rough round the edges though."

At the beginning, Jim would have risen to this and justified himself. When the insolence of the swagger became more obviously a pose, he gave the standard answer, "Fools and bairns should never see half-finished work."

The "Jimmy" grated on him, a tiresome near miss. He did not expect the obedience of his own children but felt he had a right to his due entitlement and not a rounding down that made him into Thingummy.

Barry smiled. A box of new golf balls sat on the executive desk, printed with Jack's name, and picking one up, the young man put it on the unbalanced shelf and watched it roll very slowly from right to left. "I think you've lost the bubble in your plumb line, haven't you?"

Jim could feel a contraction of the muscles from his neck into his shoulder and arm, a kind of bracing as his body involuntarily tensed to land a blow. He knew he couldn't hit him and that if they moved on to verbal fisticuffs, Barry would win because he was more unscrupulous. He stood on higher ground, young, secure and impudent, which made him unassailable. The worst abuse a man in Jim's position could hurl at him was, What do you know about it? To which Barry would reply saucily, Nothing. The same as you.

So he made Jim's blood boil, as he sat lightly on the edge of the desk flaunting his near nakedness which was in itself a challenge to masculinity. Muscle-flexing as a prompt to combat, declaring, Go on then. Take me on.

Jim put his hand into his trouser pocket, through the side vent of his overalls, and found a coin which he proceeded to put down deliberately on the desk. "Here's tuppence, son. Away down the sweetie shop and get yourself a gobstopper."

Barry looked at the coin but before he could twist a retort out of it, his father came into the study, following voices.

"You're late back. All day to play a round of golf?"

"I took my time. No hurry."

"And did you win?"

"Five and four."

Jack joined in the glee at so comprehensive a victory. "Smashed him, did you?"

"The secretary's reduced my handicap though. I'll have to lose a few rounds and put in some so-so cards."

"You're a bandit," said his father admiringly. "Anything on it?"

"A fiver."

"I ought to back you."

"They'd get suspicious if I went higher."

"Maybe so. Maybe so."

Jim, with no knowledge of either the rules or the etiquette of the golf club, had difficulty following the implications of the conversation but it left a distinct impression on him, raw ends that snagged him every time he passed. That young Shaw should also be a talented golf player seemed gratuitous enough, but that he should be able to win by the assistance of a false handicap pointed to a large flaw in the game. Standardisation of weights and measures came to mind, visible and determinable. An inch was an inch infallibly. If the system of golf handicaps was meant to ensure that everyone started out with a fair rating, it was absurd to play under the acknowledgement that it was open to the abuse of rigging. He knew most of all that he would not like to concede this young man many shots.

Barry went away to dress ready for his evening sortie.

"Cup of tea, Jim?"

"Yes, I'll take a cup of tea."

Jack went into the kitchen and made it himself, happy among

the gadgetry. The kettle boiled and switched itself off. The wall-mounted dispenser dispensed the right amount of tea. All he had to do was add one to the other and drink it. He came back with a tray of mugs and biscuits and sat down behind the desk.

"Coming along. You will be finished by the middle of the month?"

"Oh yes, I'll be over and out by then."

"Barry's eighteenth. We want to give him a proper do."

Jim thought of this, surprised in part he was not older. "Does he work alongside you?" he asked, reflecting that employment had not made itself apparent in the son. Jack worked hard at whatever it was he did. Barry worked hard to avoid it.

"No. I paid to keep him on at school." Jack hesitated. There was no one they knew in common to whom it could be repeated and Jim was in no sense a rival who might cast it up or try to take advantage of the fact, and so he admitted confidentially, "I had to do a bit more than pay. I had to practically beg his headmaster to keep him on. He's got a head on his shoulders but never uses it. Always in trouble, or nearly in trouble."

"Nothing serious?"

"Oh no, nothing serious. No charges. Nothing like that. Gives a lot of lip. Sharper than his teachers, that's his trouble."

Jim thought that yes, he was a lippy youth all right. "You should have had more family. Look at me with six. They rub against each other. That knocks the edges off."

"True enough. But it's too late now."

"What will he do when he leaves?" Now that he considered it, Jim couldn't see the young man fitting into any occupation. He had had too much freedom for too long to accept the curbs of regular employment.

"I don't know. Set him up in business, I expect. I can't have him in with me. We don't get along that well," he confessed. "A fiver for this and a fiver for that. It's all handouts. He's got to learn to balance his own accounts."

Jim tidied up the debris he had made, sweeping sawdust.

"Your girl's leaving soon, isn't she? Didn't you say she was leaving school?"

"That's true but I don't think I said it."

"Oh maybe Barry did. He seems to know all the girls round here. Isn't she blonde?"

"Yes, she has fair hair."

144

"Perhaps he's asked her to this birthday party. A hundred and fifty so far. You soon lose count. Has she said anything?"

"No, she's not mentioned it."

"Well here," enthused Jack, opening one of the desk drawers. "Take her an invitation just in case. I don't know who he's asked but she's welcome to come along. They're bound to know each other." He found a pen and paused. "What's her name? Iona. Right, Iona Stewart." And he inscribed it on the printed card and passed it over.

Jim looked at it, impressed by its formality. "Thanks very much. Very good of you."

"Oh that's quite all right. My pleasure," the man expanded, swivelling in the leather-studded chair.

The aura of munificence stayed with him as he watched Jim walk away down the drive to where his shooting brake was parked. He made a mental note of its age with rivulets of rust spreading from the door-trim where rainwater had collected over the years. He recalled a rusty car he'd had himself, the first. At least Barry would never have that to contend with. He was having a new automobile delivered for his birthday, as a surprise.

Jim made the box with care, jointing it with diagonal insets in afrormosia which showed up on the outside as richer than dovetailing, and were arguably stronger. He found a piece of piano hinge and chiselled a groove for it so that it lay quite flat and invisible. Then he chamfered the top edge and the thing began to look handsome as he waxed and buffed it. He made a wooden lining from a piece of paper-thin mahogany, itself an old bit of panelling from the bank in Princes Street they had refitted. The lid as he moved it over the lining was such a perfect fit that there was a small sound of a vacuum being broken every time he opened and shut it, and the suction of resistance he had to counteract. A tray rested on this lining which he subdivided into small compartments, again working in mahogany. The box became more and more intricate as succeeding decisions about its construction and finish evolved from each other but diminished in scale. It was its own logic, consistent to the last detail.

It had taken him hours, a hundred hours at least so that the box when he had finished it was priceless and unsaleable, because nobody could afford to pay for his labour, certainly not himself.

145

It was the best piece he had made, approximating to an apprentice chest by which his workmanship could be judged, a sampler of textbook skills. He was inordinately proud of it.

When it came to parting with it mentally, however, to actually viewing it in the light of a gift, he saw it had the most glaring fault, a built-in limitation of such significance that he couldn't understand how he had overlooked it. He had nothing to put in it and moreover, neither did Iona. There was not a single piece of jewellery she possessed, brooch or ring or necklace. The present seemed to reinforce this lack and constituted a gross tactlessness on his part, a box for nothing, a box compulsorily empty.

He wondered if Maggie had some small pin she could bestow, but realised this would look like an apology. Besides, he wanted it to be his own donation.

He searched round for a solution, knowing anything from a jeweller's shop was beyond his means. He put his head towards the displays in some of the windows, and took off in fright at the staccato price-tags. Then quite by chance, he passed a charity shop that kept trinkets and small pieces of finery on a separate stand. In amongst these, he noticed a pair of earrings, the most valid feature of which was the fact that they cost only a pound. They would do. Whatever they were made of, they were something to wrap up.

When he got them home, however, and looked at them more carefully, he found they were better than he'd imagined. Pearl droplets. Not real pearl, but they did not declare their artificiality from a distance. They must be reasonable quality because they were mounted on silver clips and came in a leather-covered box. It pleased him to put a box inside a box and he foresaw her successive unfolding of the package.

Last of all, he remembered the envelope with the invitation to the party for Barry Shaw's eighteenth birthday, which fell a fortnight after her own. A bitter thought passed through his mind as he fetched it from a drawer. These invitations had cost more to print than the entire sum spent on Iona's celebrations. It upset him to think that, a measure of what he could not provide; no matter how long or how hard he worked, he could not give her that. An invitation to someone else's event was the nearest he could come.

The card presented him with a dilemma. It fitted perfectly into the bottom recess of the box and seemed an added handsel in providing a continuing surprise. But did she know young Shaw already, and if she didn't, would he really want to act as agent in bringing them together? He did not approve of much in the Shaw household, fabric or people, and thought that what he himself had invested in the place was the best there was of it. He did not want to add his daughter to the fittings. The flourish of a party embodied all that he distrusted about Jack's set-up, too much too soon, an example of the boy's upbringing which alternated strictures with indulgence. Spoiling and waste. He consoled himself that he'd had many troubles but not with his children.

So he couldn't decide whether to tear the card up or not. It was an opening, of sorts, and he couldn't resolve whether it was his place to make the choice for her. She might enjoy being asked even if she decided against going. He advanced and retreated a hundred times, thinking she would need a dress and might be expected to take a formal present, prices subtracted from pleasure, and could not arrive himself at balance point.

Chapter Seventeen

"Do you like Chinese?" he asked one evening.

"Chinese what?" Iona wondered.

"Chinese food."

"I don't know. What is it?"

"It's anything. But cooked in Chinese fashion. Which means quickly as a rule. In a wok."

"What's a wok?"

"I'll show you, if you're interested in eating it. You'd better go home and say you're dining here this evening."

Dining. Dining! When she got back, he'd already started to peel the vegetables while strange packages lay on the kitchen table. Bean shoots. Peppers he called capsicum which bore no resemblance to the peppers that she knew. All round on the table were ranged kitchen knives, precision instruments, and a set of copper scales for which the weights went down as low as a quarter of an ounce. He moved skilfully among them, measuring and chopping with deft movements of the hand.

"When you're trying out the cuisine of a country for the first time, you've got to understand the social conditions as well. In Scotland there's always been plenty of fuel but not much meat. So you have long, slow cooking of boiling chickens and bits of brisket and mutton. A traditional meal was the broth served first and the meat and vegetables separately, as the main course. And that meat was expanded with cereal in the most typical dishes. In China, meat was every bit as expensive for working people, but there was also a premium on fuel, so you have everything chopped very small for fast cooking. Crisp vegetables. Cubes of meat. And fish and rice to pad it out."

She took a turn at stir-fry.

"No, more quickly. Really don't let the vegetables settle for a second on the bottom." Sparks flew up as particles of oil, distributed through the air, caught light, illuminating her face

149

and hair in flashes. She blinked involuntarily, leaning away from the source of heat. Impatiently, he put his hand on the handle above hers. "Like so." He shook the pan more vigorously.

She withdrew, letting him take over. "I'll watch for now. Do you do this every evening for yourself?"

"Eat? Yes, it's a bad habit, I know. But I haven't found an alternative."

"Cook."

"They're synonymous, aren't they, cooking and eating?"

"With all this palaver?"

"Artistry – yes. I don't cook much, but I cook complex when I do. The idea of beans on toast is sufficiently repugnant to make it worth while."

She ate with him in this way maybe once a week. She surprised him, some time after Christmas, by having a meal ready for him. Goulash, carefully culled from a recipe book and weeks of saving. He thought it was good. He began to look forward to finding her there at the end of the day and hoarded bits of information or gossip to pass on to her. Each day was transmuted in the telling to something witty and more interesting than it had been in the living. She drew him out about his customers, laughed at their foibles and his, sympathised with Mrs Forbes for having to put up with both of them.

She was very discreet, even guarded, and never abused his hospitality. He noticed that she invariably used the back stairs and stayed closeted in the servants' quarters unless he invited her to sit in the lounge. But as a rule, they ate or talked in the kitchen. He said he wouldn't touch the room she used and so she was at liberty to leave any books or papers she wanted wherever she happened to be working.

Once or twice at the beginning, he went in to check but found she kept the room dusted and clean. Looking round, he saw that she wasn't a desk student at all but lay on the bed to work. The pillows retained a slight impression and very gradually, other signs appeared, marks of her habitation he didn't hurry to erase. An umbrella left behind when it turned fair. A pencil chewed at the end which she laid down in passing. An old notebook, which she sometimes used for leaving a message on.

BABYSITTING. SEE YOU TOMORROW.

His disappointment was acute, but he left it there as a promise of return.

It was true that Iona had the freedom of the house, but she used it sparingly. She would not go into rooms when he was absent but limited herself to stairs and corridors, passing places. Occasionally, if there was a blink of sun, she would go out into the terrazzo where even in mid-winter there were pockets of heat and line herself along a wall like a lizard to soak it up.

The corridors and stairs were entertaining in themselves, and she could see into almost every room, even if by a personal restraint she was inhibited from entering them. She liked his house and its pervasive silence, feeling both alone and accompanied in it because the empty aspects went on declaring his presence and his taste, like clothes on hangers which were recognisably their owner's. The house was beautiful; it taught her everything about beauty. The furnishings were the English country house tradition modified, subdued to fit into a miniature. Each object that he bought was the epitome of such objects, its finest example. He would have empty space rather than fill it with an ugliness.

She wandered along the landing, privileged by her curatorship. A museum, full of artefacts of which she was the trustee. Why he should entrust them to her care, she didn't know. Perhaps because she knew better than to touch. It was a museum, but a private one. There were the stands, the exhibits, the cabinets – but there were no visitors. No people came to view, so that she started to wonder who he was preserving the pieces for. For themselves, to keep them intact? It seemed an eccentric way to live, for the benefit of posterity, or to maintain his own afflatus as the guardian of the past. Who would inherit them? Would he donate all this to the museum in Chambers Street or make a collection to fill a derelict mansion? "Bequeathed from the estate of Innes Hamilton Esq." written on cards. It was strange, that vicarious thrill, hoping to live posthumously not through your deeds but through your donations. Did he not live now? Had he not lived some time previously? She caught herself in the act of doing what she accused him of, patronising those who had a different standard of existence.

The shepherdess went on sleeping on the elongated table, raised above her surroundings. She was a lovely creature and

151

Iona bent over to admire her. Lovely, delicate thing. Bone fine. Unfleshed. Unreal. Even the sleeping features epitomised the transparency of the emotions of the piece, derobed of consciousness. She saw now how foolish they had been to imagine that the third figure of the boy could have been the child of the couple. They were too young themselves for adulthood, embalmed in a kind of unworldly prime, less developed than Milo or Discobolos after all. Their Grecian bodies were at least fully sexed, capable of maturity which was the ability to breed. These little people on their stand could not be so untidy or uncouth.

She leaned forward to the somnolence of the attitudes. It had no grandeur, only grace. Diminutive, not life-size. Such pretty nothings but they were not and never could be real. A tear or indeed any evidence of emotion on the face of the shepherdess would be a catastrophe, or merely sentimental in the context of such artifice. She admired its finish, was staggered at its likely cost, but did not covet it.

A speck of dust had settled on the shepherd's face, spoiling his beauty like a blemish. Iona was inclined first to brush it off, and then wondered with what. A cloth duster, shedding lint? A feather-headed brush? Her own fingers would transfer a follicle of skin like a worse imperfection, or a touch of sweat or possibly a grain of clay, clinging to her pores. She dared not make direct contact. Nevertheless, the speck affronted her and so she blew, letting the air from her breath dispel the offending mote. Better that, to leave no trace behind.

One evening she brought him a piece of paper to read. She put it down tentatively on the kitchen table and watched while he scanned the contents.

"So what does that mean?"

"It means my portfolio passed for Edinburgh and Glasgow colleges. They've both accepted me for next year." She underlined the words with her finger like a ruler.

"Self-evidently." His eye in these moods became hard and analytical, narrowed to a point. "In precise terms, which will you take up?"

"I don't know that yet."

"Well then, who can if you do not?"

Iona had rehearsed the phrases to herself for a long time, not necessarily thinking she would try to explain the options to him, but working out her own attitudes to the choice. She had pretty well arrived at her own conclusion, but hoped for his ratification of it, confident that he would see things through her eyes. He would lend weight and authority but would not countermand her decision.

"I know what I want. I don't know if I'm good enough."

He got up impatiently from the table and filled the kettle. "That's up to you, surely. Working harder. Good enough only means dedicated enough."

"What about talent?"

"Oh it doesn't take a great deal of talent to open a book."

She realised she was expecting him to draw correct conclusions from incomplete data, but at the same moment it was clear she had put things in the wrong order. She should have built up to confessing the ambition long ago. Saying it now made it into an impromptu remark, arising from a rash impulse. She sounded more defensive than she felt. "I mean I want to work as an artist. Or an artisan. I think I want to be a sculptor."

He didn't laugh, but his face went through such multiple contortions that he might as well have done. "That's pretty esoteric stuff." She didn't know what this meant although the tone of his voice betrayed his feelings as if he'd said pretty outlandish or pretty well impossible. "You mean statues?"

"Or heads."

Eric Gill and Henry Moore came to mind, and very few other names. Did she have the muscles for it? He saw her lumping around limestone and marble slabs. "Not much demand for that nowadays. I mean it must be practically impossible to get started. Church work and a few public monuments, but really very rarefied." He measured the hazard for her, more afraid than he would be of a business venture or a change of occupation because it was also the unknown for him, the huge adventure of self-projection.

She shrivelled. The scale of the ambition was preposterous after all. She did not know how much she wanted his approval until he withdrew it. " I was thinking more of plastic sculpture. Clay heads, and bronze casting eventually."

"Portraiture in the round? Well, maybe so. In earthenware?" He paused to fill the cups. "I would have thought that you could do something finer."

She was dismayed that the curvature of his thoughts should

after all lie in an arc so contrary to her own. Fine, what was fine? What external gauges could be applied to the impulse to create in one medium or another? Was he saying that if *The Night Watch* were painted as a miniature, it would somehow be finer? Refinement surely did not apply outside the drawing room. He might as well say "nicer", but she knew the criteria of niceness did not relate to her. She felt immediately rough and coarse-grained, a blob of creation which had still to be purged of its impurities. She did not know which was more acute, the disappointment in herself or in him. At any rate, she did not berate him but answered obliquely.

"It depends on whether my grades are good enough. The choice may be taken out of my hands."

"You'll aim for the University course, naturally?"

"Why naturally?"

"That's best."

At one time she would have cowered under this ruling and abided by it silently. But he'd taught her something, if only that he wasn't infallible. "It may not be the best for me. I want to work at art more than study it. I want to do things and not just write about doing things."

This was unfortunate. He compressed his lips and she realised she had blundered, but an apology to his sensibilities was too obvious. It would hurt them even more. What she could not appreciate was that he might object to the Glasgow option simply because it was Glasgow, and more distant.

"Well," he retracted a moiety, "the combined course would be wider and more useful in the end. The academic world does provide a safety net. Doing it half and half that way isn't so bad."

"So bad as what?"

"As going to the art college."

"Why is that bad?"

"Among all those long-haired hippies."

She smiled at his prejudice, older and wiser. "You might think differently if Rembrandt walked among them."

He measured the reproof. It did irritate him, like the accusation she made a moment before that he was a very good critic, a good judge, and not much else, that he had lost any joy or belief in the talent of others because he was bereft of talent himself. He was stung by the evidence of his own cynicism and this goaded him into the kind of aloofness which he took up whenever people

154

offended him or pointed out his shortcomings. He became worse. He flaunted prejudice and disdain, which was a false reaction because it didn't effectively say what he deeply felt.

"Rembrandt? You're touchingly hopeful. I can assure you that there are no Rembrandts any more and never will be again. The world has lost its innocence of vision."

She couldn't dispute that except by her example, which he chose to overlook. She was wounded by the words which, like a paste of powdered glass rubbed in by the hand of an expert, afflicted her with a fine and subtle abrasion.

Chapter Eighteen

They realigned, shifting ground as they went.

Innes doubted his own impulse to share a room, a roof long-term with anyone. A dozen weeks was long-term and he wished he had the power of retraction. He realised that in previous arrangements he had left himself an opt-out clause, which was the facility of saying "Go away". Against his better judgement, he had allowed a stranger to utilise his house and on such terms that he could hardly withdraw without explanation, and tremendous loss of credibility. That she was a nuisance, or interfered with his peace of mind hardly mattered when set against the positives of her advancement – even if it were an advance towards something he did not hold in high esteem. He tasted compromise and did not like it overmuch.

Iona was less tempered. The difference in stance brought his attitudes to a head but diffused hers. Unlike her mother, she could not sigh and say "Just a thought", as if the proposal were not a cherished dream. It was too generic to herself. The word studio produced a kind of ecstasy in her imagination and to deprive herself of its energy entailed suffering. Withdrawal meant something different to her, not retiral into self, but separation from herself and a balanced state of mind, making her nervous and edgy. So they moved in different directions, gratingly.

A weekend and a snowstorm made them rethink. Battling with the elements seemed enough. On Monday morning, a late train with no heating and no first-class carriage sank their differences temporarily. They shivered together. They were meek, and afraid of the truth inside the mental allegations they had made against the other of intransigence or ignorance or petty-mindedness, knowing secretly each might apply to self.

"My mock exams start next week," she told him.

"Oh do they? Will you be very busy?"

"On the days when I go in. But that's not every day. I'll have several days at home."

He took her cue. "Just use the house then, during the day. It doesn't bother me."

She wished he'd put it differently for whatever else she felt, it bothered her. It bothered her all the time to be under his patronage and be denied the warmth of feeling that went with it.

The weather turned worse. Every day it seemed an adventure getting into the city, but it was an adventure they tired of quite rapidly. Points that were iced over made for choppy journeys, jerking along in instalments. Everyone grew fractious and Iona was relieved on the days when she didn't have a paper to sit but could slip next door into a warm house and spend her time reading in sublime peace under the coverlet. It had not escaped her attention that he put out an eiderdown when he guessed that she worked like this. The pleasure of the place was increased by the pipes being frozen at home and the plumber was unable to promise an early visit with so many emergencies on hand. She hugged the heat gratefully, converting therm and calorie into turned pages.

One day, he came back early, much earlier than usual in the middle of the afternoon and let himself in, half forgetting that she might be there at three when the schedule of the previous weeks had been so erratic. He went upstairs heavily, still wearing his overcoat as he made for the bedroom. He was absolutely staggered, as he turned on the landing, to see her come out the bathroom, wearing his dressing gown and vigorously drying her hair on a towel.

They stood and stared at each other's apparition.

"What *are* you doing?" The emphasis was so authoritarian that she complied with his expectation in her answer.

"I'm skiving today."

"Playing truant," he amended. But to do what? Her suggested nudity was shocking when he was dressed for outdoors. The context made it seem more indecent than it was, while the pounding in his head drove out a rational appraisal of a girl simply washing her hair. The inferences at that moment were entirely sexual and compounded by his distrust.

His eye moved up the dressing gown. So she did take liberties when his back was turned. God knows what she got up to on her own. The thought leaped into his mind, Who else had he opened his door to besides her? She could have had her friends in, anybody, even that gyppo's brat. He had visions of him sneaking in the back way, up the stairs, throwing his leather jacket on the kitchen table as he passed. He could see it all in detail, static moments of seduction, one leading to the other in a series of framed stills. He saw her entertaining him in the back bedroom, under his covers so thoughtfully provided. And he was paying for the heating, paying for her to romp about. He imagined he was keeping her off the streets by giving her a room, well, off the grass verges at any rate, and the gesture rebounded on him. She brought her intimate indoors.

To make matters worse, she stopped towelling her head and with both hands, pushed back the mass of hair from her face. Underneath, her look seemed innocent, the features stark and pale the way they were when she'd been swimming, her eyelashes wet, her skin translucent. He couldn't bear the lie, the reassumption of naivety when she'd probably been groping with that lout an hour before. A bath. Well. She needed baths all right.

He turned away disgusted. Disgust registered in all the lines of his face at her lack of virtue, and her exploitation of his kindness.

"I'm sorry." She came after him up the passage. "I would have told you. Our heating's gone off altogether while the plumber works on it and I was dying to wash my hair. There didn't seem to be any harm in having a bath. I would have told you. I used my own towels."

So she did. So she did. She'd come prepared.

"Go and get your clothes on now."

"What's the matter?" She picked up his note of despair but it made no impression on his turned back.

He looked back at last outside the bedroom door. "I feel bloody awful, that's what. I've got influenza." He was probably the last person in the country not to call it flu and so she took a second to realise what it was he meant. "I'm going to bed now. Let yourself out." And he dismissed her with a hand. He had a way of flicking his hand, as though she were a waitress who'd been clumsy with a serving dish and he snapped her away from his table and further damage.

She went back to her room and shook for an hour, instantly ill herself when she'd given so much cause for displeasure. She stood and shook, her hands trembling, her body refusing to go into its familiar clothes, everything sticking, wet and uncomfortable as though they weren't her things at all. Why was he so angry? Why was it unforgivable to have a bath? He hadn't said anything she could define, or take umbrage at; he had just looked scathing. Did he object to her wearing his dressing gown? Maybe. Maybe that was it. He was very particular about his clothes. She picked one of her hairs off the collar as though it were an unspeakable offence against propriety.

She sat shivering in her underwear, too stricken to go on dressing. Night fell outside, and the streetlamps came on. She sat immobilised by the fact that he didn't care for her any more, didn't love her. To the phrase "He's not bothered", she added the supplement, "He doesn't love me" and this seemed intolerable because now that she was unhappy, it was easy to convince herself that she had been happy once and that he had loved her in the past. To be cast off gave her a glimpse of how pleasant they had been with each other, how much at home. The sailing, the drives to town, the evenings and the meals together ended abruptly. When she left this evening, she would never come back again. He was always humiliating her in his way, degrading her by finding fault with what she did or said. She was going to rebel.

She was.

She put on her skirt and sweater and walked up and down, feeling determined. She wasn't going to be trodden on, made to feel silly and young and irresponsible by his superior attitudes. She would show him.

Her hair was nearly dry and she brushed it out vigorously, ordering herself to walk away. Leave him by himself. That was what he liked best, wasn't it? But however she tried to work herself into a state of venom, the constriction in her breathing told her it was no good. She didn't loathe him. The reason for her emotion was that she couldn't bear it when he seemed to loathe her. There was no point in retaliating. Her eye fell on the eiderdown and the desk he'd moved nearer the radiator and the chair he'd brought through from another room so that she'd be more comfortable. Hostility melted in the face of fact. She couldn't deny that she'd been comfortable here. He had all the appurtenances of wealth but the fact that he shared them with her was worth all of them. When it came down to it, he was neither selfish nor isolationist.

Give him another chance. He was ill. He couldn't help being cranky when he was ill. She'd give him another chance to make amends.

He slept.

About seven she heard him get up and go to the bathroom, then back to the bedroom again. There were no lights on. He'd think she'd gone away. She went down to the kitchen after she heard his door shut, and made up a tray for him, nervous over details. She washed the spoon twice, eliminating every reason he might have to complain.

The light showed under his door. She tapped gently. He took a long time to answer it but eventually said, "Yes. What is it?"

Hardly auspicious.

She went in. He was back in bed and looking sorry for himself, tousled and more untidy than he normally allowed himself to appear. The bridge of his nose was sharp and white.

"I made you a drink," she said.

"Thank you," he gave back, sounding reluctant over gratitude. "I was dying for a drink but didn't think I'd make it there and back."

"It's hot lemon and honey. I wasn't sure if you'd be hungry. There isn't much downstairs. But I made some toast."

He looked a little more cheerful at this. The toast was hot and every spot of butter had melted. She'd cut it interestingly, neither in half nor in fingers, but obliquely in three triangles, one larger than the others, making a mainsail and two foresails from one square. This shape on the plate was quite irrationally pleasing to him, more than the nourishment it provided, and he went on mentally arranging the pattern to make geometric outlines. The drink she made was good too. It hit the back of the throat where it was raw and after the first shock, soothed it.

"So you stayed."

"Yes I stayed."

She got up while he ate and made the room more comfortable round about him. Put his clothes, which he had cast off in a hurry, more neatly on the chair and drew the curtains across the window and the door to the balcony, carefully overlapping them the way he liked, tight shut. He watched her phlegmatically, still pouring out huge draughts of scorn in her direction. Knew a good thing when she saw it. The main chance. On the make.

161

And other cheap phrases to go with cheapening attitudes; he hadn't known he knew them.

"Have you been working?"

"No. I couldn't work."

"So why didn't you go home?"

They both took deep breaths to launch into their disagreement but she was more practised at making a compromise with other people's feelings and could move very delicately through the quagmires of anger or frustration. "My hair was wet," she said and it was such a simple fact, he almost laughed.

"What did you do today?"

"I cracked the Reformation in Scotland. I think I've got it right, but really all those different Prayer Books. Orders enforced and rescinded. Worse than the Civil War. I felt so pent up after a hundred pages of that textbook, I would have gone for a swim if it hadn't been February." She lingered a moment, connecting with the dousing she had had. "I'm sorry about the bath."

"Don't apologise." Which was his way of saying he wouldn't, but he became less disparaging in his thoughts.

"Oh look," she said, coming back to his bedside. "Take these before you finish all the lemon. The chemist said they were the best thing he had for flu. I don't know if you've had them before." She handed him a packet of capsules from the back of the tray.

He turned them over. She had carefully removed the price from the reverse. A present. No settlement was due. "Did you go out specially for these?"

"Well yes. How else would I have got them?"

He read the instructions as though he were making sense of a foreign language, then started to cough with the breath breaking hoarsely in his throat. "These are expensive, aren't they?" He sat turning the packet over and over in his hands. She could not read his expression. Suspicious or angry or touched, she didn't know which.

"Yes, you were in luck. I didn't use my lunch money this week, so I had some on me. Usually I'm skint."

The frankness of her admission was so direct, he couldn't believe she'd made it. Skint. He'd been skint once or twice in the past, had to actually look at his bank statement at the end of the month, but he would never admit it. She'd had one single pound

162

in her pocket and put it all on him. Gone to the end of the High Street over snowy pavements to fetch him medicine. What was it, a quarter of a century since anyone had done that much for him, alleviating the double misery of illness and solitude. Being ill was something he dreaded, enforced rather than voluntary solitude when the normal pleasures of being alone, reading, listening to music, going sailing were debarred and he was forced back on absolute, dead-still loneliness, which was himself. She'd reduced that. Coming home on the train in the last few weeks, he'd thought, She'll be back there before me and will have something to say. And even when he sent her away in anger, his head was occupied with her, because she did not come to see him and make forgiveness instant. He was not deeply alone when she was by.

"What's the matter?" She sat down on the edge of the bed, frowning that he didn't hurry to slip the wrapper off. "Shall I do it for you?"

But the cellophane was tough, glued in place. Her fingers made no impression on it.

He put out his hand and stopped her.

"Don't you want them?"

His face was skeletally pale, bone white. She felt the many layers of skin were made transparent by illness so that she could see straight into him. She saw the equipoise of the two states of mind in him, wanting to trust her and refusing to believe that she was trustworthy. And it was an equipoise: neither could predominate over the other.

He put his hand under the hair at the back of her neck, shaking his head. Words wouldn't come through hoarseness. Then after a few moments of acute anxiety on her part, he said, "If I weren't ill . . . " and started to cough again, interrupting his speech. "If I weren't ill, I wouldn't be talking to you like this. Have I been unkind to you, Iona? I think I have been unkind. I could be a very sour-tempered individual if I put more effort into it. You didn't do it, did you? And why should I condemn you anyway? By your age . . . well, it's such hypocrisy, isn't it. Thou shalt not, provided I can."

She leaned forward and felt his forehead. She'd have to get some capsules down him and reduce his fever that was making him rave. He reached up for the hand on his brow and bending it open, kissed its palm. She was moved by the tender act. She remembered the other kiss that was bestowed; a kiss of hands for which this gesture of gallantry seemed in part forgiveness. So they were quits. They started out again on equal terms. They sat together for a long moment in communication.

"No. I'm not delirious. I don't know. Maybe I am, one way or the other."

Illness wore away the glaze of his restraint. She came raw against what he was made of, touching the substance of his need. He clung to her. She might have been dismayed by this reversion, the head laid on her shoulder, except that she was familiar with sickrooms and sick boys who unaccountably turned from robustness, despising contact, to a weak and enervated state, sorry for themselves. She knew exactly what to do about it. She smoothed his hair against his head, rubbing from fontanelle to crown in the most primitive gesture of comfort and compassion. She did not know how she knew it. It was like all lovingness, instinctive, endemic to herself.

In spite of this, he went on making such terrible sounds, coughing or crying hoarsely as if the comfort which she tried to give him were an additional distress. What else could she do to solace him? She stood up and pulling back the covers, slipped into the bed beside him and put her arms around him, clamping him to her body. And all the time she said, "Shoosh, shoosh," applying to his hurt the massive antidote of love.

She cooled his forehead with her hands, compressing and removing her palm in turn. The whole of her body seemed cool and he felt comfortable only where they made contact, transmitting to her the fevers of the skin which she absorbed and dispelled like a heat conductor or a flask of crystals that could dehumidify the air, leaving it fresh. Her hands were a form of therapy, healing incorporate.

They kissed almost by accident and then kissed again lingeringly. It was kind kissing, new to Iona and maybe new to Innes. He was continuously surprised by the novelty of the sensations in which he found himself an innocent. This feeling was something unprecedented, emotion and touch intermingled, a real feeling which was painful as much as pleasurable. As he caressed her, she came closer to him in a physical embrace that for once was out of his control because it was dependent. He was shaken by the simplicity of her reactions which arose from wanting and from knowing nothing. Her naivety was contagious and he shed

164

the protective layers of inhibition, reaching back to a former self. Her eyes in the half dark held his and repeated reassurance. He was neither dispassionate nor objective about her open tenderness so that the moment when he entered her was one of the most felt of his experience, as if he were the virgin. Making love was only making believe. What he discovered in her arms was not simple pleasure, hedonistic, momentary but the radiant effusion of something rare, at least to him, the sensation others termed happiness.

He fell asleep while Iona, charged with the responsibility of his person and his house, kept watch over them as long as possible. His weight was soporific. The room dimmed round her, as every now and then she would make an effort to rouse herself to go home to her own bed but the meagreness of that portion was a deterrent, quite apart from the cold and the departure from his encircling trust. She guarded him late into the night.

Chapter Nineteen

When he woke up, Innes was alone. The curtains were still drawn but the lamp had been switched off. It was the atmosphere of the sickroom, heavy and enclosed mid-morning. Then as he struggled to mobilise his limbs, his head began to clear from sleep and medication and he was shocked to realise that he slept further over in his bed than usual, making space for someone else. She really had lain there, spent the night technically in his bed.

He got to his feet thinking she must be somewhere in the house but going to look for her, was impeded by a contrary motive: whatever would he say to her, face to face? And then he thought it was all a feverish invention. She had got up and gone home. Or she had not come up to his room at all, walking out when he dismissed her. Sitting down again on the edge of the bed, woozy from too much sleep and the confusion of his thinking, he caught sight of the tray she'd brought him and on it, the opened packet of capsules. Her ministrations remained.

At that, the embraces they exchanged came welling up. Such odd embraces, she the protector, he the child comforted and loved by a larger understanding than his own. He faltered at the consequence. Surely not. Surely he had not made love to her. It was a dream, like the one where he embraced a living statue in the courtyard. He tried hard to dispel the impression left by fantasy that it might be true, because this involved an accusation against himself that he had transgressed his own code of virtue and decorum by an abuse of the girl. Though he was puzzled by the power of subconscious wanting that could make it seem so real. His own emotional dependence came back at him, mirrored in the vividness of his images which were not visual as much as sensory, burned into the tissue. He looked at his hand to see if it had altered in awareness but it appeared the same hand as he lay down with, unchanged by whatever act of intimacy it had propelled. He found it hard to accept the picture his imagination

167

presented him with because he repudiated the causal need. Only a delirium, a temporary weakness of the mind or the product of wishful thinking. He distanced himself.

He opened the curtains and a window for some fresh air. It was a grey day that blurred the horizon. The air was thick and heavy with moisture, threatening more snow. The only event outdoors was the white rill on a wave, blown up by a choppy wind. A dreary prospect that did not enliven the interior one.

Tentatively, he bathed and dressed, feeling all along that Iona must be about but was keeping tactfully out of his way. He noticed that his clothes after only one day's starvation seemed loose on him, and in the mirror his drawn expression and hollow eyes made him a ghost of himself.

He tapped on her door, then when there was no reply, put his head round it and went in. Most of her books had gone but sheets of paper lay around and a cardigan hung over the end of the bed a little lifelessly. He went downstairs to the kitchen to return his tray. It was completely tidy, almost consciously so. A rinsed mug sat draining by the sink. He had a moment of elation when he thought she might have written a message on her notepad, but there was none. No explanation. No promise of return.

He wandered through the house, vaguely hoping she had done the exceptional and started to use one of the other rooms. He went into each with an enforced casualness, but they contained successive disappointments. Emptiness. The alcoves still were empty, waiting for Daphne and Apollo to stand side by side in the captive state of alabaster. The drawing room was propped open by pink Carrara and through the panelling an east wind blew. No change and no movement and no human being.

He waited all day.

The suffused light of a winter's day reached its low meridian and subsided. A little snow did fall, lying patchily on the ground. It fell into the sea and was absorbed instantly, returning to its own medium without trace. He watched it compulsorily, impatient with his other activities and impatient with the drag of time.

She would come in between four and five. He settled on the minute and waited, but it came and went without her. The twilight thickened and he realised it would not be that day. He wondered if she had taken fright, or was possibly ill herself, catching his infection through prolonged contact. Many

168

possibilities suggested themselves but had not been resolved by midnight.

As the days passed and she didn't come, he started to put a more serious complexion on the absence. It must be deliberate; a mental division giving rise to the physical one. He thought once or twice of going to the door of her house and making the simple enquiry, "Where is Iona? How is she?" Anticipating the action, however, he realised how difficult it would be to knock or to go over their threshold. Lack of experience made it impossible to judge his likely reception, so he saw himself hanging about looking a fool while the family stood by, baffled. A child might ask the basic question, "What is he doing here?" It was too obvious an act, seeking her out, and yet when he lay in bed his senses were at straining point, listening through the partitioning wall for evidence of her, well, sick, hostile, it didn't matter as long as she were alive.

One evening over a week later, the bell rang and he leaped to answer it, but the optimism died when it was only Jim Stewart standing on his doorstep.

"Oh. Come in."

Jim followed the scant invitation up the hall, saying, "I've come to collect Iona's things. She left some bits and pieces behind." His expression as Innes tried to examine it was deliberately non-committal.

"Well, yes. I think she did." He hesitated at the bottom of the stairs locating the scattered objects mentally, but like a commentary binding them was the more demanding question, why was she choosing to abstract them? "Do sit down and wait while I go and find them. There's not so much." Hardly worth coming to call for them, he thought petulantly, but found a holder and put the few items in, even the notepad, the pencil and the umbrella which she had probably forgotten herself.

Jim was sitting by the window when he got back and did not immediately rise to leave, so Innes joined him to obviate the pressure on him to go away, although he wanted him gone.

"Is Iona well?" he asked.

The other man took a long time to say, "Well enough. She's gone to stay with my wife's sister in Edinburgh. Until she's finished out the year and taken her exams. That way she won't have to spend time travelling up and down."

169

"Oh," said Innes. "Very sensible."

"Perhaps we should have thought of it before, instead of troubling you. Having Iona here in the evening."

"No trouble."

"No trouble," the visitor repeated with a note of acrimony which made Innes look up.

"I really didn't mind her working here," he asserted as if Iona had gone home and complained that she was being made to feel an intruder and they had advised the removal to spare him hospitality. It was said defensively, because he regretted it if he had communicated that indirectly. What was worse than to bestow a gift and then reclaim it? He was ashamed of his own mean-mindedness if this was what it had brought about.

"We've sent Iona away," Jim said, "because we never thought you'd take advantage of her. Maybe we should have been more wary about your offer. It just seemed good of you to help her out. I mean, we knew you took her sailing with you and sometimes drove her up to Edinburgh but we didn't expect this."

Innes was alarmed at the sudden demise of his own good standing, and seized on negation rather than admit guilt or weakness. "What this?" he asked. "I don't know what you mean. It seems to me it's Iona who's had the advantage." These were expedients, not lies. When pushed into arrogance, his voice had a way of flattening out into a monotone that was light but insistent, like the dismissive gesture of his fingertips.

"You won't deny that Iona spent a night here last week. If that's not taking advantage of the girl, I don't know what is."

"I beg your pardon?" The force in this was so incontrovertible that Jim, who had come ready to be assertive, found himself daunted.

"Iona came home the next morning. She didn't try to pretend she hadn't been here."

"No reason to pretend." Now that he had taken up a mental stance of denial, that became the truth to Innes. The words themselves sent out a dozen waves that obscured the original meaning. His reactions were so diverse that he could hardly marshal them. He wanted to know specifically what it was that Iona had said, though he resented transmission through her father, and therefore placed the onus of proof on the other man. His suspicion that he was in some way being framed or blackmailed pushed him into the attitude of self-defence. "So Iona has accused me of seducing her?"

Jim looked tired, disheartened by finding no ready acquiescence in either party. He did not know what to make of appearances. He consoled himself that he'd had no trouble with his children and suddenly a catastrophe loomed. He could have twisted his reply, but he was strict and honest. "No, she didn't say that."

"So what did she say?"

"She said she slept here." He waited and then added, "You're not denying that, I see."

"Sleeping is not seduction."

Jim could see he made no progress along the line of fact, because he had nothing concrete to offer. In that vacuum, he refused to insult either the man or his daughter with imputations he could not substantiate. The words of slander would not come to him. Instead, he opened up his own emotion. "I'm asking you, how would this look to you? We had high hopes of Iona and it's not been easy. Well, you wouldn't know about that when you've only got yourself to consider, but it all costs, Mr Hamilton. It all costs."

Innes hated the Mr Hamilton. It made him into a squire, as though he had exercised his squire's rights. Ius primae noctis. He felt like a sexual glutton, rushing for the first grouse or the new beaujolais of the season, brought to the—at any price. He saw himself clearly in the other man's sight, selfish and self-indulged. This did not incline him to justify himself, however, so he remained silent.

If it were true, why had Iona not denied it more stringently? Perhaps it was possible that they had made love. Was it? To make love without conscious remembering. He certainly could understand that women imagined they had been the victim of a seduction, accusing their priest or their doctor or their tutor because the emotion engendered by sympathy had been so intense. He remembered how Iona, looking at the statue of the shepherdess, considered the boy might be the child of the imagination. Very likely, when the act was of the imagination also. But he did find it ironical that he was accused of the thing he had striven to protect her from. Taking her into his house to shield her from exposure to young Shaw and negligent parents, he laid himself open to the charge of corruption. Exposure, well

171

he was the one who turned out to be exposed, made vulnerable by his own philanthropy.

Looking over at the visitor, changed into much-mended trousers, his shoes creasing at the stitches, Innes underwent a double repugnance. Ally himself to that? But instantly following on the reaction was self-hatred that he should be so superficially swayed. If it had been Major Forbes, say, who sat opposite and hinted gently that his daughter might have been compromised, his own disposition would have been very different. Major Forbes's daughter would have been marriageable; a straight trade-off and they would have used gentlemen's terms in arriving at a bargain. To Jim, however, he refused to accede equality of speech, which might reside in the unspoken, but attempted to make him grovel and demean himself by hot-headed accusations.

The man did not grovel, and neither did Iona. If it had happened, the girl's protection of him was odd and affecting. An ordinary creature would have shopped him, but on all counts she was superior. He felt his own character and prejudices wane in respect of hers.

Jim sat in an equally reflective mood. The chair where he sat was a Louis Quinze. He could put a name to it because he'd mended one, a long time ago but he remembered in every jointing how it was made. He thought it worth its reputation. The panelling of the room intrigued him too, not the way it had Iona, for its purpose, but the expertise that went into making it. The beading, the mitres, the angled quadrant used to finish it off, not bought by the yard or poured in plastic mouldings. Custom-made. Hand-carved. His eye took them in one by one and he respected the joiner, who was anonymous except for this legacy, as a fellow craftsman. The thing was made to fit like a lining to the chamber, and the proportions of the panel were scaled to suit the wall, six panels to a side. They grew in place. He felt a huge regret for the passing of the age of skill and the wealth necessary to indulge it.

This man was wealthy. Every last detail declared it, so wealthy that Jim was at a loss to put a figure on it or even guess approximately what he was worth. It was quiet and dignified, this room. He couldn't help comparing it with Jack Shaw's excesses, and thought Iona had chosen a second home wisely. Reluctantly, he admitted to himself that both these men could do

172

more for her than he could. His only bequest to her was life and maybe skill, whatever was innate. There would be no other inheritance, no working capital, no start in life, no handouts. He was fired by the injustice of it and would have felt no qualms about exploiting either of them if it would have brought her an advance.

He thought of the young man whose card he'd torn up after all, an invitation by proxy being worth less than nothing. Perhaps he saved her from a kind of temptation. Registering that she was blonde indeed; out of a hundred attributes the colour of her hair was all he could remember. Perhaps all suitors were unsuitable but for a moment he found himself wishing that Innes Hamilton had compromised his daughter so that he could bring pressure on him to make amends, sealing her up here safely out of harm's way. He longed to say, "You have defiled my property" and quizzed his daughter for hours to that end, hoping to establish his advantage, a pressure point, a leverage for compensation so that for once he could have the upper hand in bargaining.

He gave up. He didn't understand girls at all.

To settle it finally, he said, "You are a man of honour," as if it were not in doubt. "I can trust your word?"

"I hope so. No one has questioned it to date."

"Well then, we must leave it at that."

In Jim's head, the commendation "Seems a decent bloke" reverberated emptily.

Innes put on an overcoat to go outside. There was a nip in the air and by early evening, a hoar frost started to settle on damp areas, an angled roof or a hedge, anything exposed. His breath turned into a freezing vapour through which he walked, dispersing his own weather.

The town was quiet with everyone indoors and he paced his way through the streets with vigour, enjoying the barrenness of shapes unconfused by human disorder. The frost was cleansing. His head began to clear. The blockage of his cold, together with a kind of stunning from the visit, started to thin out and simplify.

So she had gone and he was implicated in the mystery of why. He did not know why any more than Jim, but he made guesses which were less satisfactory in themselves than the fact that he made them, expending energy in the pursuit of the futile.

173

He walked along the sea-front of the eastern bay, following its natural arc. He'd come along here since he was a boy and knew the layout of the houses and the shore as intimately as Iona, a landscape which was fused with childhood and so unforgettable. His favourite place? Yes, it was his favourite place because he knew it stone by stone.

The cold air made a bond between the sea and land, and though the North Sea was not likely to freeze, it had a sluggish iciness about it as if the specific gravity had increased, bringing it nearer the density of earth. A crag that stuck out halfway along the bay seemed not a promontory of rock under these conditions but an encrustation of salt, a sea stalagmite frosted with rime. The water lapped round it silently, either wearing it away or adding to the strata. Hard to tell. The extremity of the bay was pitted with rock and pools as the cove swung out towards, and ultimately joined, the headland of the Leithies. There were some deep caverns in the causeway where oarweed and sugarweed hung in long straps that were exposed at low tide but today lay eight fathoms under, steeped in brine.

This tidal action of deposit and abrasion was alarming, and although he knew and understood the maritime charts, he never could be free of the threat of change. High and low tide, plotted so accurately on a calendar, must defer to the unpremeditated, a sudden squall or a freak wind or a cold so intense it even combated the influence of the moon.

He reached the track that led to the golf course and then stopped, looking out across the Forth to Fife and westwards, to Edinburgh. The air was diamond clear and the city lay gleaming and winking in prismatic sharpness. The night had edges from which he protected himself, cold invading his trachea and forcing him to move on. Memories were anxious. This was the path to which he'd raised his binoculars; Iona slept that night in a safe house. Jabs, making him wince.

Ahead, the twin lighthouses sent out their intermittent signals, flashing at variable intervals so that shipping could distinguish between them, at night or in storms, the Scylla and Charybdis of the channel. He thought of the lonely life of the men who acted as wardens of the lantern. Two months on. One off. Living a third of the year on shore and the rest on a rocky outpost. One's own life like the beam, visible for a shorter time than the following dark interval. It was the lack of choice or variety in such a life that

174

engaged him. Other occupations seemed self-indulgent by comparison, and whatever heroism or taste for solitude it called for, he didn't have it.

He walked no higher but turned back and cut along the shore. It had an added crunch, a glost on which his footsteps rang clear. It was very many years since he'd first walked along here, the town rising and falling in change, a grain attaching itself on the outer edge, a new house, a new face, the tide grinding the rocks to powder but all still substantially the same within the scope of one lifetime. And himself, ageing from boy to man to a future senility, did he make any difference? It had changed him but he did not think he had changed it. Not one whit. If he had never come into existence, what would have been different? Some objects might have been dispersed, swept out rather than collated. But as for human dynamism, he did not think he'd made much of an upheaval. Not a go-getter. Not a breeder.

Too late was it, to make the change? Belief in one's own adventure. Belief in the efficacy of kisses. What else was there to believe in? Without some compelling certainty and the power of fusion, he was nothing but cullet scraped back into a wastepile ready for refiring.

He knew that much about himself – I need a fixed point in this welter of uncertainty – but when he came to the moment of adhesion, his mind slewed away. He watched it happen. Time after time as he approached a crisis, he dodged it by temporising. Let us wait, let us see, became an attitude of mind hardened into perpetual postponement. Allied to intense mental and physical activity, this could nevertheless give him and others the impression that he was in a state of progress. Action the flow, lack of purpose the ebb – and going nowhere beyond giving the simulation of it.

So when it came to facing the problem of Iona – problem, there he went again, making confusion in a relationship – he avoided the shape of responsibility. He found himself mentally running back over the dialogue with Jim Stewart, checking his answers and assuring himself he had not committed a blunder or given anything away. He congratulated himself on having got the better of that argument. He thought this deeply dishonest of himself, cheating the man of the truth albeit of his uncertainty. Why was he trying to blot it out, this commitment to one human? To protect her or to enshrine one moment from the grubbing of most sexual encounter. Evasion or hypocrisy. The characteristic he most despised in others was crowningly his own.

He reached the end of the bay, passing the children's paddling pool which was filled and renewed by the tide, an empty quadrangle out of season, and pressed on to the harbour. It was quiet and still along the wharf. Some lobster crails were white with hoar which made them luminous in the dark, an unexpected lace. He had an image of robust seamen netting with twine on bobbins. It made a giant tatting like the lace that women put on linen handkerchiefs.

It became obvious as he drew up to the edge that the harbour was not empty. One trawler was there, with a row of car tyres over the bows which made an admirable fender. There were other ramshackle boats, indifferently guarded against the winter. Jack Shaw's was an all-weather craft and it too lay at anchor. It was lit, surprisingly, but the curtains were drawn over the cabin windows, diffusing the light. Jack entertaining on board? Strange. He could think of more comfortable venues than a water caravan mid-winter.

He drew alongside the cruiser's rails and for a moment actually thought of joining the poker party or whatever game was played on board. Human company, however facile in interchange, was appealing. Jack ushering him in, huge and hearty and generous with the casual visitor. A glass of whisky to keep the cold out, a portable fire of paraffin or calor gas, fuming the air and making him drowsy. What seductive temptations after all.

There was a laugh, a female laugh. Jack did not play mixed hands and Innes started to misgive. The light was abruptly extinguished to the sound of voices that were not angry but bantered in a querulous tone he recognised as sexual. A teasing will you, won't you. He walked away quickly over the freezing jetty but behind him, the boat rocked gently at its moorings, making a contraflow against the incoming tide.

His quickened footsteps matched his heartbeat. He did not know why he should be so angry. For Jack, because he was misguidedly trusting with his son. For himself, to be affronted by the sounds of misalliance even on a starlit evening. Perhaps for the boy who was already sated with easy access. But most of all, he was angry for the person who was not there but might have been, giggling and posturing in the dark. No, she wouldn't have done it that way, she really wouldn't. He recognised that if Iona were not safely in a suburban terrace somewhere in Edinburgh, he would be in a state of paranoia wondering if he should play Galahad and rescue her.

The thought came uppermost, Rather me than him. Save us from the upstart Shaw. He saw the voracious energy that consumed money, time, boats, cars, girls without a visible return. A spendthrift in the making.

Was he any better? Had he ever been any better? Why should he sit in judgement on Jack's son for displaying tendencies that were identical to his own? It was no good protesting that he was a totally superior animal when the margin between them was a hair's breadth. He searched for the categorising distinction. Culture. Civilisation, or civility at least. But he dismissed these shibboleths as bestowing no moral quality. Honourable intentions? He thought of the long line of beauties stretching back to his own coming of age and couldn't find anything very honourable in the proliferation. He couldn't affix smug labels to himself and say – prime example, rare model – when he ought to be something more than artefact. He would need to prove the intentions were honourable before he could designate himself better in kind rather than degree.

He angled across the beach and passing in front of the Stewart house, stood for a while looking up at the windows. Jim had done as he hoped, renewed the paintwork so that it was glossy. Lights shone through from the back rooms, without the curtains being closed, like the lamps inside a toy, a theatre or a child's house, innocent because there was nothing to hide. One window was blankly unlit, and that he guessed was the room Iona shared with her sister who lay alone this evening, as he would.

Chapter Twenty

It was May before she came to see him. Hope and belief had worn thin, a transfer decoration to his character rather than an under-glaze. Better to have been without them altogether, instead of carrying shoddy remains.

She thought about using the key she had hung on to, coming in quietly by the back way, but decided against confronting him so unexpectedly though he was more shocked than she could imagine by the figure at his door. She had changed out of all recognition; his impression of her was fixed but she moved on to create other impressions. He realised that this was due to appearances. She wore a two-piece suit, dark and severe and it aged her. He reflected that he had only seen her in uniform or summer clothes, shorts and bathing dress so that the contrast was startling, a few months spanning a decade of maturity.

To his politeness, "Let me take your jacket," she turned with almost practised ease and let him remove it from the shoulders so that he was left holding an empty garment while she walked away. He noticed there was a brooch on the lapel he considered cheap and nasty and in his mind he replaced it with something valuable.

She made herself at home and looked natural in the setting, more so than he did when he was suddenly tense, seeing himself in bas relief. He talked about nothing and she was silent, noticing that under the shirt and the voice there was a tremor of some-thing too rapid that suggested lack of control. Yes, she draped, superb drapery of female and clothing in the classic style. He lifted his eyes and dropped them again continually in a kind of reverence.

"You're sailing again?"

"Yes. I may race this year. How were your exams?"

"I think I passed them all. What about your handicap?"

The questions came in no particular order and with as little logic as the replies, the only effective outcome being a wariness of the central issue which they circled tentatively.

He made tea for her as if she were a visitor but on his return, found she had moved into the terrazzo, passing her hands along the frieze as though she were memorising it.

"Come and sit down." He dusted the bench with his hand, a rustic setting after all and not wrought iron.

She obeyed, stretching her legs into the sun.

He poured from a china vessel into a china cup. It rattled gently on the saucer as he passed it. It was hard to think, as she stirred the grains of sugar into the liquid, that she would not shatter the eggshell thinness of the bowl.

There was no subject that was not fraught. The weather was reminiscent of other weathers, spaces of earlier habitations, objects of innocence before they had a past. And so they sat in silence which was conscious on her part and baffled on his; as if he probed mentally up creeks and found they led to nowhere, forcing him back to a stagnant but connective silence.

"Why" loomed large in all his questions, but it did strike him that enquiry after reasons was impertinent when he had no right to ask. Iona was not so inhibited and let him wait to the very limit of forbearance, when his sense of manners and breeding were stretched, before she said the obvious.

"Did your flu last long?"

"A few days. The tablets you bought were good." He let the question roll. "Did you catch it?"

"No. I didn't."

The night came back to both their minds, urgent with emptiness.

"I missed you."

"I know."

The sun circled, finding a chink between garden wall and roof, and slanted in her eyes so that she lifted a hand to shade them. She could see out of this penumbra. He could not see in.

"Did I offend you?"

"No." She shook her head. "Quite the reverse."

He knew if he pursued the statement too avidly, he would dispel its elements. He stumbled repeatedly over the impediment to discussion of the key question, which in other men might have

180

been resolved by a caress or an emotional closeness he found it impossible to generate.

"Well then."

"When I went back the next morning," she started, "I thought nothing in particular about it. Yes, it was exceptional to stay here, but so were the circumstances. That you were ill. And that I fell asleep." She searched back for old feelings. "However, I was met by such a barrage of questions you wouldn't believe."

"Such as?"

"Oh everything. Where had I slept? Where were you? Had I slept with you before?"

"And what did you say?"

"Nothing. I would say absolutely nothing. It was my business and if they didn't trust me, spelling it out for them wouldn't change that."

The accusations brought them closer in complicity, and fact. It did not escape his notice that he had made the same assumptions about her, or had the same fears as her parents.

"Why didn't you ask me to say something?"

"I waited. But when you didn't come in the next few days, I knew you never would."

He remembered the cause of that unwillingness, and his mind slid away from his own diffidence. "You could have been more emphatic, instead of letting them think the worst."

"The worst?" Her eyes came out like luminaries from the dark. "You talk like them. It did not seem so bad to me, extending warmth."

"Nor to me." But he made a huge concession in saying that.

"What struck me most was that they wanted to have a hold over you. They actually wanted it to be true so that they could force some reparation."

"I don't believe that."

"I wouldn't have done, but it was true. They were almost indifferent to me, or whatever I felt when I was something they could haggle over, buy and sell."

The statement of the purchase price was imminent. The worth of the artefact was a bond of honour he must fulfil.

"Maggie said at one point, 'If you play your cards right, you can land him.' I didn't know what cards I had to play."

"Would you have married me?"

The phrasing of this question in the subjunctive and the past

181

surprised her as much as the rapid bargaining itself, opening with the highest bid.

"I don't know what you mean by that."

He changed the mood and tense. "Will you marry me?"

She looked so genuinely bemused that he made a final emendation.

"I am offering you my hand in marriage."

She made a long assessment of the terms. "Only your hand."

"The usual contract."

She remembered how hurtful it was to have such aspirations mocked, and tried to approach the question seriously. "So I have a choice. I would like it to be possible. But I want more."

"I can't offer any more. There isn't any more."

"Oh yes there is. Tempt me."

"How?"

"With words."

Words failed him. He could not put his mind to any seductive image, or even to a humorous one. He had delivered an ultimatum, served honour and there was no advance on that. He wrapped himself in hauteur.

"I think I understand why you make the offer," she helped him out, "but you must know it's impossible."

"I wouldn't ask if I thought that." He felt he had offered someone a job, a regular income and light duties, only to find the candidate turned it down. Not in the script at all.

"Innes to Iona, maybe. But there are a dozen people inside us who might not agree."

"Who? What do you mean?"

"Why didn't you try to see me when it was obvious I wasn't coming back? You couldn't bring yourself to ask the simple question, Where is Iona? How is she? Imagine that on an everyday basis. Think how you'd introduce me in the future. Iona Stewart, my neighbour's daughter. Why, you'd be so embarrassed to make the affiliation, you'd probably pay for them to move house. Or move yourself. Anything to put a distance between the me you want and the me you don't want."

The perception in this was so specific and so just, he couldn't argue against it. She got up and moved among the objects of the terrace. She looked well among them and so he did regret the hint that in associating with her, he had traded down the social order. Beauty was beauty, from whatever source.

182

"You would, you know," she intervened. "I would infuriate you. The way I do things. You'd be trying to improve me, but I can only improve myself."

"Aren't they the same?" He leaned forward earnestly.

"No. Not when you'd put me in a glass case and dust me down from time to time."

He laughed at the accuracy of this picture.

"No, it's not funny," she admonished. "I'd shock you all the time, by being vulgar. I am vulgar. I don't care. I want to be vulgar if vulgar is being real. Look," she said, stopping dramatically by the wall. "Even the flowers grow in pots. I am more earthy. I need a bigger soil."

The girl who said this puzzled him. Images of growth came to mind, prompted by her comparison. Some plants were always miniatures of themselves, the first leaf supplying a pattern for subsequent ones; others were more devious. The initial show was a misprint and kept you guessing through a series of changes until the form was established, finally. Or like the cotoneaster towards which she extended her hand, interesting because it had a different phase for every season. She was a more diverse being after all, and he felt her emotional strength bearing down on him, intent on her own evolution which did not take account of his.

Iona was thinking of the woman he saw in Edinburgh, but did not dare to move on to more personal matters. She might jibe a little at his belongings, but his slender emotional ties were forbidden territory. It did seem preposterous that a man could offer a union, of sorts, and leave out of account the other unions he would have to break. Or would he? Would he intend carrying on with the formula of his life as before, a man who could readily sift the element of child wife from woman mistress?

Commenting on the pot-bound vegetation, she began to see the environment he created as an artifice. The transplanting of Italianate styles into a northern climate was effete and maybe pretentious. The terrazzo was not cool, but sun-starved. His windows did not look out, but inwards on themselves. She designated its faults and his, regretfully, seeing his future as enclosed but her own divergent, full of hope.

"So, what will you do?"

"I'm going to Vienna. I won't go back to school. There's no point. And then Rome and Paris. For six months."

"To do what?"

"Oh, I'll go round the galleries. I'll go to the Rodin museum and see the bronzes for myself."

He recalled his own visit to the rue de Varennes, many years before and not alone, not impecunious. "Do you want money? I'll give you anything you need."

"No, I don't want your money. I'll go under my own steam."

"But how will you survive?"

"The same as everyone else. I'll work my way."

He saw her serving at tables, living in hostels and shabby lodgings, rubbing shoulders with the disreputable masses. He feared for her as she made the huge leap into the dark, casting herself out with wilder and wilder gestures over the edge. Worst of all, he foresaw her marrying the first man who would buy her out of it. Tomorrow to fresh woods and pastures new? She simply had no idea of the impediments to idyll.

"Can I come and see you?"

"No." She gave it cursory consideration. "I don't want that."

"Well, can I write then?" He amended the haste. "May I write?"

"There's no point, Innes. I'll be on the move. And you'd expect an answer. I'll drop you a postcard."

He opened his hands and looked at the empty palm. "How will I manage, not knowing how you are?"

"Oh, you'll manage. You did before."

He sat for a long time after she had gone and felt the terrace cool, stone by stone, until he started to petrify into position himself. His legs locked when he stood up, in an attack of cramp, and he stamped on the paving slabs to restore circulation.

It was not so late. Somewhere the sun still shone even if its heat did not reach him. He was not desolate, but cold.

He went upstairs in search of a pullover to combat coldness but putting it on, found he was more vulnerable to desolation. They had not talked of love once. They had not talked of love ever. He wondered if it was that mortal affliction that assailed him now, nothing more than the yearning to be different from oneself and hoping that the change could be applied externally in the shape of another human being. A fond ambition. As it faded, became just a thought, a dream, something occasionally to be remembered, he felt that against the current of his own dispassion, he had actually wanted that fulfilment very much. Craved it perhaps,

184

but suppressed the craving as animal and basic. But it was basic at its origins. Did he not want it? Did he not! What would he not give for his own elements to be regenerated in the primordial way. For her to bear his children, so that they were fruitful and increased abundantly, and multiplied, and waxed exceeding mighty; and the land was filled with them.

Her, or someone like her. That was the nucleus of the problem. There was no absolute of identification. Bringing himself to the focal point of one and one only was so hard – choosing a definitive example – that it drove out pleasure. He saw he had not expressed any pleasure in her, had not in the traditional sense wooed her at all. The two arcs of his dilemma, liking her but being unwilling to indulge himself romantically, which was too high a stake, and thinking it was time he settled down and took a wife, refused to flatten and come into alignment, to fuse into one.

His disappointment was sharp. He had misbid, mistimed his entrance but knew that at auction or on stage cues there was no rerun scheduled.

He came along the landing, not really knowing where he went. The objects which had formed a framework to his self-containment, the Davenport, the torchère with its shepherdess, a Tiffany lampshade which drew them into a grouping, seemed disconnected, merely objects. It was a museum indeed, interesting to assemble but worthless afterwards because there was always a larger collection in Chambers Street, the Victoria & Albert or the Musée de l'Homme. He would have been better adding to what was representative of self, investing his money and his effort in some foundation, putting himself through the eye of a needle to disburse his assets in a cause larger than the individual.

He looked out of the window at the terrace which with the onset of evening was totally in shadow. Enclosure and privacy, its prime assets, lost their allure. Instead of the enticement of aesthetics, he felt a form of claustrophobia, like a mollusc in a clam. The walls did not protect so much as crush and he could have stood like Samson between the pillars, not to bring down the Philistines, but to keep his own temple from caving in.

Leaning with his arms on the sill, he caught sight of the tray, left outdoors. The tea cooled with the day, a useless brew. Dregs in a basin for throwing out. He felt the massive futility of objects

185

without people and without the function which human patterning imposed on them.

He wanted to bring it crashing down, to be nothing and to have nothing. On an impulse, he picked up the dormant shepherdess from her stand and almost without reflection, dropped the statue out of the open window onto the paving stones below. As soon as he let go, he regretted it but he could not have it back. He watched her fall helplessly the second he released her from his grasp. It was a frozen moment and he looked down mesmerised by the impact.

The figurine smashed with great elegance, like a drop of water caught in slow-motion photography. There was a circle of points that rose to form a crown, then a column of dust like a nuclear surge from which the fallout seemed never-ending. It smashed to smithereens and parts bounced to the furthest corner of the terrace. The dust and ashes of the explosion he had generated would not stop falling. The breakage went on and on and on, for minutes it seemed while head and arms and body ground to a powder, man and child and woman dislocated from each other and from themselves.

The sleeping shepherdess was no more. There was a white patch at the centre of the detonation but hardly enough debris to sweep up. Gone. Two centuries of rarity wiped out. He thought as he went downstairs that he would have to write and inform the British Museum and the curator in Frankfurt that one of the rarest and most perfect examples of that factory had met with an accident, one of the last of its kind which he had certified by his own act was daily becoming rarer.

The
Arcade

Only after they had been married a year did he notice from a top window that there was a view of the church and the churchyard. He couldn't exactly see the headstones but he knew that they were there. He wished he hadn't noticed there were people buried within sight of the house – but it was too late to change it now.

His wife learned to avert her face from the view as well and looked into the mirror of her dressing table. She put on a suit of business-like efficiency and smoothed the collar of her blouse to lie neatly under it, smoothed and patted all extrusion flat.

At breakfast, which they always took together in the dining room, over a newspaper and Baxter's marmalade, she put on her reading glasses to scan the print. He did not like these spectacles. They put him out of focus, distinguishing close from distant, unable to combine the two. His own eyes were still perfect and he went on defying the lapses which his body might make into senility, doubly resenting the symptoms of middle age in her. They sat to all intents and purposes behind separate screens, he of the *Financial Times*, she of the *Scotsman*, from which she would occasionally read the pithier sentences to amuse him. During the course of the day they would trade papers with each other, so as to be fully informed.

"Have you an engagement this evening?" he asked, spreading a wafer of toast. A week before Christmas should have had an air of festive communality.

"Oh yes. I told you last week. Andrew and I have a client to take out to dinner this evening."

"Again?"

"Business, I'm afraid." Business was the irreducible claim, as if she said "Breathing, I'm afraid," and so he did not try to combat it with argument, or even persuasion. "He's pretty anodyne, this character. And tight-fisted."

"You mean he looks at the small print before he buys?"

"Something like that."

"Sounds a sensible fellow to me. Some of the small print can be so very small before you buy and so very large afterwards."

She did not reply, though whether she examined the things he said minutely or dismissed them, he could never tell. Her mind ran off at tangents that had ceased to fascinate him. They were simply tangents. He realised the circuits of her brain, that had seemed complete at one time, were small explosions made by terminals that did not meet correctly. The bursts of her thinking became tedious when he had expected something more sustained and maybe even sustaining.

"I do believe business is going to have a tremendous boost in the New Year."

This might be apropos of the customer they were entertaining to dinner, or the article in her newspaper, or the imminence of a change in Kalends. He plumped for the last. "Why? What resolutions have you made?"

"The new shop in the Arcade is going to make all the difference. What's really gone against us in the past is getting solicitors to act as our estate agents. It's all so slow and so sedate up here. Gentleman's agreement is binding. I ask you. Hopeless for new property. Now that we've got our own window, things are going to take off."

She believed so fervently in her own sales talk that sometimes he was drawn in by it. "Do you think?"

"Hm. Absolutely. We've seen an increase already. The boutiques are giving the right customer-orientated environment. The architect's done a marvellous job with the layout. Very up-market, don't you think? The people we're getting with enquiries are a feed-off from the precinct. Precinct is wrong, isn't it," she considered to herself. "Arcade is so much better. Overtones of Burlington and Regency colonnades, maybe even a hint of the Pantiles. A touch of inspiration."

He was not sure if this was hard sell or soft sell, but it did remind him of brain-washing techniques that alternated punches with caress, even mentally. Andrew delivered the punch of facts, contract details, pricing and then she came in with the attractive packaging, the enhanced life style which it was possible to buy into, a heritable trust. They worked well in tandem. Most buyers found the couple irresistible. He'd fallen for them himself. Fallen. Fallen.

"If the operation develops around the concept of inter-changeable units, we're onto a winner. Actually," she drawled for long enough to give him time to wonder at what point he had started to notice the particular stress of her intonation, and resist it like sand-blasting on his nervous system. He did not know which was more grating, the voice or the catchpenny phrases. "Actually, at this moment we are showing the largest percentile increase in turnover in the last five years."

"You don't need to sell to me," he reminded her. "I've already bought."

She chatted on about the Arcade. She and Andrew had been lucky enough to secure one of the units in a new market, under-cover, all-weather, security guards etcetera. High rentals ensured only the most lucrative concerns settled under its arches. When he visited it on opening day, to champagne and caviar, he found it a dreary, soul-destroying place. Smart enough. Too smart. All glass and stairs and fountains with greenery to create the aura of vastness and opulence. Gigantic, wall-to-wall mirrors created a false depth so that the Arcade was an optical illusion, doubling the floor space at minimal cost. Without daylight or solid structure, it became an ephemeron, a fantasy environment like a gambling casino where exposure to realities of cash, loss, value or time were scrupulously excised. It was a world apart. Nor was it properly functional. To his knowledge, the escalator which was the pivot of the design, had not worked on more than half the days since its inauguration.

She, on the other hand, was carried away by it all and became unaccountably excited by such things as whether photographs of the properties looked better on cream or blue mounts with scientific surveys on colour response, divided between the sexes, to back up her opinion or contradict his. In total, he was reminded of one of the best puns he had ever come across, when Rhett Butler suggested slyly to his wife that her new store should bear the legend EMPTORIUM. He did not specify its derivation from "Caveat Emptor", a witticism that would also have been lost on her, but stressed the variant of emporium which might appeal. Innes found the word a huge, if hollow, joke and often chanted it silently to himself.

"Do you?" she asked suddenly.

"Do I what?"

"Have an appointment this evening?"

"Nothing arranged." They planned their schedule carefully, so that no more than two evenings per week were spent in one another's company.

"Why don't you come along?"

He did not consider this question as serious and shook his head automatically. Her breathing was her own.

"What will you do for dinner then?"

"What I usually do. Cook it myself."

"As you please."

He wondered, in percentile averages, how much difference they had made to each other's life. Five per cent, or ten? She resumed her reading glasses, changing focus to the newsprint. She had a way of scanning the columns that was rapid and paced out, a regular stride eating up miles of words without too much consciousness of the passing scenery. She seemed to have no power of retention, however, and he could not recall her once referring afterwards to an event or fact that had been recorded in her paper. Why do you read the newspapers, he once made bold to ask. In case I miss something, she replied. But in truth, she missed everything. Saw the words and not the meaning.

"Oh look," she said, "how terribly interesting."

He put the paper down and paid attention to her.

"Iona," she explained.

"Who?" he stammered.

"The island Iona," she replied with distinguishing emphasis. "Apparently there's a demand to be buried there, in consecrated soil. A return to the homeland, even in death. How extraordinary. They're selling the island now as burial plots to rich Americans, a metre at a time. What a marketing coup that must have been. Not many overheads. And there's a waiting list. I wonder who had the agency for that?"

"Isn't it part of national heritage? Inalienable, or something of the sort?"

"Seems not. They're using Arran as an overspill. What a wheeze."

"So much for private enterprise. It extends even beyond the grave."

"Oh come, you must admit it's a brilliant idea."

She choked him. "Must we have this jelly stuff for marmalade? I thought oranges grew with peel. I like peel in mine, not all sifted out."

"I must fly." She glanced at her watch, an accurate timepiece. "Three showhouse visits booked this morning."

So the island was carved up in burial plots for tourists who still went on travelling when they were dead, buying a square of the ancestral homeland they did not know, to be interred in for the remainder. Dust to dust. Ashes to ashes. He was so outraged by this parcelling of beauty spots, and of ground sacred to religion as well as sacred to heritage, that he felt he was the victim of a personal insult. Iona. The crux of the nation; seat of its Christianity, home of its kings. Awful. Was nothing out of bounds to property developers, intent on making a quick buck and salving their conscience with the thought that somebody wanted it and so it was permissible? Bending to market forces. He'd heard the phrase on his wife's lips many a time, an edict which was inarguable, because it found expression. The bottled bathwater of the famous, shreds of pop stars' clothes, useless memorabilia of cults and fads and movements: these were the holy relics of the century. Give them museum room. Put them in glass cases. Someone had touched them, neither illustrious nor talented in the larger sense, but famous fleetingly. O tempora, O mores. Civilisation had gone over to the worship of kitsch. Christie's and Sotheby's opened up their door to plastic, alternating with fine art. Who made a distinction between the real and the unreal? Only cynics. It was all collectable, saleable, had a mark-up value. He wondered who confirmed the status of these artefacts. What spurious pedigree or catalogue entry did they bring with them in the way of provenance, or was someone prepared to say, I personally cut his waistcoat up into fragments, exactly one-inch square, authenticating the worthless? It was wonderful stuff, if you had a taste for the bizarre. He remembered Chaucerian cheats like the Pardoner, symbolising a generation of religious pedlars who made a trade from hawking fakes as splinters of the true cross, to prey on the weak-minded. The holy made unholy by transubstantiation into curios and idols. Pigs' bones indeed, purporting to be sancta. There was nothing new in extortion after all, or in the sale of indulgences.

Quite sensible people he knew who at one time would have devoted themselves to good works, charity, fund-raising for societies, turned instead to making their own shrines from scraps hoping, if nothing else, to win a place in a book of records for the feat. He knew a man who boasted the world's largest collection of cigarette cards. It was laughable, or ought to be. And another who sifted through jumble sales for rare first editions, elbowing his way up queues to do it; not because he cared about the book or the writer or even the rarity, except that it pandered to a fashion, and could be converted into profit. He admired the genuine collector but scouting for merchandise was somehow disreputable, an activity bereft of pleasure which seemed to belittle the originators.

> Seven wealthy towns contend for Homer dead,
> Through which the living Homer begged his bread.

Who could afford a Van Gogh canvas nowadays? But at one time they were going cheap enough in Arles, for the man hadn't managed to sell a painting in his lifetime. He would have gladly traded one in for a meal. Somebody could have made a killing out of him. Yes, it could give rise to madness for there was no morality in these standards. Say it was rare and it became rare. Who could not despise mankind when it showed as little sense of judgement as the swine of the Gadarenes, and was driven by these compelling fashions, possessed – yes, possessed by demons.

The article stayed with him all day, adding to a despondency that was both external and internal. If the sun had shone brilliantly, he would not have noticed. But it didn't. It was grey, a grey descent into the city.

They travelled separately. He took the train: she went by car when her routines were so diverse. It was not always convenient to give him a lift and so while she hurtled up to the capital taking the roads the way she took the newspapers, he continued to travel at leisure and alone.

Towards five, however, she made a reappearance in the Grassmarket. He knew even by the opening of the door that it was his wife who made her entrance. She did not open it modestly, enquiring what might lie behind the carefully arranged displays and the oyster-coloured velvet, but pushily, with a proprietorial air. He didn't put a foot towards her or smile when she said, "I came to see if you wanted a lift back. Andrew booked at Greywalls, so it seemed sensible to go home to freshen up and change."

194

"Yes. Half five." His regular closing time was not to be accelerated.

"Not any later," she warned.

He retreated into the bay with his papers and catalogues. These seemed more than ever a haven from commercial frenzy. He adhered to the symbols and markings of the trade, like the imprimatur of the Mint, for they denoted a coinage which could not be debased. The wheels and crosses and initials stamped on the base of an object became more and more compelling. They were too difficult to forge and in that lay their superiority to falsehood.

A late customer came in, a man. Such men were often serious buyers for they didn't browse idly, a pastime for which they had neither leisure nor inclination. He knew he could safely leave the sale to Mrs Forbes. Like Markheim, this customer wanted a Christmas present for a lady he was courting. He heard the terms of the commission from inside his booth with ironical understanding. What the man really wanted was something that looked good but wasn't too expensive, something that smacked of Valentine. He thought through the stock in hand and mentally sorted out half a dozen items that were suitable. Sure enough, Mrs Forbes offered them. A cupid. A pair of lovers on a stand. Sèvres they were and rather pricy. A Staffordshire couple, glazed but uncoloured. Slightly lumpy and unimpressive. Two separate figurines which he knew in his heart of hearts were not a set, and would have admitted it to an informed buyer. But they passed muster, from the same factory and period, a cobbled pair. And finally, a rather dreadful musical box which had only come in the day before, itself traded in for other Christmas gifts. He would not have taken it in the way of normal business, but thought the folly of the amorous season might find it a ready buyer. And here was one already.

Each was handled, turned, assessed. The buyer did not know the lady well enough to know what she would like and was uneasy anyway in the middle of women's objects, and of women. Mrs Forbes and Hamilton stood by, encouraging and drawing him out so that the man, bemused by his situation, confessed he hoped to make a rich marriage. Yes, thought Innes, a rich marriage was not a thing to be neglected.

For once he wished he were alone to do the serving. He swivelled round so that he had a sidelong view of the intending

195

buyer and husband. A man beyond the age of idiocy at any rate, though he had to confess idiots were not all young. On the verge of handsomeness and youth, the visitor nevertheless looked raddled. He had lived hard, taking a toll of his vigour and his years. Innes was curious about what saving features this marriage and this prospective lady wife might bring with them. Was she so well favoured that he could break the habits of a lifetime for her sake, so rich, or had a bout of ague confirmed that old age needed nursing and companionship, unpaid? Wifedom was many things. He hoped earnestly that the stranger might be rewarded with at least one of them.

His hand went back and forth indecisively. He was inclined towards the Sèvres lovers, thinking the richest gift might be returned in kind. The cupid he did not like. Too sweet and cloying, dimples and all. Its stylised infancy mocked at real, hard-headed courtship. Bad taste. Bad policy. Staffordshire he rejected at once. He lifted the lid of the musical box which was decorated with china flowers to resemble a market pannier and let its sound out into the darkened atmosphere of the shop. Mrs Forbes had wound it fully up and so for maybe three interminable minutes the notes of "My love is like a red, red rose" tinkled out while all three of them went on analysing what he might or might not buy for a woman he might or might not marry.

The sound was unendurable to Innes, for the rudimentary organ lacked quarter-tones and what came out was a rough approximation to the melody. It had lost its lilt. The metallic sound of prongs vibrating against a barrel of spikes bore no resemblance to the song as given by the human voice, full and glorious and rich. Besides, he remembered all the words as the machine wound down through verse after verse.

> Till a' the seas gang dry, my dear,
>   And the rocks melt wi' the sun:
> And I will love thee still, my dear,
>   While the sands o' life shall run.

It contained the most potent sadness. He wanted to lean over and close the lid again on those romantic aspirations which they each believed in and fell short of, as musical boxes fell short of music, creating a discord which was worse than silence.

196

Alone, he might have had the courage to say to the newcomer, Go away and forget about it. Don't think of this makeshift marriage but go on being defiantly whatever it is you are. The presence of the women was an inhibition to that. The man had come intent to buy, and would not be deterred even by a genuine well-wisher. He put his hand at last on the ill-assorted pair of figurines, a compromise choice. It did not make too large a demand on aesthetics, or on his wallet.

Mrs Forbes wrapped the purchase up quickly before he changed his mind. It was closing time and she was anxious to shut the door and make her own escape into the suburbs.

"I hope you have a lot of pleasure from it," he heard his wife say ingratiatingly to the purchaser as she opened the door to let him out. He hoped so too.

"How is the major?" she asked, turning round without a second's interlude as though the question were already prepared to fill a gap in conversation. "Is he better?"

Innes had not been aware of Major Forbes' malady and listened with growing interest to the symptoms. The man was as little known to his wife as to himself, and yet here she was discussing his temperature and his medicine with feigned intimacy. The dialogue of women made such comforts accessible. He put his head into his hands.

The women locked up ceremoniously and he got into the car for the homeward journey. He was the passenger more often than not, content to let her drive when it effectively absorbed her attention, leaving his free to concentrate on the radio.

"Are you sure you won't come along this evening?" she offered. "Might be rather jolly. We can easily change the booking."

Royal, conjugal or epistolary we?

"No, thank you. I've a deadline to meet on an article."

"Nonsense," she retorted. "That isn't due till the February edition. Heaps of time."

"My own deadline, then."

She shrugged and listened with him to the news.

Underneath the tally of disasters, for happiness was not found often enough to record, he heard a recurring note which the man in the shop had struck unconsciously in his bargaining. It was the note of last-ditch optimism; do or die. Innes puzzled at what emotional or financial extremes had driven him to make the uncharacteristic move, believing against previous experience that the woman he espoused, or her income, would put an end to his own insolvency and fill the void. The twin nature of the problem forked him too. He identified with the man's emotional dilemma, but found in the pecuniary embarrassment, a mirror of his wife's.

Whyever had she married him, succumbing to his own rebounding moment of weakness, except for money? He thought it very calculated now. A skilled baiting and he was hooked. They had drawn up an orderly contract, verbal and legal, whereby as a wedding settlement he bought her business partnership, a double jointure. Maybe he bought her business partner too. On that he never would be sure. The two of them were amorphous while he provided the vital cementing ingredient in the mix, cash, and was now in eternal bondage with the pair of them. Technically he owned half. He had the status of a guarantor, a professional underwriter who ought to be good for a few thousand. He wondered if they had looked into his books before they settled on him. He was better than an insurer who could be located through a brokerage, or a bank expecting high returns. He could hardly put up the premiums to indemnify against bad management, or withdraw. He had the satisfaction of knowing that his profits went on subsidising her losses in the Arcade. She had her cut.

So he felt alternately pity for the stranger's emotional incapacity and scorn for his monetary one, casting himself by turns into the role of exploiter and exploited.

She sat at her dressing table and brushed her hair, cut in its sculptured shape. She sat with her back to the window but even through velour curtains she could feel a chill, making her shiver.

Like her husband, she wondered about the late buyer and the woman he referred to, their counterparts. She wished she knew the woman, could put a face or at least a name to his intended. At that very moment, was she too sitting in front of a mirror, putting on an appearance for a public engagement, or a private one? Did they hold hands at dinner? Did they look at each other and were the speeches more lengthy than the intervening silence?

Her husband came and passed behind her. He went to the window and lifted the curtain to look out into the street. Some shops stayed open late to catch the Christmas trade. Several had

198

"Men only" evenings when the devoted and attentive could buy presents for their lovers without risking discovery. He would not make one of them.

"Don't," she said.

"Don't what?"

"Open the curtains. It lets the draught in."

He obliged, letting the mass of material fall to the ground but at that moment the clock on the church tower started to chime the hour and she shivered again.

"Not cold surely?"

She did not reply and he came over to the table, watching with some fascination the fresh paintwork she applied to her face. Emollient, deflocculant, gesso, impasto. A wonderful veneer of colour and glaze, renewable by the hour if it should start to slip and smudge under the effect of heat or water.

"Are you sure you will not come?"

She did not look at him directly but in the side mirror of the cheval. By moving a fraction, he could put himself out of the range of the eyes which he still found disturbing. Eyes of celadon they were, composed of iron whose oxides lent a peculiar colouring, blue or green or grey like water. He felt she tried to trap him in the mirror, making him look at her or even at himself. But he was expert at avoidance and she did not succeed in catching his eye.

"The third time of asking? No. We'll stop at that. I am sure you will enjoy it more alone."

She did not contradict him. "I may be late."

"As late as you like."

He noticed that the jewel box on her dressing table was open and its contents were spread out indiscriminately as she searched for something at the bottom. There was a pearl necklace with a clasp of diamonds he had bought on their engagement. Real pearls. Imagine, deep-sea divers risked their lives collecting oyster shells so that women could wear a string around their neck. She seldom put them on. They lay now, discarded, and some of the pearls were tinged with make-up where she had been careless in removing them. Grains of powder clung, as coarse as sand. He remembered reading that some women were unsuited to wearing pearls. Their skin was too acid so that contact with the natural enamel made it dark, like teeth when the root has died. Grey instead of lustrous white. Strange that, he thought, and picked up the double row to see if he could detect premature signs of discoloration.

The chimes from the tower had finished striking but the peel went on reverberating and they both heard the knell of hours thinning into silence.

She hurried mentally from the sombre place, eager to make her escape. She anticipated the hotel which would sit like a focal point of light, attracting and transmitting it, in the middle of the winter evening. The foyer would be thronged with guests in evening wear, on their way in and out of the dining room, the library, the sun lounge to the rear where drinks and coffee would be served. The chandelier picked up the colour of the rooms and the people and intensified it, adding the spectrum from crystal droplets, so that the occasion was brilliant and enlarged with glitter. She warmed to that magnification. A meeting place. A social event. Andrew and the client waiting for her before they could begin, while the moment of suspense hung on her arrival to propel it into action. She thrilled at the idea of demonstration partly of herself, preened for display, partly of the package in the folder. The challenge of selling them, somehow, using one as the framework for the other. This is me and this is what I believe in, attractively put together. She enjoyed the power of influencing decisions and of seeing minds in balance tip in infinite gradations to her side.

"Done now?" he asked.

"As well as can be," she replied, checking finally in the three-way mirror. "If your light is out when I get back, I'll sleep in here."

"As you please."

She went, leaving a vapour whose composition was heat rather than smell. But the aroma did not fade and he got up after a little while and found she had left the bottle of perfume open. It was expensive perfume, too expensive to waste and so he put the stopper back, entrapping her essence. The small squeak of the ground glass made him flinch.

He did not put the lights on in the sitting room but stood at the window for some time, virtually in the dark apart from a little light shed from the lamp-post at the end of the street.

There was an occasional beam from the lighthouses as they went on flashing at their intermittent rate, east and west of his position. It was one version of chronometry. They began to irritate him, those rotating lenses, like eyes out of focus with each other and yet it was self-defeating to try and bring them into alignment. They must be variable to make sense, the long and short of Morse code which was still subtle enough to build into a sign language. He could time the difference in interval between Bass and Fidra if he stood there long enough, taking the pulse of two creatures out of synchronisation. Flashing or occulting, he couldn't remember which signal they used, whether light or dark predominated. He admired the sporadic rhythm, if only because the two beacons tried to regularise what was immeasurable in its flux, time and tide. They were an expression of faith, or a safe point, and would carry on signalling in perpetuity, to the end of recorded time. He bowed to that. Those conjugate foci represented all that anyone could do to indicate the natural hazard: they did not reduce it but they warned shipping on its way up the Forth of the imminence of rock and sand bank, markers above a water graveyard. A just precaution.

He settled down to eventide, waiting for night and the other hours to strike.

The
Choice

He noticed the young woman browsing through the display downstairs, probably putting in an hour before she picked her children up from school. He noticed her as soon as she came in because she had an air about her he couldn't define, or even instantly absorb, and so he went on trying to establish what it was while she threaded her way among the objects that were offered for sale.

It was a craft centre and Iona had stumbled on it by accident. Small rooms downstairs were opened out and converted into cubicles where different artists worked, and in the middle their products were displayed, small embroideries, hand-dipped candles or beeswax tapers, carved ornaments, boxes and some small pieces of metalwork. The garage was a forge while in another outhouse, an etching artist kept the tanks of acid for dipping his metal plates. Not all of these positions were filled and considering the number of places provided, there was comparatively little for sale. Iona guessed that it was a secondary place of work for some, who used its facilities occasionally, the forge, the kiln or cutting equipment, but that the majority of their output went elsewhere to more lucrative showrooms.

She lifted the pottery with a critical eye to perfection, knowing the effortless and inspired from the mundane. Two potters worked here; one a natural designer with lazy attitudes to finish – a glaze uneven, the base on a pair of vases not identical, but the other, though meticulous in workmanship, had no eye and favoured gaudy finishes. Neither was likely to tempt the coins out of her pocket.

"Have you seen upstairs?" the man asked, interrupting her exit. "There are paintings and other displays on the upper floor."

"No, I didn't know there was another floor."

"Well, let me show you," he offered.

The man who approached was familiar, though she didn't

know him personally. He wore a hessian apron of marsupial dimensions. She couldn't understand why the apron was the symbol of domestic constraint, a man in apron strings being tantamount to a child in leading reins. The apron ought to have the status of its craft when it was essential for the stonemason or an outdoor carpenter to store his tools, and was really a toolbag tied around the waist. Though it was many other things, a dust covering, an impromptu glove for handling tongs and irons in the firing hearth, a duster to remove an imperfection; the garment he wore brought a wave of nostalgia for the years she spent at Glasgow art college, dropping in on other people's specialisms. Laughing at disasters, proud of achievement communally. That was why he was familiar. His working habits were inbred in her.

He walked back down the length of the room again and indicated the staircase in a recess. She met his eye and it concurred. Yes, she would mount, and he followed her to the upper level. The premises had been converted from a house. Downstairs the rooms had been removed, but upstairs the wall divisions remained. This was advantageous for picture-hanging. There was more wall. Additionally, the rooms created a form of privacy, as though it were a private house and this a private showing, him and her.

Iona took the tour. It was a darkish afternoon mid-season and so he switched on the light in each of the successive rooms and landings of the showplace to accentuate one or the other item which she might choose.

She stood in front of a fashionable piece of art, done in a strip which ignored the proportions of the golden mean. A bit of canvas blackened and then a painting of a town, any town would do because the fineries of architecture were blurred. This one might be called Mont St Michel or Île de la Cité or anything else modish, drawn out of a hat. It could have been built up from a stencil or a template, so crude and basic were the shapes.

"Most people go for these," he prompted.

Indeed, she thought of acquaintances who had them on the wall. Nouveau de nouveau. That was up to them, but they talked about these pictures as though they were art and imagined that because they bought them from a place designated "gallery", they were making an investment.

"Not me," she said.

"No," he agreed. "A money-spinner. I'm disappointed with the way this painter has turned out. I'll have to stop taking his work. Too commercial."

It was an unusual assembly all the same, something unexpected when the place was off the beaten track. She wondered who might come this way to buy from the collective, but its continuance was proof that someone did. In the middle of each of the rooms was a display made up of simple boxes to which scrim had been attached. Iona was not greatly taken with the artefacts but found that the actual collection and framing of the groups was handsome. Colour, placement, lighting, even the small folded cards of the price-tags were pleasing. They carried the name of the piece and the artist. Whoever made these out was a fine calligraphist. An italic nib, black ink, forty-five-degree angle to the paper making light and dark strokes. Such handling.

She picked one up, enquiring more of its author than its inscription. "What is this house?" she asked.

"It's owned by a consortium of craftsmen. East of Scotland guild of something or other. I can't remember what we call ourselves. A bit pretentious." He smiled wryly.

"But whose idea was it? Somebody must manage it."

He did not like direct questions or ones that pointed to a factual answer and so he walked away a few steps to straighten a piece of stained-glass work. "I'm the warden, I suppose. I live," he laughed, "in the stable block. Only half a dozen people work here at a time, so I'm afraid it's become a bit of a showroom. I'd hoped for more of a community."

"How long has it been open?"

"A couple of years."

"So long? I'm amazed I haven't come this way before."

There were lengthy silences into which he did not wish to propel an opinion, because enquiry into her life or how long she had lived nearby or why she had not come down that road before, seemed an intrusion. But when she commented on the selection in the rooms, he was driven to ask, "You've studied art?"

"Yes, I did."

"Do you paint yourself?"

"Not now. A lapsed faith."

"So you may go back to it," he said so rapidly that the speed of his response caught her off guard. She had not made that connection when she said it. It was a swift inversion, showing her two sides, a seal and then its impression struck in hot wax. It was so long since she had met that quick-thinking faculty that she was confused in her reply.

"Sculpture. I stopped when I was married."

In both their minds there arose, at the same moment, the equally contrary proposition that she might start again if she were unmarried, one being the impediment to the other.

She lost a little breath and hesitated in her walk to regain it. His was not a burdensome presence. She was immediately comfortable with him, as if his body as well as his habits were known to her. He had the almost emaciated leanness she liked in men. She had discovered that broad-faced men were always self-sufficient, needing women only as ancillaries, not spinal to their life. Thin men remembered, everything. They were intense. In everything. And there arose in their minds the same proposition at the same moment.

Hungry he was. He was hungry.

In the furthest room was a collection of silverware, marked *Not for Sale* and going closer, Iona could see why. It was made up of church plate and sacramental vessels, spoons with twisted handles and one bearing the insignia of a church patron, like an apostle spoon.

"These are yours?" she judged.

"Yes, I am a silversmith."

Round the rim of the collection plate he had inscribed the symbols of Christianity, the cross, chalice and a candelabrum as well as the name of the church to which it was dedicated, and in the letters she recognised the proportions of the calligraphist. She foresaw its station on the altar and the bags of coins which had been passed along the pews coming ceremonially to rest on it. The sacred offering. Given the rarity of new churches, he must be considered an exceptional craftsman to be given this commission.

"This is not for communion surely?" She held a bowl of traditional shape, thinking it did not belong with the rest.

"No. I only put it there when I had finished it. All this is going to Edinburgh to the silversmithing hall for marking. I wait until I've got enough to make the trip worth while."

"Is this a christening cup then?"

"It's a quaich. It's any kind – even a loving cup."

"But it's not for sale?"

It was, from the mass of objects that her eye had lighted on that afternoon, the best, a raised bowl with two flanges or ears instead of conventional handles. A quaich. Yes, she remembered now. It had a Celtic beauty about it, a shape as natural as a stone for fitting in the hand. Two hands. A loving cup. The surface was smooth but she perceived the complex conversions by which it had arrived at that simplicity. By analysis she could take it back through soldering and planishing and hollowing to its incipient state of sheet metal.

"No. I can't sell it until it's been hallmarked. It seems strange I could give it away without the authentication, but I can't dispose of it by way of trade. So they say."

"And what happens to it after it comes back from Edinburgh?"

"I put it back here and hope someone comes along, one afternoon, and buys it."

She put it down and they turned towards the staircase. He switched off the lights after her, a careful energist, and she became aware of how long they had spent in the chamber by the depth of the shadows that fell. She should go. She really should go. Her boys would be out of school and waiting for her.

"If I give you a deposit, that would hold it until it is hallmarked?"

He put his hands into the empty pocket of the apron and considered her suggestion, walking steadily towards the room where he worked. "You're sure?"

"Of course."

They came to a halt by his bench on which the organised clutter of his work made a sequence she could read.

In readiness, she opened her purse and found several notes from which she took the largest denomination and laid it on the bench. He did not hurry to pick it up and in the heat of the powerful lights, it seemed to curl a little.

" 'I promise to pay the bearer on demand'?" he said disparagingly of the terms. "No, I don't need that. I'll give you my receipt." He found a piece of paper and with the slanted lines of the italic pen, jotted some words on it and signed it. He folded the paper over and put it in an envelope with her ten-pound note. "It'll be waiting for you if you call. In about a month's time."

It was only afterwards she realised they had not arrived at a settlement of cost.

She drove along the lanes of East Lothian impatiently, or rather hurrying in time but languid with her thoughts, dream-like and seductive, on which banks and cross-roads and hedges hardly impinged.

Her boys were waiting for her, accusing her with the delay. She'd promised to take them to the shows which came to Longniddry for a week in the autumn, and they stopped to put on Wellingtons in case it was wet underfoot, and heavier coats.

"Come on then," said the older boy, quickly reseated.

"Allan's having trouble with his boots. I think they're too small for him."

"Slowcoach," he said and fished in his school satchel for a toy to play with while he waited.

"I don't remember that car," she commented over her shoulder once they were under way. "Did your father buy it?"

"No."

"Your grandfather?" His pockets were always filled with presents for the boys which she tried to curtail, or confine at least to special events, but when they all colluded in the indulgence it was hard to keep track of what her children owned.

"No."

The boy had never lied. He just didn't volunteer the truth, so she often had to act like prosecuting counsel with him.

"So where did you get it?"

"I swopped it."

"What for?"

"A Dinkey tractor. I had two. I gave the old one away," he explained as if this were an important qualifier, to keep the better for himself.

She struggled with the moral distinctions of fairness and equality but did not feel up to them.

"Do you think his mother knows?"

"Doesn't matter," he shrugged and ran the car defiantly along the back of her seat. "He swopped it."

"But yours wasn't such a good car."

"He wanted it."

They wrestled with each other already, in long and hard and silent bouts. Eight! What would he be like at eighteen? Iona

210

thought of the brothers she had managed with such ease, such simple happiness when they confronted the external factors, not each other. It seemed a wicked fate that this boy was a trial to her. She learned not to argue with him because he triumphed in every debate, with more and more unreasonable tenets based on the validity of what he wanted, no other standard being logical to him.

She wondered uneasily if some bullying had weighted the barter to his side. He was bigger than his age group and she could well imagine him literally twisting a classmate's arm. She did not know what to do about this incipient fault in character. "Hunger is the best sauce," her father used to say, but deprivation as a panacea was a notion in which she knew the flaw. It did not solve problems, or not as many as it created. A year of penury might be therapeutic for this child, but who was going to impose it? His father or his grandfather? They would say she was insane for suggesting any such restriction. They had everything, and he would have everything too. That was their pleasure and their privilege. Besides, she could put him in an empty room with a dozen others and at the end of a year, he would be king. In possessions or in authority, he would be king. She saw and admired his young potential, but worried that without formal discipline it would turn sourly to greed instead of generosity.

"It's barrie," said the child and dangled the flashy sports car in front of his brother, who was not allowed to touch.

"What's that you say?" asked Iona.

"Barrie. That's what the boys at school say."

"What does it mean?"

"It means braw."

Braw. Barrie. The boys were always trading in these words and she wondered about excising one more solecism from his vocabulary, under the ambitious project of making him a gentleman.

"I don't think I like that word, barrie."

"It's a good word," he retorted, and went on chanting it softly in her ear.

The fairground was pitched on its traditional site, on the foreshore between Gullane and Longniddry. The lights had been switched on, though it was only a little after four. Multi-coloured lights in thousands were strung between the attractions or fitted into holders on the canopy of merry-go-rounds. She put the boys on the more juvenile whirligigs with miniature horses or child-size buses and planes, but the older boy grew tired of these imitants and went alone on the fast rides, speedway and rollercoaster. The younger clung to her side, dizzy, watching his daredevil brother who might be terrified but would not flinch, going faster and faster round the circuit with gritted teeth and hands clutched to the rail.

In the background, barkers called out the going rate for their stall, refined to winning averages, one in fifty. Was it possible for these hoops to go over these objects, and even if it was, did she want the prize? A statuette of cartoon characters in plaster of Paris. Her boy did. He took minutes to assess the angles of each game and for such a youngster, had unusual motor skills to land a dart every time on a high-staked card. The stallholder who had started out with a patronising "sonny" and a smile, soon lost his humour when the boy carried off three prizes in a row. Iona became tired of carrying them around like a porter.

Each attraction was its own hypnosis of light and sound. A hurdy-gurdy played a travesty of popular tunes, drawing them in out of the night and the cold air to the jollity of things shared. She let herself be carried along, following her children. She liked to watch their faces, eager with the momentary thrill of being tossed in the air, and the downward plunge, the winning and the losing, the exaggerated sensations of being a child.

"Can I have more money?" the boy asked.

"But you've had such a lot already. Allan's still got some of his."

"Allan's a scaredy. He won't go on half the things."

"Well, he's younger than you."

"My grandad gave me an extra pound."

This was true. He had slipped her money for the treat, but she did not know he had been injudicious enough to tell the child.

"And that is what you've spent," she said firmly.

"Can I have what you were going to give me then?"

Oh to plead simple poverty. You cannot have it because we have not got it. It was a fine corrective after all.

She gave him one more coin which he traded in against his brother's small change. "That's the finish," she said. "No more."

He walked purposefully towards the covered area where the pintables and slot-machines were kept. He could not resist the

212

penny arcades and the lure of putting something in and hoping to get more out. He was a systematic player. He didn't put his coin in the first machine and pull the lever at random just for the sake of it. He studied form. He watched other players intently before he risked his stake, watched the combinations roll so that he could guess the sequence. The showman turned a blind eye to so junior a competitor when it was likely to put money in his pocket, and walked to the other end of the tent.

The boy won. A shower of coins fell into his hands and Allan scrambled after one or two that ran loose under the duckboarding.

"Shall we go now?" she asked.

He looked at the bonus. Bright silver money. Shingle in his pockets, making him heavy and important.

"Just one more go."

He fell into the compulsion of more, a self-promoting compulsion when more was endless.

In the evening when she was alone again and had a quiet hour for reflection, she went and found a dictionary and sat down to locate the word he'd used. It wasn't in the English dictionary, however, and so she got up again to find a Scots one, not hopefully when it was likely to be a piece of undocumented slang.

But she was in luck. She found the entry. Barrie: fine, big, smart in appearance. It was the derivation that made her start. Of gypsy origin. Well, well. The Romany tongue finding a new, twentieth-century application. She wondered why or how, who had first broadened the base of the word, taking it out of its parochial locality. Barrie indeed. She knew she had been right to have mistrusted it, sound and meaning.

With the book still on her lap, she had a piercing memory of the only man she had ever met who was concerned with these neologisms. "Manufacture". She remembered his wrath at the corruption of the language, a dozen years on, a corruption in which she felt compounded at the time because she was young and indiscriminating in the use of words herself. Unconscious youth. She smiled, under the reading lamp, to think how his lip would curl in displeasure.

Though it was the book and the word brought Innes to mind, she realised that he had been ubiquitous in her thinking that day.

The silversmith came very close with the same delicacy of appraisal in handling objects and the hint of strength behind, making a torsion in the character. The two men came and went in her imagination, one near, one far, but linked by the generic similarity of type. Her type, when other surface attractions had worn away, the only type she could admire because they were individualist.

Innes. He came back very often to pass a judgement on what she had done or said, and the asperity of his criticism was not reduced by time or by removal. He was as caustic about bad taste and manners as ever and often she found herself putting something back on the shelf because it had failed to reach his standards, which by borrowing became hers. She was much indebted to that man and felt churlish that she hadn't had occasion to tell him so.

Sometimes, emulating the best of him, she feared she had incurred the worst. This bowl now, a handsome working, but did she need it? It seemed to have a function but in truth it was a function that belonged to clan gatherings and trencher boards, a skeuomorphic fancy in the twentieth century. It was irrelevant to her way of life and in promising to buy it she was guilty of the indulgence of personal shrine-making, hoarding objects so that she could make a statement about who she was and the quality of her taste. Odd, how everyone was convinced that his own taste was good, or superior to others'. No one voluntarily said, "I have bad taste."

Or was it simply middle-class acquisitiveness taking a hold on her, an advance warning of middle age, the double threat she was convinced that she would cheat? Surely she could resist the tendency to calcify through possessions, and remain fluid in her attitudes.

She got up to put the dictionaries in their place and while she was on her feet, remembered the receipt which she hadn't had time to look at since she left the craft centre. She opened the envelope nervously because she wasn't sure what he had written. A strange receipt it was. On the page she found a variant of her own bank note. "I promise to sell the bearer on demand the silver quaich." Her bill seemed an affront to such a statement. No wonder he had despatched it. His was a genuine document, a guarantee of good faith signed with his full name, a declaration of intent. The antithesis of cheapjack, nothing hidden.

She recalled the definition of sterling silver, a pure metal or one that was minimal in alloy, and how this warranty became attached to the national currency. One pound sterling. No counterfeit. No clipped edges. No fool's gold. It was true, high-grade silver had that in-built patency about it, a sheer honesty in its mirror finish. It might tarnish but a buffing would restore the lustre.

Oddments accreted in her mind about the mediaeval guild of silversmiths and goldsmiths, members of a worshipful company who were entitled to wear their own livery which became the most prestigious, from wealth as well as the emblematic honesty of guildsmen. It was Charles I who had seized the assets of the Mint so that the company of goldsmiths formed their own guarantee of deposit, and were the forerunners of merchant bankers.

Well, he did not look anything like her idea of a merchant banker, the silversmith.

It was enticing to have one side of his nature revealed to her in detail, his expertise, his appearance, and now his name, snippets of information that did not make up a man but were a collage of him, placed out of order or with some clues missing. She guessed at the omissions. She knew she flirted with him mentally, an innocent pastime but when her mind progressed to the day of settlement, she knew she should have arrived at a decision. If she went back and bought the cup, or had it gifted, the man would become her lover.

So the piece of paper with the contract was far from simple. Adultery was not simple, however easy, and before she agreed to one, she must envisage the consequences of the other. But the reverie was agreeable, charming as long as she stayed at fantasy, a stylised action vitrified in her head, and did not hurry on to enact a consummation, which was to admit the possibility of yes.

She let her mind stray off into hypothesis. If she had taken up Innes' offer, would she be contemplating adultery after a decade? And her boys, if they were Innes' boys instead of her husband's, how would they be different? Less extreme anyway, one wilful and the other weak. His and hers divided even when it came to progeny. She thought that Innes' children might have been the kind to whom it was possible to say, "There is the sand. There is the water. Mix them or separate them, but that is all there is." Children who could entertain themselves with

215

nothing, or what was in their head. Children of the imagination.

There was a large element of regret in her reminiscence. She should have conjoined with him, one way or another. A Grand Tour, bringing back a taste for the ornamental way of life, standing beside him in his own shadow in the rue de Varennes. That was something. Maybe it was everything.

It was a selfish tally she arrived at and she was not satisfied with its imbalances. Consciously she stripped away the indulgent elements, the quaich, the silversmith, but found even so denuded, the experience of the afternoon held something of adventure. It was the place itself, the moment of recognition as she walked in. And then she had it. The workshop had brought her into contact not only with the man whose craft she could respect and the community of artists, but with the person she had been and almost forgotten, the young and ambitious and creating self.

The dream came out of soft focus when she perceived that as well as the silver bowl and the man, there might be a change in her way of life. Not simple adultery at all but the cataclysmic change of one being on another. New potential and new relationships fired her.

She was stirred by the old excitement. The foundry where she had worked as a student came flooding back, the clay mould, the cradle to hold it while she poured the metal in and the particular smell of bronze heated in a crucible inside the furnace. A kind of roasted chalk, with clinker and breeze cooling out of the ash. It charred the membrane of the nostrils and made even breathing hot. Magnificent it was, juggling with the elements. She felt stuff on her fingers again, clay or cinder or the grit of sand, and longed for the tactile experience.

Why should she not be one of those who worked in a cubicle, alongside other craftsmen? There was no other sculptor there whose work she could oust. She could join on her own terms, use the kiln, display the finished heads in clay or bronze – each piece hallmarked with her own initials underneath.

So she twisted the piece of paper, like an invitation to the future, this way and that in the light, noticing how the ink of his pen dried in a colour between blue and black and was faintly iridescent, like coal, an ore for mining.

216